SORROW
TO THE
GRAVE

*Then shall ye bring down my gray hairs
with sorrow to the grave.*

—Genesis 42:38

"**D**an," said Mary Fernald.

Sergeant Daniel Valentine made no response. He lay somnolent on the warm sand beside her, eyes shut. Mary inspected him; she didn't think he was asleep. She sighed and sat up, thinking it was about time somebody checked on Garm. It was illegal to let a dog loose on the beach, but this lonely little cove up the coast past Malibu was their own discovery and still remained theirs during this summer of '63.

Garm was toiling toward them through the sand. He'd been rolled by an unexpected breaker and his thick shaggy coat was water-logged. At the best of times an odd-looking dog, very large, with a round, shaggy, flop-eared head and plume of a tail, a dirty-tan coat with an Airedaleish black saddle, but soaking wet he was even odder-looking than usual, his wasp waist and bulging shoulders undisguised. He came up, laid a very ancient tennis ball at Mary's feet, and beamed at her.

"Well, where'd you find that, boy? All right," and she threw it down the beach for him. Garm panted after it. "Dan."

Valentine lay still. "You're *not* asleep," said Mary severely, looking at him. And wondering (not for the first time) if he'd ever ask her to marry him—and what she'd say if he did.

There was quite a lot of him to look at, stretched out like that. A long, long man, with good brown shoulders and chest, good mat of black hair on the chest, thick waving dark hair above thin regular features, long upper lip and straight mouth; he looked tranquil and unaware. *Was* he asleep? He didn't, she reflected, look much like a policeman. Not really.

Garm came back with the ball and she threw it again. "Dan!"

No response. "You're shamming," said Mary, and scattered a handful of sand over his chest.

Valentine grunted and opened his eyes. " 'I began to understand,' " he quoted, " 'why it is sometimes necessary to kill women.' Damn it, I *was* asleep. I didn't get in until three A.M."

Mary said automatically, " 'The Village That Voted the Earth Was Flat.' " She had grown a good deal more familiar with Rudyard Kipling since she'd met Valentine, and could usually identify his quotations. "Look, I've got a question for you. I just remembered Brenda asking about it."

"Who's Brenda?" Valentine sat up with a groan and fished in the pocket of his jacket beside him for cigarettes.

"A girl I went to school with, Brenda Sheldon. She's somebody's secretary—a nice girl, I always liked Brenda."

"What about her?"

"Well," said Mary, "we both belong to the alumni association—UCLA, you know—and know some of the same people, so we see each other now and then. And she knows I know you, that is, a police officer. And—"

"Whom you just keep around to pick his brains for your plots," said Valentine. Mary was a middling-successful writer of crime novels.

"You do come in handy. And remind me to tell you about

the latest utter absurdity that idiotic editor— But about Brenda. I ran into her at the Cheyneys' last night and she asked me to ask you about this, if you could tell her what to do, who to see. It's this old lady she knows, a pensioner, who is—maybe—being defrauded or robbed."

"How?"

"By her nurse—a practical nurse."

"Old woman any relation to the Sheldon girl?"

"Oh, no—she just lives near her, I gathered. From what Brenda said, it all seemed rather up in the air, I thought. Apparently the nurse is a little too officious, and nobody likes her much. She's keeping people out, Brenda says, not letting the old woman's friends in to see her, on flimsy excuses."

"Well, there's not much in that," said Valentine. Garm came panting back with the ball and Mary threw it for him again.

"No. The old woman's on pension, as I say, and Brenda wondered whether maybe the Welfare Board would investigate."

Valentine inhaled, coughed, and shook his head. "No authority has the power to investigate a private citizen like that, unless there's an official complaint laid. In this case, which doesn't sound like much, by the old lady. If she isn't complaining—"

"Yes, I see. I rather thought it'd be like that. I'll tell Brenda."

"In any case," said Valentine dryly, "I shouldn't think it'd be very profitable to set up a pensioner as a mark. Even if California does pay the highest old-age pension."

Mary laughed. "There is that."

He got up, yawning, kicking sand over his cigarette stub. "Now you've waked me up. I think I'll have another little swim. Coming?"

"Too lazy."

* * *

11

Mary duly passed her information on to Brenda Sheldon the next day; being downtown shopping in Santa Monica and knowing where Brenda usually lunched, she found her there— and an empty stool beside her at the counter.

Brenda looked incredulous and angry. "You mean nobody could lift a finger? I tell you, that nurse is up to some funny business."

"Well, you can see how it is legally," Mary pointed out. "By what you've told me there's no real evidence of anything wrong, legal evidence, I mean."

"Oh, forget legal evidence!" said Brenda impatiently. She was, Mary thought, a very pretty girl, and even more so when she was angry. Like most people, Mary didn't think much of her own looks—she was so used to facing her dark hair, fair skin, and green eyes in the mirror. Very ordinary, really; but Brenda made Mary, at five five, feel as tall as Valentine. She was a trim, very small girl of Mary's own twenty-seven years, who always looked very neat. She had dark copper hair in a fluffy short cut, and eyes almost exactly the same color under winging brows.

"Well, before the police can start to investigate, they have to have something besides a vague suspicion that something's wrong."

"I see that," said Brenda reluctantly, "but I'll bet if they did look, they'd find plenty of evidence that something *is* wrong. Thanks anyway, Mary." She looked broodingly at the remains of her tuna sandwich. "What can I do? I suppose you could say it's none of my business, but—"

Brenda Sheldon rented a little three-room frame cottage that sat in the backyard of Mr. and Mrs. George Hawkins's house on Royce Street in Ocean Park. It was a street of older modest frame houses, and there were few young people. Most of the householders were middle-aged to elderly. Some of the

12

houses were poorly kept up because their owners were too old for the work and couldn't afford gardeners or painters. It was the first block down from Lincoln Boulevard, and the little shopping section around on Lincoln was a great convenience to many of those elderly people. There was a dairy store, a small market, Mrs. Cass's real-estate office, the dress shop kept by Jacqueline Devereaux, a variety store, a hardware store, a drugstore, and a bakery.

The Hawkinses were typical of the neighborhood, in a way. In their late fifties, with three married children and five grandchildren. George Hawkins was a skilled mechanic, with his own gas station. He kept their place up pretty well. Across the street lived John and Elsa Wilanowski; he was a carpenter, and all their children were grown and away too. There was Mrs. House, a widow who lived alone; and another widow, Mrs. Johnson, whose schoolteacher daughter lived with her.

Brenda had rented the little house two years ago, when her grandmother died and she moved from the over-large house they'd rented. She hated apartments; they gave her claustrophobia. The little house didn't look very fancy, but it was more private than an apartment, and she had her own little strip of yard. The bus was only a block away, she could be in downtown Santa Monica, where she worked in the office of a large jewelry-manufacturing firm, in twenty minutes.

Of course, in the two years she'd lived there, she'd got acquainted with several of the neighbors. The Hawkinses were friendly; Mrs. Hawkins persisted in the delusion that young working girls didn't know how to feed themselves properly, and often came in with a cake or a plate of cookies. Brenda also did a good deal of her shopping in the little shops around on Lincoln there, and met other habitual customers.

That was how she'd first met old Mr. Foster, in the little dairy store. The old man had been friendly, in a stiff shy kind of way, and she'd asked Mrs. Hawkins about him. He was so old.

"Oh, the Fosters, everyone knows them. They've lived here so long. Such brave old things."

She'd got to know them too; and about them. As half a dozen people in the neighborhood did, she occasionally stopped in for a little chat with the Fosters, offering to do any shopping. Generally, people could be counted on to be kind, and everyone rather admired the Fosters.

The Fosters owned the little two-bedroom frame house next to the Websters, on the same side of the street as the Hawkins house. It was hard now for the old man to keep the lawn cut, the shrubs trimmed, but he did the best he could. A couple of years ago, he'd saved enough to hire some high-school boys to paint the house, and it looked better than some of the other places on the block.

The Fosters had come here from somewhere in the Midwest—Iowa, Kansas?—nearly twenty-five years ago when the old man retired. He'd run a machine of some kind in a factory. Talking with him, you knew he'd run it the very best he knew how, never been a minute late for work, and been pointed out as an example to wayward youths. He'd said once to Brenda that he'd been on his own since he was fourteen, working. He might have had six or seven years of education. He was a tall, very thin old man, bent with arthritis and getting a little deaf, and his false teeth fit badly so that he slurred his words for hanging on to them; but he had a dry, rusty sense of humor. He liked people to call him Clyde instead of Mr. Foster.

"One thing about gettin' old," he'd said to Brenda, "and outlivin' everybody your own age—nobody left to call you by your own name. Y'know? A lot o' folks younger, they figure it don't sound exactly right, call an old codger eighty-seven by his given name. But it's one o' the things you notice, know what I mean?—bein' just Mister to everybody."

It was a thing she'd never thought about, but she understood how he felt. It must seem odd. To most of the people she knew, she was Brenda; it would seem strange, nobody left to use her name—to be just Miss Sheldon.

Mabel Foster was eighty-eight, and she shared her husband's sly little humor. "Never caught up t' me yet, all these years," she'd say, her little dark eyes twinkling. "Comes December, he gets to be as old as me, but right off next April I get ahead of him again. He was right put out when he found I had nearly a year on him—didn't let him know till we was married, I didn't!"

Mabel was a little, round, cheerful woman, probably very pretty once. You could guess that before she'd had arthritis, she'd been quick at everything, and neat, and particular. She'd graduated from sixth grade, she confided to Brenda, back in 1887. She was twelve, and worked as a maid before she married Clyde Foster.

She'd started to have the arthritis six or seven years ago, and it had, as she put it, slowed her down some. But she could still get about the house, get the meals and keep the place dusted. Mr. MacFarlane, who owned the hardware store, had fixed a ramp down from the back steps of their house so she could get out in the yard to hang up her laundry. The new automatic washer had been a real godsend.

Mr. MacFarlane had told Brenda about that. He shook his head over it—a very remarkable thing that they'd managed to save up so much money, just on the state pension. But they were thrifty, careful people. "If you'll believe me, they live on the one pension check and put the other one in the bank every month. It must take some damn close figuring, you know—taxes up too, the last couple of years—but they make do on that. Kind of a lesson to us all."

Brenda agreed. California paid the highest old-age pension of any state, but even so, eighty-nine dollars a month wasn't much for two people to live on in the sixties.

"He asked me to go with him when he got the washer; he

doesn't know much about business of any kind." MacFarlane chuckled. "Said he'd count on me to see he didn't get cheated. They're funny old souls, but you kind of have to admire 'em. Independent, you know."

That they were, and there was all too little of that around these days. They could have gone to one of the county medical clinics, but old Mr. Foster said sturdily he didn't hold with taking charity while he could still pay his just debts. Besides, he'd rather pick his own doctor. So as little things came up, Mrs. Foster's arthritis worse, or one of them coming down with flu, they'd gone (Mrs. Hawkins said) to young Dr. Clarke over on Dewey Street. But he'd recently moved away, and Dr. Robertson had taken his office. They didn't like Dr. Robertson much; he wasn't much interested in old people.

The Fosters had been young, they had known all the young things in life, when every feeling was new and exciting— they had loved, and made love, and had fine plans and hopes; and things had changed, life had changed, for them together. Once they had hoped for children, sons and daughters to raise and see married and having children of their own—and to look after them in turn as they grew older. It hadn't happened that way. They had gone along, humdrum, happy enough, pleased with small joys, expecting little, for long years; and in the end it had come to this, a little house bought with savings and a small legacy from a bachelor uncle—and the old-age-pension checks.

They were simple people; you could call them ignorant people. But did it make all that much difference (when you came to think of it), the good or bad grammar, the book-knowledge, the job—at that end of life? Simple people, through no fault or intention, alone.

Brenda thought wryly that it would be easy for a psychiatrist to explain her feeling of sympathy for old Mr. and Mrs. Foster. All association—selfish association. An only child, her parents killed in an accident, she'd been brought up by her grandmother, dear Gran Kilpatrick.

It had been five weeks ago that Mr. Foster had the stroke. ...Everybody who knew them had been saying for some time that if one should go, the other couldn't possibly carry on alone. They had to help each other in almost every way. They had the county nurse in once a week—you didn't have to pay for that unless you could: They did. She would give Mrs. Foster a bath and straighten up the house a bit. They managed as best they could. Their own little house, a painfully accumulated bank account. The privately paid doctor. The penurious grocery bills—never more than seven or eight dollars a week, said Mrs. Cass, who drove Mr. Foster to the nearest supermarket on Saturdays. Whatever Mrs. Foster couldn't do, Mr. Foster managing somehow. One of the pension checks put away safe in the bank each month, toward the taxes and the medical bills and any little luxuries... "It's all I can do to keep myself from it," Mrs. Cass had said to Brenda. Mrs. Cass was a transplanted English countrywoman, and in moments of emotion her accent thickened into the lush North Country dialect of her childhood, "All I can *do*. They do like their liddle fresh oranges that much, you know—and times, they'll be up a penny or two a pound, and the old man shaking his head and saying, Too dear. I'd dearly love to say, Oh, do have them, I'll pay the difference! But they're that proud, you know." Her three chins had quivered and her vast bosom heaved. "What can you *do*?"

What indeed. But they had saved enough, just this year, to buy a small portable television. They so enjoyed the old movies, and that awful western thing....

Inevitably, she thought—when she heard about Mr. Foster's stroke—inevitably, in the minds of everyone who has anything to do with the Fosters now, there will be a faintly impatient overtone. They had gone on living *too* long.

17

You seemed to be here for an appointed time, reason or no reason. Those who survived incredible dangers, in war and so on, and then slipped on a wet pavement or something... Not that she was so terribly religious, but there seemed to be a kind of rule about it.

And were you to blame, did you suffer any less, if you went on tediously living to be ninety? Even alone and poor?

2

Mr. Foster had his stroke on a Wednesday. In the next few days, most of the neighbors had called, as well as Mr. MacFarlane, Mrs. Cass, Jacqueline Devereaux, Mr. Purdy from the dairy store, and Mr. Da Silva from the little grocery.

Brenda went to see Mrs. Foster on Thursday evening; and by then the old lady was realizing that they couldn't go on like this, with just the county nursing service.

She looked older, and sad, but also reconciled. Perhaps at eighty-eight you lived so close to death that it didn't seem so frightening or shocking. Yes, of course the Fosters had known that this day was inevitable too.

She rocked a little in the shabby old platform rocker opposite the love seat, and her small mouth drooped. "I know it's best it should be Clyde first. He'd be just awful helpless, alone."

Brenda said nothing.

"Well," said the old woman, gaving a sharp little sigh. "O' course he's still hanging on. Doctor came this morning. But—I'm not afraid to say, tell the truth an' shame the devil—better for him if he wouldn't, if he'd just slip away like. You know.

He'd be mostly helpless, and need a nurse by him all the time. And that'd mean the General Hospital, I guess, or a county home. Neither Clyde or me ever fancied a home like that." And because that was true, and there was nothing to say about it, Brenda was silent. "But whichever way," said Mrs. Foster, "it'll mean a change. I come to see that." She looked around the little living room and sighed again.

The only new things in the room were the ugly little blond-finished television and the carpet, a blinding-bright cheap American Oriental pattern. There was the late-Victorian "set" they had probably got when they were married—love seat and two chairs, the gentleman's and the lady's; originally horsehair-upholstered, now in a faded tapestry. There was the platform rocker, and a couple of straight cane-seated chairs, remnants of a dining set, and a marred marble-topped table with a cheap ceramic lamp on it. There was an old-fashioned floor lamp. A too-colorful lithograph of a farm scene, framed ornately in gilt, hung over the love seat, and a charming old banjo wall clock over the table. The walls were papered in a bright blue-and-pink flower pattern. It was an ugly room, and Brenda could guess how bare and ugly the bedrooms would be: very likely brass bedsteads, sagging mattresses, cheap painted chests. But these were the old woman's things, making up her home, and she was seeing them taken away from her. Seeing herself taken away, for some unknown new place. For, as she said, whether the old man lived or died, this meant change.

She did not ask for pity, or grieve aloud; she just rocked a little, her eyes sad, and looked at her familiar things. She said everybody had been nice and kind.

"Coming in, and all. Not that there's much anybody can do. Mrs. Cass was real nice, we had a long talk. I hadn't paid all that much notice, you know—Clyde always took care of the bank business and all—but she did make me see, we can't afford the county nurses." The nurse had tactfully removed herself to her patient. "It means three of 'em a day, you see, and we can't noways afford it. There's a bit over a thousand in the bank, but—"

And Brenda thought ruefully, more than I have. How had they managed it? The automatic saving and scrimping, because they'd always had to be careful.

"I won't have Clyde in the hospital. If he's going to die, he'll die at home, where he wants to be. And that's that. And 'twouldn't make any difference really, you know, Miss Sheldon—because if they took him off to the hospital, why, I'd need somebody here just the same, to help me. There's things I can't do. No, Mrs. Cass said what we'd best do is find a practical nurse who'd come and live in and look after us both—till we know...I can still get the meals, it's just till—"

"Yes," Brenda interrupted, "I expect that's the thing to do. But it's not so easy to find a good practical nurse."

"Mrs. Cass said she'd have a look around. Sometimes they advertise in the paper, she said, and there's a kind of agency too."

It was the sensible thing to do, until the old man died or recovered as far as he could.

Brenda received a daily report from Mrs. Hawkins, who usually went up to the neighborhood shops once a day. Evidently Mrs. Cass was having no luck locating a practical nurse; the county nurses were still with the old man, up to that Saturday.

On Saturday night, Brenda went out for the second time with Leonard Bristol, who was assistant personnel manager at a local department store. Again, she told herself that she liked him all right; he was, well, all right. He was thirty-four, and in spite of a slightly receding hairline, not bad-looking. His manners were good, and he gave her that just-slightly-too-attentive courtesy that betrayed real interest. He took her to a good restaurant, and a new play that had received flattering reviews. She felt a little ashamed to notice that he had a very broad sense of humor, and missed a couple of literary allusions.... Funny, she thought, looking into the mirror in the bathroom as she creamed her face, how life never quite measured up to expectations. She was reasonably good-looking, she was still young, she wasn't hiding herself away in a job where she never met men, but somehow no one had ever come along who was worth much interest or attention. Am I too particular? she wondered. Probably. Anyway, she told her cold-creamed face defiantly, she wasn't going to take one like Leonard Bristol just to have a husband.

Especially one like Leonard.

The interesting ones had all gone away somewhere apparently, or were already married. She thought about Mary Fernald. It didn't seem fair, somehow—not only a successful writer but pretty. Very pretty, and unfairly having quite a lot of brains too. That matte-white skin and jade-green eyes. Going around with that police officer on the Santa Monica force, a plainclothes detective. Brenda had never met him, but she'd seen him once. The first time she'd been out with Leonard, there'd been Mary across the big main room of the Fox and Hounds. And Loretta had said Mary wasn't dating anybody but her policeman these days. He didn't look the way you'd expect, but good-looking, in a scholarly, intelligent sort of way. Tall and dark, and his face came alive when he laughed. Of course, as per the old saying, looks weren't everything. A man could be interesting in other ways. She wondered how it would feel, having a policeman as a husband.

She hoped (as always) to sleep late on Sunday, but (as always) was awakened at seven o'clock by the Websters' old dog demanding breakfast. She lay in bed awhile thinking lazily about Leonard Bristol. Then she got up and started water boiling for coffee. Sometime today, she thought, she must mend that slip, and wash a couple of blouses, and do her nails....

In the afternoon, on the way to the drugstore for nail-polish remover, she stopped at the Fosters' and found Mrs. Cass there. Mrs. Cass was very pleased with herself. She had found a practical nurse.

"She's to come tomorrow. Only seventy-five a month, and she's experienced, a nice motherly soul she looked." No, there wasn't much change in Mr. Foster's condition; he was a little weaker. "He's not eating, you know. But that's only to be expected."

Probably, thought Brenda, in the hospital he'd be having intravenous feeding by now: all the modern rigmarole, to keep his tired old body alive a little longer—for what? Mrs. Foster said little, rocking and looking depressed. "It'll be easier about the money," she said, "no question. What was it you said her name is?"

"Slaney," said Mrs. Cass. "Mrs. Josephine Slaney. I'm that pleased to have found her. You'll like her, Mrs. Foster. She's a bit of a diamond in the rough, as they say, but nice and kind."

"I hope so," said the old lady. "It was nice of you to go to the trouble."

The practical nurse came on Monday morning. Brenda, walking up toward Lincoln at eight-thirty, saw the strange car parked in the Fosters' driveway, a two-door blue Ford about ten years old, looking as if it had seen hard usage. She thought, I hope she's kind, I hope she's good to them.

She didn't meet the woman for nearly a week. She was tired when she got home, had things to do, and she knew other people were being kind to the Fosters, dropping in, offering to do shopping, bringing small gifts—a cake, cookies. But the following Sunday, her conscience pricked her and she walked up the block in the afternoon.

The Ford was in the driveway. The grass was brown and tall, neglected: the rosebushes bore many dead blooms. Already

23

the place looked shabby. She pushed the bell, and was a little startled at the promptness with which the door opened.

"Oh— I just called to ask how Mr. Foster is, and if Mrs. Foster—"

"She'll be pleased for a little company, come in! We was just havin' a nice glass o' iced tea, dearie, plenty left for visitors!" The door swung open invitingly. "Haven't seen you before, have I? I'm Mis' Slaney—pleased t' meet you—beg pardon? Miss Sheldon—come right in." And there was Mrs. Foster in her rocker, dressed in a neat clean housedress, her sparse white hair combed, smiling and nodding at Brenda.

"It's nice of you to drop by, sit down. Clyde, he's about the same. Only getting a lot weaker, nurse says. I guess we're that lucky, have Mrs. Slaney to look after us."

Brenda looked at the nurse. She was bustling about, fetching another glass, stirring the ice in the pitcher, proffering a plate of cookies. "You like a little lemon, dear? Sure?" She was an immensely fat woman, but not soft; every inch of her looked firm and solid as rock. She might be fifty-five; she had a lot of rather obviously dyed black hair, and a round florid cheerful face with little round cheerful blue eyes and a rosebud mouth. She looked jolly and, as Mrs. Cass had said, motherly, and very competent.

"Oh, we're making out," she said, beaming at Brenda as she sat down opposite her. "We're getting on fine, aren't we, dear?" She beamed at Mrs. Foster.

The old lady gave her a faint smile. "That's right. Nobody needs to fuss that we're not getting took care of."

"Even if you will keep on doin' too much, all the cookin'." Mrs. Slaney's hearty laugh echoed in the little room. "What I'm here for, take care o' you!"

"Oh, well, you've got plenty to do, with Clyde," said Mrs. Foster. "I know that. I like to keep busy as I can, that's all."

"Hafta get a collar an' chain for you, honey, you try to do

too much. But I must say, Miss Sheldon, all the neighbors been just awful nice—comin' by, bringin' cakes and so on. I say to Mis' Foster, they sure do spoil her!"

"Folks have been kind," said Mrs. Foster.

"Well," said Brenda awkwardly, "you know we're all so sorry, and—"

"That's right," said Mrs. Slaney heartily. "A lot o' friends you got, dear. Take another cookie, Miss Sheldon, they're just fresh baked."

"Folks have been kind," repeated Mrs. Foster quietly. "But I'm just sorry it's being so long—for Clyde. He wouldn't want it like this. Just lying there helpless, and not knowing me or anybody. We always did hope it'd be quick, for both of us."

"Now you don't want to fret, dear," said the nurse. "It's no good a-tall, the Good Lord knows best like I'm always tellin' you, you got to trust in Him. I got a boy's a minister," she added to Brenda with pride, "and he's forever remindin' me of *that*. You know, Miss Sheldon, little things goin' wrong, bills comin' in, and you say, drat it anyways! But my Jason, he always says, Ma, don't you quarrel with what the Lord sends you. His way is best, and you'd best just go along with it. He's ordained, you know, but he hasn't got no church of his own yet. You like a li'l more ice in your glass, dear?"

"No, this is fine."

"They say maybe next year he'll have his own church. It's the Church of the Enlightened Believers he belongs to, they all useta be Holy Brethren but they had a fight with that preacher, see. I don't mind sayin' I'm right proud of Jason, Miss Sheldon."

"Of course, you must be."

"He's a smart boy. I never had much schooling myself, make no bones about it, but Jason's dad, the late Mr. Slaney, he went through high school. Take another cookie, do."

"Oh, no, thank you." Brenda stood up and began to make polite farewells.

Certainly a rough diamond, she thought walking home, but apparently a jewel, polished or not. Mrs. Foster neat, clean, cared for; the room tidy and dusted. Probably she gave the old man as good care. And she'd be sleeping on the couch (that enormous bulk!) or perhaps with Mrs. Foster in the second bedroom? For seventy-five a month it seemed too good to be true. Brenda had had a vague idea that practical nurses expected a good deal more than that now. The woman could earn far more at other, easier jobs, but maybe she just liked nursing. The Fosters were lucky to have Mrs. Slaney, for all her dearies and honeys and hearty ignorance.

She forgot that, thinking of what Mrs. Foster had said, so quiet in her dignified grief. *He wouldn't want it like this.... We always did hope it'd be quick....*

But things happened the way they happened.

Mr. Foster had had his stroke on the twentieth of August. He lingered on for nearly three weeks, eating practically nothing and growing progressively weaker. But he was well cared for by the practical nurse; despite her girth she was a hard worker, and kept him clean and comfortable, kept the house immaculate and old Mrs. Foster as comfortable and cheerful as might be. Everyone agreed that she was a jewel. They were lucky to have her.

On the twelfth of September, with the summer reaching its worst heat and Brenda's third date with Leonard Bristol coming up (why on earth had she accepted?), old Mr. Foster died.

There were perhaps five people who were genuinely concerned—who really grieved—other than his wife. Brenda, because in a way it brought back her Gran's death, dear indomitable cynical Gran. Jacqueline Devereaux, because she was a lonely woman and understood loneliness. Mrs. Janet Cass, because she was a sentimental, loving woman with a large sympathetic heart. Mrs. Hawkins, because she was very simply sorry for Mrs. Foster. And old Mr. Da Silva of the little grocery, because he and Clyde Foster had been much of an age, and had liked each other.

Everyone else said warmly, I'm *so* sorry, the poor old man— and poor old Mrs. Foster!—and forgot about it. They *were* sorry, but inevitably they thought too, Well, eighty-seven . . . a good age . . . pity the old lady will have to go into a rest home now, but people that old—.

Inevitable. Of course.

No one could say, afterward, exactly when the practical nurse began to change.

Up to the time of Mr. Foster's death, everyone agreed that she was wonderful. She was that phenomenon, a genuinely un-selfish, generous person. No one thought it was very odd that she should take it on herself to make the funeral arrangements. The Fosters had no relatives and obviously Mrs. Foster wasn't up it. George Hawkins went to volunteer ("least we can do") and found the matter already in Mrs. Slaney's large capable hands.

Brenda attended the funeral, mostly because she knew there wouldn't be many people there. Several of the oldest neighbors could no longer drive; others, younger, would not take time off from work. It was at the funeral that she felt the first faint warning hunch of (how to put it?) Something Wrong.

It might have been the hasty, impersonal funeral of an unknown buried in potter's field. There were only three wreaths, and no music, and no minister—only a brief reading from Psalms by an unctuous undertaker's assistant.

That was another thing there'd been some talk about. The

Fosters, in the days when they could get out and about, had been faithful attendants at the same church every Sunday for years. They'd managed it only very occasionally the last few years, but all during Mr. Foster's illness, not one soul from their church had come near them, not even the minister. It was a large church, yes, with a large membership, but you'd think— Disgraceful had been Mrs. Hawkins's word for it, and so it was. These good Christians...

It was probably the cheapest funeral on the undertaker's list; and there could be reason for that too—there was, of course, very little money, but—

Mrs. Foster was not there. That bothered Brenda. Mrs. Hawkins, beside her, whispered, "She's just too dazed and shocked and weak, the nurse said. Even when she knew it was coming. You know how it'd be. Old and frail like she is. Mrs. Slaney said to me, she wouldn't take the risk of her having a stroke, trying to bring her today. Just a terrible ordeal."

And that might sound plausible in a way, but, Brenda thought, the Fosters had been old-fashioned religious. Simple-orthodox religious. Mrs. Foster's weakness hadn't affected her mind; she was thinking and feeling as she always had, just a little slower. Brenda thought that to a person like Mabel Foster—old-fashioned, simple—the idea of staying away from her husband's funeral would be shocking.

Or—? She had been reconciled to his death; she had accepted it. Even so, it would have been a shock after all those long years together. And she was so old. People had said wisely that she probably wouldn't last long now. With old folk like that, when one went, the other wasn't long following. The shock, and the prospect of change, might have taken some of her well-preserved faculties from her.

But, Brenda thought...

No one could say, exactly, how soon after that the nurse changed.

It was not at all obvious. She was as hearty and friendly as ever to everyone.... Only, said Mrs. Hawkins to Brenda the week after the funeral, nobody was getting in to see Mrs. Foster anymore. Not at all.

People talked; quite a few of the neighbors were in those little shops three or four times a week, and Mrs. Cass and Miss Devereaux, even in business hours, wandered down to the drugstore for ice cream or coffee—and gossip.

Mrs. Hawkins retailed it all to Brenda.

"What it comes down to, seems like she's keeping people out on purpose. I mean, you know, you can't tell *me*—and Mrs. Cass said the same thing—anybody as bright as Mrs. Foster, even at her age, is goin' to go downhill overnight, to get senile. It wouldn't be natural. You know how she was talking, before the old man died—sensible as you please. But comparing notes like, that's how it looks the nurse is making out. Mrs. Cass went up on Tuesday, and there's a little note on the door, PLEASE DO NOT RING BELL. So she goes to the back door, to catch Mrs. Slaney and ask how Mrs. Foster is, you know. And she sees her, and the nurse says the whole thing's been such a shock to poor Mrs. Foster, she's not right in herself at all, needs a lot of rest and so on, and she's sleeping right now so Mrs. Cass better not come in and wake her up. And Miss Devereaux, next day, she gets the same story. And so do *I*, when I went up with an angel-food I baked special. Nice as pie, the nurse is, but you don't get in, see? As far's we can make out, nobody's got in to see Mrs. Foster since the funeral."

Which did indeed seem a trifle—just a trifle—odd. But of course it could be true, that the shock of her loss and the threat of change had, overnight, reduced brave old Mrs. Foster to something less than she had been.

The nurse, so very friendly and welcoming, before. Brenda, who liked detective novels, thought suddenly, Creating the good impression?

She then thought blankly, But why? For what conceivable reason? What was there to get out of old Mrs. Foster, who now had only one eighty-nine-dollar check a month, to live on? Out of that, she couldn't pay the nurse's seventy-five and have enough left for herself. She'd have to dismiss the nurse and go to a county rest home.

Yet the nurse stayed on. Every day, the blue Ford was seen sitting in the drive.

Impotently, not quite meaninglessly, the talk rose among those who were friendly to Mrs. Foster. Brenda heard it from Mrs. Hawkins, from Mr. Purdy, and at the drugstore.

The nurse was keeping everybody from seeing Mrs. Foster. There was that sign over the doorbell all the time. If you did ring the bell, there was the jolly fat nurse saying, She's napping, but I'll tell her you called. And, Thank you for the cake, or the ice cream. What was it all about? Why should she stay on? But then Jacqueline Devereaux did get in; she was persistent and pushed her way in, and there was Mrs. Foster lying on the couch and talking (she said) very vaguely, asking about the funeral. Not at all like her old self.

Well, that happened, Brenda thought. People as old as that, they deteriorated rapidly sometimes under shock, or change, or for no reason. . . . But Miss Devereaux said no. She'd done some practical nursing herself, she said, and she knew a person under sedation when she saw one. That nurse was keeping the old lady half under with some kind of drug, she said.

Brenda was interested and concerned enough to try to see Mrs. Foster herself.

She walked up the block on a Saturday afternoon. There was the sign; PLEASE DO NOT RING BELL. She rang it defiantly; bringing the nurse to open the door.

She was vast, beaming, red-faced; she said at once, "Why, Miss Sheldon. It's right nice of you to call, but if you'll excuse it I won't ask you in. Poor old dear's just dropped off to sleep—

I hadda give her one o' the doctor's pills. She's gone down sadly since The Death, you know. Old folk like that, they will."

"I just wondered how she was getting on," said Brenda. She looked at the woman through the screen door. She could see into the living room dimly; no sign of Mrs. Foster.

"Oh, as you might expect, way I say," said Mrs. Slaney cheerfully. "Poor old dear, wish I could do more for her."

"I'm sure you're giving her good care," said Brenda; and in the September heat felt gooseflesh.... For she realized suddenly that though the rosebud mouth turned up in a jolly friendly smile, and the fat cheeks creased with it, there was no emotion in the tiny pig's eyes at all. Not even coldness; just nothing.

She came away convinced that the woman was up to something; but what? Mrs. Foster couldn't afford to pay her now. What with the doctor's bill, medicine, the funeral expenses, that bank account must have dwindled in this time. Why was the nurse staying on? She was up to something. A thankless job, even for three times the wages, taking care of an old invalid woman...

That night, meeting Mary Fernald at the Cheyneys' party, she told her about it; possibly Mary's policeman might offer advice. And what Mary told her—no reason to investigate—well, she could see that legally they'd need something more to go on, but it seemed wrong somehow just to sit back and do nothing.

By now, only a few people were taking any active interest in old Mrs. Foster. Out of sight, out of mind. George Hawkins said, "Oh, talk, talk, talk! What the hell harm can the woman do? Maybe she just likes old folks, feels sorry for them. You ought to be thankful she *is* staying on—way you was all saying before, how terrible for the old lady, have to go in a home."

"But nobody's seeing her, George. Why, that Slaney woman might be doing anything to her, from what Miss Devereaux said."

"Don't be a fool, woman. What for? She took real good care of her before, didn't she? So Miss Devereaux says the nurse was giving her drugs—maybe the doctor prescribed 'em."

Which of course was quite true.

He said another thing, too, which probably others were saying. "Look, if there *is* any funny business, well, it's got nothing to do with us, and we'd be fools, stick our necks out—maybe get her suing us or something."

Everybody had their own business to think of. Mrs. Cass went on trying to see Mrs. Foster, as did Jacqueline Devereaux; and a few people went on talking about it. They all agreed that it was a puzzling thing, but nobody did anything about it. What could anybody do? And who wanted—in George Hawkins's phrase—to stick his neck out?

Brenda, after rumination on what Mary had said, called a lawyer she knew: the one who'd drawn up Gran's will and had been a friend of Brenda's father. She explained the situation to him and asked his opinion. "I don't know what the woman's up to, but I'd swear *something*. The poor old thing, she's got so little— I still think the Welfare Board would do something."

"About what? On what evidence?" asked Mr. Whitney. "If the old woman's in possession of her faculties—"

"She certainly was," said Brenda cautiously, "the last time I saw her." She was remembering what Miss Deveraux had said.

"Yes—well, in that case, if *she's* making no complaint, no one else has the right to step in and do so. Even if you had much more evidence than you have that the nurse is up to something."

"But, Mr. Whitney, surely you can see how odd it looks—"

"Certainly," said the lawyer. "It's pretty obvious what's going on. The nurse has got your old lady completely sold on her, and she's working on her to hand over everything she's got."

Dell Shannon

"But she hasn't got anything!"

"You said something about a house? They owned it?"

"Of course, I'm a fool," said Brenda slowly. "Why didn't we think of that? The house. Yes, they did—do—own it. I'm sure there isn't a mortgage. Mr. Foster told me once they'd bought it with a little legacy left to his wife. Real-estate values were awfully low then, you know. I think he said it was only a little over three thousand. Now I suppose it'd be worth, oh, at least ten—maybe more."

"And it was probably held as community property," said Mr. Whitney, "so it passed to her automatically on his death. She could sign it over, or sign a power of attorney, at any time, and the nurse could take everything legally. It'd be very hard to prove undue influence. You said there are no relatives at all. No outsider, or even a friend, would care to stick his or her neck out and get involved in a legal hassle that'd cost money, on a deal like that. I'll tell you the only thing anybody could do. Go down to the Public Administrator's office and try to get the old woman declared incompetent. If you did that, you'd have to sign an agreement that you'd be entirely responsible for her in all ways. Then you could get rid of the nurse."

"I see," said Brenda. Of course nobody—not in the circumstances all of those concerned were in—would be willing to do that. Sorry as these people felt for Mrs. Foster, none of them could afford to do that. And if that was the situation, Mrs. Foster trusting the nurse so implicitly, she would scarcely appreciate it if anyone did.

"The contents of the house would be worth something too," he said absently, and suddenly added, "There's just one point—if either of them was ever in the General Hospital as a charity patient, there'd be a lien on the house until a nominal fee was paid. In that case, the old lady couldn't legally sign it over."

"There isn't," said Brenda bitterly. "They were very proud

34

of not taking charity. Always went to a private doctor." That was something else suddenly in her mind. This Dr. Robertson, who wasn't much interested in old people...Mrs. Cass had been quite indignant, and with good reason. When Mr. Foster had had his stroke, Dr. Robertson had at first refused to come to the house. Only after Mrs. Foster had called Mrs. Cass, and Mrs. Cass had gone to his office and argued with him, did he come. Afterward, he'd only come two or three times, leaving it all up to the nurses. Consequently, thought Brenda now, he probably was not attending Mrs. Foster—probably no doctor was; and Mrs. Slaney could indeed be doing anything she pleased. What Miss Deveraux had said—was the nurse keeping her under constant sedation, something like that?

"Mr. Whitney? If that happened—her signing over the house, or a power of attorney—and she was under sedation at the time, well, isn't that illegal?"

"It certainly would be, but it'd be very hard to prove after the fact, you know. The nurse is preventing anyone who knows her from seeing her, so you'd have no opportunity of judging. Quite a nice little racket, isn't it? Something over ten thousand, for a few weeks' work. And no legal way to touch her. I'll bet this isn't the first time your Mrs. Slaney has worked a little deal like this. I'll bet it's a regular racket with her. The ordinary person wouldn't stop to think about it, but there must be thousands of old people around with no relatives to reckon with. The pensioners—you know how they flock here because of the high pension. When you try to divert really big money into your own pocket, there's always somebody to raise a row—trustees, lawyers, interested parties—but pick people like your old lady, with anything from a few hundred to a few thousand, and no relations—well, who's going to get involved just out of altruism? Quite a little racket," he repeated almost admiringly. "You think about it, even pensioners like that—even those not as careful as your old lady—there'd be pickings to be had. Some of them

35

would own little cheap houses like this one. There'd be a little savings, maybe old jewelry, furniture—and everything'd be grist to this nurse's mill. This case, she might only get five hundred or so, that case, a thousand—I'll bet this represents a sizable killing for her. Quite an ingenious racket."

"And what would she do *then?* When she'd got it?"

"Oh, that'd be easy. Tell the truth to the Welfare Board. Indigent pensioner, no relations. And the board would stick the old lady or gent into one of the county homes where they're looked after for the eighty-nine a month. So what if the pensioner complained, said Nursie'd promised to take care of 'em for the life savings and so on? Nursie'd just smile benignly and say the poor old folk were senile. With the number of old people the board's got to look after, who's going to investigate?"

Brenda felt a little sick after thanking him and hanging up. Nice old Mrs. Foster, to end like that—after all their planning and saving. Like a lot of old people with her lack of education, she wouldn't know much about what she'd call "business things." Trusting in the nurse, she'd sign where she was told.

And those nursing homes—there were standards, they were inspected in theory; but the proprietors knew the inspection days and could have everything slicked up. So easy, if a patient complained to an outsider, to say, Oh, she's senile, doesn't know what she's talking about. The old people crowded in together, cheap communal meals, a minimum of personal possessions allowed...

Everybody saying, What a pity and How terrible, but nobody wanting to stick their necks out.

Well, damn it, thought Brenda, sometimes you had to stick your neck out, to stay by any principles you owned.

She sat down and thought. In spite of what Mr. Whitney had said, she thought that if it could be shown that this—this jolly nurse had worked this racket a number of times before, the police would be interested. No legal offense: but there ought to be some way to stop her. In the past, legal loopholes had been spotted and sealed up because some situation like this had been publicized. Meanwhile the police might—what was the phrase?—lean on her a little, let her know she was being watched. Maybe.

How many helpless, trusting old people had she robbed this way?, Brenda thought.

Brenda made a little plan. It wasn't a very good plan, she knew, but the only one that had occurred to her at the time. On the next Saturday afternoon she determinedly started out for the Foster house. She intended to get in and feed the nurse the most fulsome flattery she could manage—how wonderful a nurse she was, how sympathetic to these poor old people, and so on—and try to get her chatting and make some mention of other cases she'd had, and where. If she did, then Brenda could do a little detective work tracing those other cases, looking for similarities.

In spite of her sympathy for Mrs. Foster and her indignation at this racket, Brenda felt rather excited. This was going to be—in a way—fun. Brenda Sheldon, girl detective, she thought.

When she got to the house and turned up the front walk, she noticed the Ford in the driveway and another, newer car in front of the house. As she pushed the bell, beyond the obscuring screen door she could vaguely make out several people moving in the living room.

A man's voice, colorless and formal, said, "That finishes it, then. . . . Thank you. I'll see that it's filed—"

The nurse's vast bulk appeared behind the screen. She smiled her jolly smile at Brenda (the little eyes quite empty). "Why, how-do, Miss Sheldon."

"Hello, Mrs. Slaney. May I come in to see Mrs. Foster? How is she? You know, I do think you've given her such wonderful care and been so good to her—" Brenda forced herself to return the smile.

"Oh, well, now," said the nurse, "it's not every young girl like you'd spare the time or thought for an old woman—long as we're exchangin' compliments," and she laughed, showing her dentures. "We're just finishin' up a li'l business, but come right in, sure—old lady glad to see you."

With a sinking heart, Brenda stepped into the small room. There was Mrs. Foster, in her platform rocker. There was a strange man, middle-aged, colorless as his voice, correctly dressed, just fastening a worn briefcase, and beside him a plain, tailored-looking woman with "secretary" written all over her. His gaze passed over Brenda uninterestedly.

"I think that takes care of everything then," he said to the nurse. "Very wise to get these matters legally straight before—um, yes. Good afternoon."

A lawyer, at least, Brenda thought. And he was out and gone, with the secretary—and Mrs. Slaney hadn't even called him by name, to hand her that much of a clue. She looked at Mrs. Foster.

The old woman was lying back in her rocker, her eyes vague and fixed. Brenda touched her shoulder. "Mrs. Foster?"

The eyes remained vague, trying to focus on her. "Oh, hello—I know you, just can't put a name to you, but—"

"I'm Brenda Sheldon, Mrs. Foster."

"Brenda—Brenda. Of course, child. Nice you come to see me—folks don't seem to drop by much anymore." Her voice was thick and slow. Brenda could have sworn she was on a drug of some kind.

The nurse was beckoning her in large gestures toward the kitchen door. Brenda went to her, was drawn into the kitchen. "You can see how the poor thing's failed," said Mrs. Slaney in a stage whisper. "It's a funny thing, but you'd be surprised how often it happens like that with old folks. Long as they're together, spry and chipper as you please; but let one be Taken, why, t'other seems to go downhill all of a piece, right off, you know. I can see you're that shocked, and no wonder. You just set with her a spell, while I get us some nice cold lemonade."

"Yes," said Brenda. She went back to the living room and drew a chair close to the rocker. "Mrs. Foster. Did you sign some papers just now?" She kept her voice low.

The vague eyes turned to her. "Papers—there was, yes. Where he put the cross, to sign. I—I always think, best get all these things done 'n' off your mind. Josephine said. I guess 'tis all for the best. I know you—know your pretty face, but I just couldn't say the name—"

"What kind of papers, Mrs. Foster? Was it a power of attorney? Was it the deed to the house?" Brenda's tone was insistent. The old woman only shook her head helplessly; and here was the nurse bustling in with a tray bearing glasses.

"Now this'll taste fine, won't it, dear—such a terrible hot day, and worse to come as we all know! Can you manage, dearie, or shall I hold the glass? *All* righty—that's fine!" She sat down with a thud of her big body and beamed at Brenda over her glass.

Brenda contrived to beam back at her and look idiotically ignorant at once. "Was that man a lawyer? I suppose about Mr. Foster's will, or was there one? I never heard."

"Just a li'l needful business," said Mrs. Slaney cryptically. "How you getting on, dearie? Here, better set that glass down a minute, if you find it a mite slippery. *That's* right."

Mrs. Foster suddenly sat up a little straighter and smiled at Brenda with the unselfconsciousness of a child. "Going to sell the house 'n' go live with Josephine," she said. "Our own little house—our own nice little house—but—things for certain bound to change—"

"That's right, dear," said the nurse, sipping lemonade noisily. "You like to do that, hey? Well, that's sure flattering, ain't it, Miss Sheldon?" She winked at Brenda. "Maybe we'll think about it."

"Going to sell the house 'n' go live with Josephine," said the old woman. "I'm tired—I'm so tired—"

"I think you better have a li'l nap." The nurse heaved herself up. "Had a bit too much excitement, didn't we? Come along, honey, we'll see you settled all comfy." She nodded and winked at Brenda over her shoulder as she guided the old woman toward the front bedroom.

Brenda stared at her lemonade grimly. It was all working out just as Mr. Whitney had foreseen.

Quite a little racket indeed.

If he was right—and a lawyer ought to know—the damned woman hadn't done one illegal thing.

Unless—

Unless it could be proved, *right now*, that Mrs. Foster was under the influence of drugs. Oh, God, and these days so many sedatives, sleeping pills, very volatile—and the old lady wouldn't need much, it would be out of her system so soon—

When the nurse came back, Brenda was on her feet. "I mustn't stay, I know you're busy—such a care—"

"Oh, now she's settled I—"

"No, no, really, I've just remembered I said I'd meet a friend at—" She got away, and ran up to Lincoln and down Lincoln. There was a doctor—Brandon, Landon—in the three-hundred block. Any doctor—get him to come and examine the old

41

woman— She was breathless when she got to the door and burst in.

A well-furnished anteroom. A well-dressed receptionist sat behind the desk.

"Please, is the doctor in?" she asked.

"I'm sorry, the doctor's never in on Saturday afternoons. If you'd like to make an appointment?"

"Oh, *damn!*" said Brenda. She turned and ran out. She pounded on up the boulevard, spotted another doctor's office on the second floor of an office building at the corner of Vernon, wasted time gasping up the stairs—he was out too. She limped on up the street. Down one block, two blocks—no M.D.s—to Dr. Robertson's office, round the corner on Dewey.

"The doctor's never in on Saturdays—if you'd like to make an appointment?"

Desperately she turned in to a drugstore. All the public phone booths were occupied. She waited, cursing impotently, fishing out the dime. She waited ten long minutes, and got a booth, and dialed her own doctor, Dr. Tanner.... "Please may I speak to the doctor at once, Miss Jeans, it's an emergency—"

"I'm so sorry. The doctor's in emergency surgery. Can't I help you?"

Brenda banged the receiver up and stepped out of the booth. She looked at her watch. Forty-five minutes, more, since she'd run out of that house. And very likely the dose (yes, apt to be a small one, just enough) had been given to Mrs. Foster some time ago, to last over the lawyer's visit. Probably too late now for any doctor to say—by the time one got to her.

"Where did you get her name?" she asked Mrs. Cass. She'd been waiting to ask the question for some time; informed of this new light on Mrs. Slaney's motives, Mrs. Cass had been emotionally voluble.

"To think I never saw that, and right up my own street

too, as you might say! The wickedness of it—and adding insult to injury that the law can't stop her somehow! *Wicked*—"

Brenda agreed. "And maybe the law could do something, you know. Mr. Whitney thinks this isn't the first time she's done such a thing—that it's a regular racket for her, you see. I thought if we could trace it back, maybe we'd find someplace she'd slipped up. On some other case, perhaps. Where did you find her, Mrs. Cass?"

Mrs. Cass, vast and beautifully dressed as always, uttered a little hiccuping snort as she wiped her eyes. "To *think* of— And I should think those places would be careful about who they recommend!" She sat up straighter at her desk, under the neatly framed real-estate license. "It was the county agency. First place to go, wasn't it? It's a county service, you know— practical nurses put themselves on the list there. There's never enough—two or three jobs for every nurse listed, the woman said. You can see how that'd be. I told her what kind of case it was, old people, and just then she hadn't a nurse free, but a few days later she called back and said this Mrs. Slaney was available, so I went to see her. And you know, Brenda, at first she seemed—oh, a rough diamond all right, but—"

"Yes, I know," said Brenda. "Where's the agency?"

"They have offices all over. The one here is in the County Health Building. What are you thinking of doing, Brenda?"

"I don't know, yet," admitted Brenda. "But *something*."

"I never heard of such a wicked, *evil* thing. That poor helpless old soul."

Brenda went away and ruminated. The first thing that occurred to her was that this seemed to indicate, contrary to what she'd previously thought, that the county service didn't screen its list of nurses. Even if it did, Brenda thought, what would show up on Josephine? They wouldn't look at her bank account. Very likely the demand was so great that they gratefully accepted all comers; probably if there was a complaint about a nurse,

43

that she was incompetent or something, she'd be dropped, but not otherwise. That implied, though, that it would be fairly easy to get information out of them, if they were so slapdash in their methods. One thing she felt, and it was contrary to all her instincts, was that it would be a waste of time, and more than that it might spoil any chance to discredit the woman, to let her know her little scheme was suspected. To tell tales on her to the agency, or anyone, with no proof at all, was technically slander.

Not the phone, she decided; personal contact was required. She changed into a frilly summer dress she'd regretted buying—not her sort of thing at all, but it made her look little-girlish and feminine—put on more rouge than usual and a couple of dangly costume bracelets, and walked up to Lincoln to catch the bus into town.

At the County Health Building she was directed to a small cubbyhole of an office and welcomed by a Miss Whistler, who was dowdy and angular, about forty-five. "You," said Miss Whistler acutely, "are looking for a practical nurse?"

Brenda giggled and batted her eyelashes at the woman. Sweet empty-headed li'l old femininity she hoped was the impression. "Well, not *exactly,* you see, I already *know* this nurse, and she seems just wonderful—she's one of your nurses from here, you know—and I think she's just the one for darling Grandma, but if you know what I *mean,* Mama's kind of suspicious and like that—taking somebody right into your own *home*—and we want to be *sure*—"

Miss Whistler floundered after her slowly. "Er—which of our nurses—?"

"Oh, Mrs. Slaney, Mrs. Josephine Slaney. I mean, Mama says if we could just talk to some *other* patient she'd had, just to be *sure.* If you could just tell us who she was with last."

"Mrs. Slaney is on a case now, I believe—"

"Oh, yes, but we'd just love to have her, if she turns out

to be the way we think, and maybe if we offered more— If you could just tell me a couple of names—"

"Well, it's not our usual procedure, Miss—Er. Really, I don't know—"

"But goodness, it's only *natural* we'd want to be *sure*— taking her into our own *home*—" She wore Miss Whistler down eventually by volubility, and got two names and addresses. One was in Ocean Park, one in Venice. She also got the information (once Miss Whistler gave in she was quite chatty) that those were two of only three cases the agency had sent Mrs. Slaney to; she'd been registered with them only a little over four months. She had turned down one case they had sent her to, after a day or so on it, because she'd come down with flu. She had said when she registered with them that she preferred elderly patients. I'll bet!, thought Brenda.

Not for the first time she regretted her car. It had been one of the last things to go; in California, a car was almost a necessity. But Gran's illness had been prolonged and expensive; it had (even with all the sacrifices made at the time) taken her over a year to pay off the hospital bill. She was saving for a car of her own now.

Well, there was Lillian. She was generous about lending hers when Brenda asked; of course Brenda hadn't asked often. And how unlikely that Lillian wouldn't be using it herself, on a nice October Sunday!

Nevertheless, she called and asked. Miraculously, Lillian said of course, she hadn't planned to go anywhere. "You're an *angel*," said Brenda fervently. "I'll come by for it about noon." The chances were, in the afternoon she'd find more people home than on Sunday morning.

The first address was that of a Mr. James Ferguson on Naval Street in Ocean Park. Brenda wandered around awhile looking for it. It was a down-at-heel street lined sparsely with old frame cottages in poor repair. The yards were neglected, most of the houses in need of paint. The one she wanted sat back farther from the street than the others; it was a slatternly-looking place, one front window broken. There was an aged Dodge pulled up into the front yard, with a pair of masculine legs in shorts protruding from underneath it. A little doubtfully, Brenda picked her way through the tall brown grass and pushed the doorbell. Its old-fashioned angry buzz brought a woman to the door. She was as slatternly as the house, scraggly, in a faded pink sundress, hair uncombed, her face weathered-looking.

"Mr. Ferguson? Never heard of him."

"But I was given this address—"

"Never heard— Oh, say now, wait a minute. *Ferguson*. Sure, I guess I do know, come to think. See, we just bought the house, couple-three months back, it was—"

"From Mr. Ferguson?"

"Oh, no, dear, from a Mis' Slaney. But I do recollect now, first time we see over it there's this poor shaky old guy all bundled up in blankets settin' in the corner, and Mis' Slaney, she did call him Mr. Ferguson. Says he's her patient. She was a nurse."

"Oh," said Brenda. "You didn't see him again?"

"Oh, no, dear. They move out 'n' we move in."

"Yes. So you don't know where I might find him?"

The woman laughed, shrill and high. "Nor nobody else, dear—he's dead. Died pretty soon after. How I happen know, this Mis' Slaney, she took over the mortgage onna house, so she's right here, collect, every month. An' ain't she a talker. Talk the hind leg offa mule, she would. She just happened mention her patient'd kicked off. Coupla months back it was."

Brenda stared at her. "I see," she said slowly. "Well, thanks anyway."

"This is a very interesting little story, Miss Sheldon," said Valentine.

"It's a very frightening sort of story," said Mary. "Those poor old people!"

Brenda, after her visit to the second address, had driven straight back to Lillian's to leave the car, gone home and called Mary. Could she meet Mary's policeman privately and tell him something? "Well, I suppose—" Mary had said cautiously. "He's taking me to dinner tonight. Meet us back here at, say, nine o'clock? What's it all about, Brenda?"

"I'll tell you when I see you." And she was telling her story now, to an interested audience. Mary's policeman, seen up close, looked more like a college professor than a cop. But at least he was paying attention and seemed to think what she had to say was worth listening to.

"But that's not all. I found the Venice address—a Mrs. Bella Hall—it was a six-family apartment, and the tenant I talked with knew her. A Mrs. Greenspan. She said Mrs. Hall had rented one of the apartments there—she was an old lady.

'Looked about ninety,' she said. She probably didn't have much, it's a shabby old place, and I asked the manager, the rent's only fifty-five. Anyway, Mrs. Greenspan said when Mrs. Hall got sick she had a practical nurse—she remembered the Slaney woman. Didn't like her. It was only a bit over two months ago, you know. And then Mrs. Hall died. By what she said, Mrs. Hall was the sort who didn't mix much, none of the other tenants knew her very well, so they didn't take all that much interest. But Mrs. Greenspan—she lives just across the hall from the apartment Mrs. Hall had—did say that she and a couple of others were surprised and thought it was 'sort of funny' when, the day after the funeral, Mrs. Slaney and this young man came and took away everything Mrs. Hall had owned. They had a small truck."

"A young man," said Valentine. "The son, maybe?"

"I don't know—she didn't know. She said he 'looked like one of them beatniks, with long hair and funny clothes.' And just because nobody had cared much about Mrs. Hall, you see, well, nobody thought it was funny enough to do anything about. Mrs. Greenspan said she did know—Mrs. Hall had told her once—she didn't have any relatives left. Mrs. Greenspan thought maybe Mrs. Hall had left all her things to her nurse. She said it wasn't very much, a few sticks of furniture."

"Let's not be too hasty with our few sticks of furniture," said Valentine. "The woman had something, when she was paying rent, even fifty-five a month. Did Mrs. Greenspan say anything about a monthly check, anything like that? In a place like that, the neighbors can be nosy."

Brenda shook her head. "They didn't know where Mrs. Hall's money came from. The only thing she said was, Mrs. Hall had said something once about her husband leaving her enough to live on."

"Oh, really," said Valentine. "Well, money's got to come

from somewhere." He lit another cigarette. "That might imply quite a windfall for Josephine. Of course, Mrs. Hall might have been living on capital. But also the capital might have been invested. And in that case—paying fifty-five for rent—I'd deduce a capital sum that'd bring her in at least a hundred and a quarter, hundred and fifty a month. That would be somewhere in the neighborhood of—what?—have to be twenty-five, thirty thousand. In five percent common stock, say. A very nice little windfall for anybody. Of course, might not have been—might have been a lump sum of insurance money. But even so, something. Did she die there or in the hospital?"

"There," said Brenda. "Mrs. Greenspan said Mrs. Del Valle downstairs was superstitious about a death in the house and 'carried on awful.' "

"Um. Doctor in attendance?"

"Yes, a Dr. Lawrence, she heard the Slaney woman call him by name once."

"But," said Valentine dreamily, "who—even a doctor—would be much surprised at the death of somebody seventy-five, eighty? 'I'm all o'er-sib to Adam's breed—' "

(" 'Tomlinson,' " said Mary automatically).

"By the time we get that far along, practically all of us have some serious chronic trouble. High blood pressure, heart condition, asthma—and it often doesn't take much to carry off somebody old and frail. I can think of several possibilities. Just withholding some necessary medication—"

They were both staring at him in surprised consternation. "Dan, you can't be thinking—! There's no evidence that—"

"Oh, no!" cried Brenda.

"I know I've got an imagination. No, there's no evidence. I may be woolgathering, probably am. Don't look so upset, Miss Sheldon."

"*Upset!*" said Brenda. "If I thought for one minute you

49

were right about *that!* But, Sergeant Valentine, why should she? Why would she need to? Mr. Whitney said, get rid of them into a county home—"

"Sure. I'm probably just exercising my imagination," said Valentine, shrugging. "Just occurred to me. The perfect setup. Of course, there are some people—fortunately few and far between—who murder quite casually for very little reason."

Brenda had turned white. "I—look, I *can* think of a reason," she faltered. "Maybe. If this Slaney woman was forever turning old people over to the Welfare Board, wouldn't they get suspicious after a while?"

"Not much there, I don't think," said Valentine. "So many old people—so many county homes... And she hasn't made one illegal move. Quite a little racket indeed, as your Mr. Whitney said."

"But even when we're sure she's robbing all these people, you mean there's *nothing* anyone can do?" Brenda was nearly in tears.

Valentine sat up suddenly and put his cigarette out in the ashtray on the coffee table. "I do not like to see people going around thumbing their noses at law and order," he said. "Yes, I'd like very much to catch up to this jolly vampire with a legal charge. I don't know whether it can be done, but I'm going to look into it a little. In one way, it'd be very nice if the woman does put her victims, or some of them, out of their misery, because if we could catch up there, that'd be one very damn fine legal charge. On the other hand, it'd be almost impossible to prove it."

"You *will* try to get something on her? It's such a wicked kind of dishonesty."

"It's a particularly nasty sort of dishonesty," said Mary. "Like that passage in the Bible, 'From him who hath not shall be taken even that which he—' " She shivered.

"Yes. I have the feeling," said Valentine, "that Mrs. Josephine Slaney should be caught up to. That, though, would probably be the trick of the year. But we'll see." He smiled at Brenda. "We should have you on the force. You did some smart detective work here."

"I couldn't just stand by and watch. You *will* try?"

"We'll see what a little poking around turns up," Valentine replied.

He passed the story on to his immediate junior, Detective-Sergeant Dave MacDougal, the next morning. MacDougal listened in silence, fingering his mustache; as he talked, Valentine regarded him, and the mustache, with concealed amusement.

MacDougal, at twenty-nine, despite his slim six feet, still got annoyed by bartenders asking for proof that he was of age. His round, snub-nosed, pink-cheeked face would stamp him as a juvenile until he was middle-aged; and since he was a cop with eight years' service, a cop getting extra pay as a top marksman, and a fairly tough cop of experience, this considerably annoyed MacDougal. In the hope that a mustache would age him a trifle, he had started one about six months ago; the results had been somewhat startling. For a while the mustache had languished scrubbily; MacDougal was mouse-brown in coloring and it hadn't shown up much. Then it had suddenly begun to flourish, and as MacDougal couldn't bear to trim it, it had grown to impressive proportions: a bushy World War II RAF mustache. However, it didn't come out mouse-brown, but a beautiful almost-platinum blonde, with the result that MacDougal now looked remarkably like a high-school senior half made up for some part in the class play, with a palpably false mustache. Proud of its hirsute extravagance, he refused to shave it off, in spite of all the kidding he got from his colleagues.

He listened to Valentine patiently, stroking the mustache. At the end he said, "Look, I agree with you a hundred percent, I think it's a goddamned shame; this woman's a bloodsucking vampire and deserves the book thrown at her. A very nasty little racket indeed, but just the way this lawyer said, she's kept legally clean. There's not one charge you could lay on her. These people, by what you've got, voluntarily handed her the loot. Hell, it's not even a con game—it's dirtier than that—she's got it all legal in every sense of the word. If what you're guessing is so, she sweet-talks them into signing a deed, or a power of attorney—depending on what they've got that she wants—and that's that. The Supreme Court'd have to quash any charge on her."

"True," said Valentine, "but we'll do a little work here all the same. She's not really very smart, you know. Just rudimentary cunning, Dave. In this little racket, circumstances are all on her side. She's smart enough to pick people without relatives—people alone. It seems, by what the agency told Brenda Sheldon, that she left one of the cases they gave her. Said she'd come down with flu. I'd bet you it was a case where she couldn't see any pickings—loving family clustered around. And she knows enough to get the legal papers signed. But beyond that, I don't think she's a big brain. Maybe she's made a few mistakes in the past. I may be going senile myself, but I'm still thinking about those two deaths. The two we know about. That's a pretty high incidence, three patients dead in succession. I wonder if there were more."

"Oh, for God's sake!" said MacDougal. "Why, Dan? Why the hell? That's a real wild one—you dreaming up new business for us! We've got enough on hand as it is."

"And isn't that the truth," said Valentine. "But I tell you, boy, I've got a feeling—I've got a hunch this is a big one. Something like an iceberg, hell of a lot more to it than shows on the surface. I think we ought to do some looking. Because, well, there's another little something. Brenda Sheldon said, if our Josephine went on turning indigent pensioners over to the county homes very often, wouldn't somebody get suspicious? I said there wasn't much in that, and there isn't. But there's another aspect to it, you know. She must make some promises to them, that she'll take care of them personally, something like that, before they hand over the loot. And we've got no idea how many times she's pulled this, of course. So, she keeps them under sedation until she's got the nice signed documents—but if and when she shoved them into a county rest home to be rid of them, at least one or two would have talked about it? They won't all have been senile. And somebody, sooner or later, would have listened."

"What are you getting at?"

"I don't quite know. Just, I've got a feeling here. Let's do some looking at our Josephine."

MacDougal pulled at his mustache. "As if we weren't busy enough. And don't tell me, I know—I'm the boy to go looking. I'll just ask you, Danny—so we look at this all serious as a possible case, grant everything you've dreamed up is so, she's put these people away—will you tell me how and where you figure we could turn up any solid evidence on it?"

"You're asking me! Old people like that—the window left open, the medicine withheld, even a little overdose of sedative, and kaput! And the doctor, is he surprised? Is he suspicious? Happy release, he says, and signs the certificate."

"My great-aunt Clara," continued MacDougal cynically, "was an old she-devil. Lived to be ninety-three. The original miser, and for twenty years the family hung around hopefully waiting for her to die so they could divvy up the real estate she owned. She wouldn't part with a nickel, to help pay my dad's hospital bill when he had the heart attack, or help my cousin Bill over a bad patch when he set up that insurance office—we always figured he could've made it, with a little help. He went into bankruptcy instead. She kept her daughter, my aunt Betty, from marrying the fellow she wanted to—Betty danced attendance on her till she died, and died herself the year after. There were plenty of people had damn good motives for wanting

53

Great-Aunt Clara dead. And old Dr. Rowley knew it. But did it cross his mind somebody had given her a shove? At ninety-three? It did not. And between you and me I always wondered if one of 'em did—she was too mean to die natural."

"Fascinating as this family history is, Dave—and I take your point—let's get back to Josephine. I'd damn well like to catch up to Josephine. And as I say, I have a hunch that poking around in her past might turn up a few little mistakes."

"You know as well as I do, we can't spare the men to work on something all up in the air like this. All the legwork—" MacDougal uttered a rude word.

Valentine grinned at him. "Oh, a healthy young fellow like you won't mind some overtime."

"Listen," said MacDougal, "there's that Scott thing, and this gang of shoplifters. Not that it's not a damn interesting case, if it *is* a case, but have a heart, Dan!"

" 'What profit then to sing or slay/The sacrifice from day to day?' " quoted Valentine. "Kipling always has the word for it. No, it's not exactly a case as it stands—no real reason for us to go looking—but from the very little we know, I don't much like the smell of Mrs. Josephine Slaney. I'd dearly love to find a little something—legally speaking—on her. You go and look, Dave."

"Well," said MacDougal, and sighed. "If there *is* anything we could get on her, she ought to be caught up with, you're damn right. About the meanest little caper I've ever come across—pensioners, people like that. OK, I'll take a look around."

"I'll wish you luck," said Valentine.

MacDougal realized that one of his difficulties would be the necessity to keep any hint of investigation from Josephine's ears; he couldn't go poking too close to her. At the moment he didn't want to; if he could find good presumptive evidence that she was what Dan thought, only then might they close in a little. He didn't think she'd be brazen enough to charge slander or anything like that, but if she knew they were looking at her it might scare her away. Yet some of the people he wanted to question might pass the word along. Oh, well, maybe that could be got around, thought MacDougal.

He had had enough work laid out to fill the day—and tomorrow, and next day—and there'd be more coming in. But if Dan was so set on looking into this thing, get with it, give it a day, see what turned up. Himself, from the little they knew about Josephine, he didn't think any legal excuse would show up to turn this into an official case for the force. But go and look anyway, he thought.

With some misgiving, he turned over the last of the paperwork on the Scott case to Sergeant (third-grade) Andrews, who wasn't the world's biggest brain. MacDougal hoped he wouldn't have to do it all over again after Andrews had got through with it. He checked to see that he had his badge and credentials on him—everybody MacDougal contacted officially took one look at him and demanded proof that he really was a cop—and left the office.

He went up to the County Health Building and saw Miss Whistler. Introducing himself, he said he had some questions to ask her. "And I must impress on you, you mustn't gossip about this, Miss Whistler. We particularly don't want the subject to know she's being investigated. Do you understand?"

"I—yes, certainly," said Miss Whistler, looking agitated, alarmed, and eagerly curious. "Who—who is it you want to know about?"

He didn't get much there. This service was just that—a service to put potential patients in touch with nurses. Anybody could drop in and ask to have her name put on the list. Obviously, as Miss Whistler had given the Sheldon girl those names, the agency did not have any record of the outcome of cases; when

55

a nurse left a job, on the recovery or death of the patient, she simply called in to report that she was free. The agency didn't take too many particulars, Miss Whistler admitted, and didn't do too much checking up, though they did ask for two references.

MacDougal saw Mrs. Slaney's file card. It told him that she was Caucasian, a widow, fifty-six, and had had, she claimed, over twenty years' experience at practical nursing. She lived on Larman Drive in Santa Monica. Her two references were listed on the back of the card: a Reverend J. H. Hoyt and a Dr. Bruce Rivers. He took the addresses down. He asked whether the agency had, in fact, contacted the references for personal background; Miss Whistler didn't know. A space marked SCHOOL was left blank. He asked Miss Whistler about that.

"Oh, well, you see, there are schools for practical-nurse training—some of them are graduates of those, and some aren't. I can't say we have any preference exactly, it doesn't seem to make much difference, some of the graduates without experience, well, I suppose they wouldn't be as competent as older women with a lot of experience. But really, I don't understand— has someone *complained* about Mrs. Slaney for some reason?"

"I'm sorry, I can't tell you about it at this stage of the investigation," MacDougal said. He stroked his mustache, which appeared to be fascinating Miss Whistler. "Do you have that happen often, patients or doctors complaining about nurses for some reason?"

She looked shocked. "Oh, no, hardly ever. Well, some doctors are more particular than others, of course—it's mostly the doctors we get calls from, you see—but aside from that, hardly ever. I do remember once we had a complaint of petty theft, and another time—that was awful—a nurse gave the wrong medicine and nearly killed a little boy—there was a lawsuit over *that*. Awful. Of course, in both cases we took the nurse's name right off our list."

"I see. I'd like the names and addresses of all the patients you've sent Mrs. Slaney to since she's been with you, please."

"I don't understand," said Miss Whistler plaintively. "There was a girl here just on Saturday, asking about her—I thought it was odd at the time—"

"Yes, I know about that. The names and addresses, please."

"She *seems* like a nice-enough woman, Mrs. Slaney. Terribly uneducated, of course, but some of them are. Really, I— Oh, well, certainly, but I don't—"

There were only three, and two of them he knew about—James Ferguson and Bella Hall. She had gone to nurse Mr. Ferguson in the first week of May, soon after she'd listed herself with the agency. She'd been with him only a month. Almost at once, on reporting herself free, she had been sent to a Mrs. Cora Adamson, and after a day on the case had called to say she had the flu and couldn't work. About a week later, in mid-June, she'd called to say she was all right and had they a job for her? They had—Mrs. Bella Hall. She had been with her for nearly a month, and then called to say—as far as Miss Whistler remembered—that she was going to take a little vacation and would let them know when she was back. In August she had done so, and they had sent her to Mr. Foster.

MacDougal thanked Miss Whistler, again sternly impressed upon her that this was not to be talked about, and left. On the principle of tying up loose ends as he went along, he sought the Adamsons' address and asked questions there. It was about the way Dan had figured; Cora Adamson was a comfortably round grandmother with a loving family in evidence—husband and married children. She had been recovering from a gallbladder operation. The family remembered the fat nurse who had stayed only one day, but didn't remember her name; MacDougal didn't remind them. The agency had sent another nurse, a very nice woman named Yates, who had stayed two weeks.

He had already started the machinery of officialdom looking at Josephine Slaney—requested information from the DMV in Sacramento, their own Santa Monica records and the LAPD's. He didn't think she'd have a record. Now he drove out to Ocean Park, to shabby Naval Street, to question the neighbors of the late James Ferguson.

"Well, nobody knew the old man real good," said Bill Hogg. "He'd lived here donkey's years—here when we come. Hell of an old grouch. Ever'body thought he was some kind of miser, way he chased off kids and dogs, 'n' never did nothing to the yard or house. On account, for all that, he never seemed to lack nothing, see? Had a new TV—I saw the truck come, deliver it, how I know. Matter o' fact, one time a couple o' big kids—delinquents like, you know—tried to break in, after all his money, and brother, did he go after 'em! Liked to kill one of 'em, with a two-by-four, we had cops around like flies that night. O' course, that was before he got sick."

"Do you know if he had a doctor?" And MacDougal realized suddenly that it was a redundant question. Of course there had been a doctor—there'd always be a doctor. Even if there wasn't at first, if it was the patient who called in the nurse, she'd see that there was a doctor. Because automatically, if there wasn't a doctor, in the case of death there'd have to be an inquest. Whether or not Josephine was guilty of murder—that was a really wild idea—she wouldn't go around inviting inquests and publicity.

Yes, Hogg thought there had been a doctor but didn't know his name. It would be on the death certificate. . . . Yes, see the doctors and how much could they tell him? In a sprawling big metropolitan area like this, doctors were often called in to utter strangers. And some doctors—witness Dr. Robertson—feeling that they wasted their time on hopeless geriatric cases, would give them the minimum of attention.

Hogg lived next door to the ramshackle old house Ferguson had owned. He was, he said, a painter by trade. He didn't seem curious as to why a plainclothes cop was asking questions; just glad to have an excuse to quit work. He'd been mowing the lawn.

"Nobody paid much notice to old man Ferguson," he said, yawning. "I guess he didn't go out much. You hardly ever saw him. I didn't even know he was sick until there was this car sittin' in front of the place and my wife found out it was a nurse. He was real sick. Then after a while he died and the house was sold."

"Other way round, wasn't it? The house was sold and the nurse took him away—somewhere."

"Did she?" asked Hogg indifferently. "Well, he was old as God anyways. . . . Jeez, it's hot. Think I'll have a can o' beer. . . ."

As MacDougal started for the house on the other side of Ferguson's, he thought again of all the people like that—alone. Sometimes it was their own fault—as it seemed to have been Ferguson's. If he'd been friendlier, he'd have had friends, people concerned about him. But more often it was simply chance. Just the way things happened, that left people alone. Widows and widowers, bachelors and spinsters. And when they were elderly people, how likely it was that they'd have few close friends. Elderly people not able to get out and about as they once had— to church, to club meetings, among friends. Their former friends the same; and younger people so apt to be impatient (even when they were sympathetic) with their rambling talk, their crotchets. Even when they were nice old people—like Brenda Sheldon's Mrs. Foster—there was a subtle feeling that they didn't matter much. Yes, that was it. As if, being seventy-five or eighty-five, they were half out of life already—and when they did die, people said, Too bad, but she *was* eighty-five, or, Happy release for the old man.

Every once in a while, still, somebody—the meter reader, the bill collector—found a long-dead body in an empty house.

Someone so far out of touch with life and people that they hadn't been missed by anyone for days or weeks.

MacDougal, who had some imagination, for the first time in his life wished he was going home at night to a mortgaged ranch house and a wife instead of an empty apartment. Till now he'd been quite happy playing the field; there his schoolboyish appearance served quite well. He had a cousin or two, an old uncle, but every relative he had was a lot older—he'd probably outlive them all, unless he got shot. It was a fact he seldom thought about, but this business, well, it made you think.

Oh, well, plenty of time.

"Oh, yes, I remember the nurse," said Mrs. Herbert helpfully. She was a stout young woman with her hair in curlers, wrinkled red capri pants too small for her, and a dirty T-shirt. She joggled a disheveled-looking baby who drooled and stared unblinkingly at MacDougal. MacDougal detested women in pants—not from a moral but an aesthetic view—but contrived to smile at her encouragingly.

"Yes? What can you tell me—?"

"The old man was awful, of course. Yelled at Billy alla time—Billy's my oldest—for crossin' his yard and like that. I dunno what he was sick with, and it was just the once I met the nurse. Great big fat woman she was."

"Yes, how did that happen?"

"Damn car wouldn't start, see? *Steeeeeevie!*" she yelled suddenly past MacDougal's shoulder. "You leave that dog be and come straight home, hear? I was goin' down to the market and the battery was low or something, I guess. This nurse was just comin' down the walk next door and I guess I was cussing, naturally, and she asked could she take me anywheres. Real nice of her. It's only a couple blocks down, I could walk back. So she took me down there and dropped me. Oh, I don't recollect much what all she said. She did say old man Ferguson was awful sick and she didn't guess he'd last long—and sure enough he didn't. *Steeeeeevie! You hear me?* Oh, yeah, and I do remember—I passed the remark we'd just moved here from Hollywood, and she said she useta live there too. What you askin' all this for anyways? You really a cop?"

"Sorry, just routine. Thanks very much." MacDougal, replacing his hat and turning away, heard a dog yip painfully and glanced across the street, where Stevie was yanking grimly at the tail of a black-and-white mongrel.

"Steeeeevie!"

He was on the point of crossing the street to deliver a lecture to Stevie, when Stevie let go of the dog and approached a large yellow cat coiled up on the porch of that house. MacDougal smiled and climbed into his new Mercedes sports car.

Ten seconds later, as he turned the ignition key, the cat was recoiling itself in injured dignity and Stevie, sobbing, was bearing a well-scratched hand to Mama at top speed.

That business took him till lunchtime. He stopped
for a sandwich, and by a quarter to one was in Hollywood's
County Health Building asking whether Josephine Slaney had
ever appeared on their list of practical nurses. An obliging clerk
hunted, and found her name. She'd been registered with them
from approximately three years ago until last April, and in that
time had, of course, been sent out on a number of cases.

"People just don't realize what a demand there is for good
practical nurses—"

"Yes, I know."

"But why on earth are the *police* asking about her? Oh, I
suppose I mustn't ask questions, but I can't imagine— *All* the
cases she was on? Oh, dear me, Officer, that'd be quite a little
chore to— Well, yes, we do have records."

"I'm sorry to ask you, but I'm afraid it's necessary."
MacDougal gave her what he hoped was a charming smile, and
she looked at him (he could almost hear the words, Are you
really a cop?) and said unenthusiastically she'd look up the file.

It was quite a list. It would be, of course. He looked at it and sighed. Thirty-five, forty names, maybe more. On a case like this, what you needed was half a dozen men spread out. But the evidence so far didn't warrant that. The only thing to do was to take the names in order.

Something occurred to him, looking at the list. Not every patient she was sent to by any means would be a potential victim; and the length of this list made it look as if she had been working steadily as a nurse and nothing but. Probably, when by chance she got a patient who was a potential victim she'd take the opportunity; but that wouldn't be one in ten, twenty, would it? Not one in thirty or forty, maybe. Yet a few months back she'd made an excuse to get herself off a case that wouldn't offer her any pickings. Was she, for some reason, in need of immediate cash? Or was this Hollywood period the one in which it had first occurred to her there was occasional loot to be had, and was she now limiting herself only to suitable victims?

It was unlikely, taking this list of names in order, that he'd hit pay dirt with the first one. They were chronologically listed, so the one at the top was the furthest back—upwards of three and a half years ago. A Mrs. Adaline Widdemer on Banks Street.

Banks Street was substantial middle class. There was a good chance that some of Mrs. Widdemer's neighbors would still be there. He tried the house itself first: a neatly maintained California bungalow. But the young housewife had never heard of Mrs. Widdemer; they had bought the house a year ago from someone named Bartlett. MacDougal thanked her and tried the house next door.

A very pretty teenager flung the door open to him and then stopped short. "Oh, I thought it was Tommy, I'm sorry—" She flushed and became a little awkward under a strange young man's smile. "Mrs. Widdemer? Sure, I knew her. She used to live next door but she died a long time ago. Well, I don't know, we never knew her much, she was awfully old."

He tried the house on the other side. Here a minute white

63

Chihuahua defied him loudly through the screen door before a fat middle-aged woman appeared to shush him and call him Mother's Darling. The subsequent interview was conducted with an obbligato of the Chihuahua's suspicious growls. MacDougal, who liked big dogs, remembered that burglar they'd dropped on last week; and any burglar would say the same. "Any day, if there's a dawg, give me a big dawg! They don't bark right off. They got sense. They kind of investigate to see is it a mouse or something first. But them damn feisty *little* dawgs, jeez, they go off like a bomb when they see their own shadows! An' alla time backin' away so's you can't get at 'em to shut 'em up!" It had been a dachshund that caused that particular burglar's downfall. MacDougal still liked big dogs better. Even that funny-looking hound of Dan's.

Later, when he met Mrs. Cass, he was to reflect on this phenomenon again. Quite possibly the same rule applied to humans. Vast, still-pretty, three-chinned Mrs. Cass had been quite as indignant about the victimizing of Mrs. Foster as had Brenda Sheldon—but it had been diminutive, five-foot, one-hundred-pound Brenda (red-haired, of course) who had done something about it....

He presented his credentials, asked questions, was overwhelmed with questions in return, pleaded official secrecy, and gradually extracted what Mrs. Sybil Kingsley had to tell him.

"Well, of course she was a lot older than I— I didn't know her very well. Do be quiet, Chico! I call him Chico, that means 'boy' in Spanish, you know. *Such* a clever little watchdog! But it's a nice man, darling, don't growl at him. Well, she'd lived here some while, but she wasn't what I'd call neighborly. Oh, polite and all that, but not going out of her way to be friendly, if you know what I mean. I can't imagine why you're asking, after all, she's been gone nearly three and a half years. Poor soul. Very dignified sort, she was. Do be quiet, Chico darling. ...Well, I don't know what it was she died of, I'm sure, but she was old—in her seventies, I'd say. Oh, yes, she lived all alone. I don't think she had any family, but now I call it to mind, after she died there was a young fellow came round asking questions about the practical nurse she'd had. Of course I couldn't tell him anything—I gathered it was about her will, and he wanted to know if I'd been in the house, seen how the nurse treated her and so on. Of course I hadn't. I *do* know— bad dog to growl at the nice young policeman, Chico!—I *do* know what doctor she had, because I expect she'd never gone to a doctor here before, and she asked me—just before she was taken sick that was—if I could recommend a good doctor. Of course I said at once, Dr. Norvik, our doctor. He saw her, because I saw him come to the house later on. *Bad* dog, be quiet! It isn't as if we'd known her well, you see. I just can't imagine why the *police* are interested in her."

Dr. Norvik kept him waiting some time; when MacDougal was ushered into his office, he apologized, took a second look, and asked to see MacDougal's identification. "Been doing any- thing I shouldn't?" he asked, looking at the badge.

MacDougal laughed. "You should know. What I want from you, Doctor, is anything you remember about a patient of yours, a Mrs. Adaline Widdemer. Banks Street. She died about three and a half years ago. I don't suppose you keep case histories after a patient's death, but do you remember the case?"

"Mrs. Widdemer, oh, yes," said Norvik. "Sit down, Ser- geant. Yes, that one I remember, though she wasn't a patient long."

"Good. Remember the practical nurse she had? Mrs. Jo- sephine Slaney."

Norvik laughed. "How could I help it? The whole thing was a farce. A tragic farce." He sat back in his desk chair. "Why are you poking around after all this time? Oh, of course, you boys never answer questions, just ask 'em. Forget I asked. The

---

Widdemer woman came to me recommended by another patient. These poor devils, why will they do it?—all the publicity
and the lectures we read 'em—but they go on being ostriches.
Pretending if they don't look at it, it'll go away. If she'd come
to me two or three years before, I might have been able to do
something for her. As it was, she was a dying woman when I
first saw her. Internal cancer. I gave her three months. Didn't
say so—she wasn't the sort you could say it to. Dignified—
puritanical—standoffish. I did what I could—sedation and so
on—but of course eventually she got to the point where she
needed a nurse. There wasn't much money, I gathered—just
enough left of her husband's savings and insurance to get her
by, so I fixed her up with a practical nurse. This Slaney woman
was the one the agency sent out. Uneducated woman, but she
seemed a competent enough nurse. She was with Mrs. Widdemer, let's see, I'd say about six weeks to two months. Then Mrs.
Widdemer died. The first I heard of the row was a few days
later when this young fellow came to my office. I'd certainly
got the impression that Mrs. Widdemer hadn't any relations,
but he said he was her son. She'd quarreled with him years
before, over the girl he married—girl was Catholic and Mrs.
Widdemer disapproved of Catholics—and she'd refused to see
him since. Disowned him, as the saying goes. And now, it
seemed, when he saw her obituary notice and turned up to claim
his rightful inheritance, he found out she'd made a will leaving
everything to the nurse."

MacDougal laughed. "I see." And no homicide there; but
had that experience, possibly, first shown Josephine how loot
might be had?

"He took it to court, tried to break the will. But it was
shown that they'd quarreled and broken with each other years
before the nurse came on the scene—there wasn't any evidence
of undue influence—and the will held. I had to testify that the
Slaney woman had, by what I saw, given her patient good care

and so on, and the woman had a perfect right to leave her whatever she liked in gratitude."

"Yes. What would it have amounted to, do you know?"

The doctor shrugged. "Probably seemed like a fortune to a woman like that. I don't know how much money—maybe five, ten thousand, and the house. Well, you see what I mean about tragic farce."

MacDougal said he did, and thanked him.... Yes, he wondered if that had been the prototype case that started Josephine on her career. She would have been careful, after that, to concentrate on patients without relatives....

He went on methodically to the next name on his list, a Miss Mary Gilchrist, an address in Brentwood Heights, that haunt of millionaires. It proved to be an apartment house—a very expensive-looking and modern apartment house. He tried the manager first. She was a thin gray elegant woman who took several minutes to recover from the shock of finding police on her threshold.

"Miss Gilchrist? She's dead. What on earth are you asking about her for after all this time? I don't—you're a real police officer?"

Automatically he hauled out his badge, soothed her down, asked questions, but didn't get much. Miss Gilchrist had had lots of money; she had lived there ever since the place was built. She hadn't been exactly young, no, maybe in the forties, but very "social." Went out a lot, always dressed beautifully, and had lots of friends. She'd been nice too, always a friendly word, and a sizable tip to the elevator boy at Christmas. Then she got sick and died. It had been a pity, but that was how things went. The manager didn't remember anything about any nurse, and of course there must have been a doctor but she couldn't remember his name.

MacDougal looked at his watch; getting on for four o'clock. If he'd had those half-dozen men, they'd be halfway through this damned list by now. Oh, well. He thanked the woman, and drove back downtown to the Hall of Records. There, after a delay, he was shown the death certificate. Mary Anne Gilchrist, spinister, age forty-four. Cause of death, pneumonia with complications. Doctor, Earl A. Davies. After thought, he asked if there'd been a will filed in her name. There had; he saw that, took down the lawyer's name. A good many personal bequests of jewelry and so on, and everything else left between the SPCA and the Children's Hospital.

Well, well. He looked up Dr. Davies's address—fortunately not far away—and drove there. Yes, the doctor was in—he was lucky, the doctor'd just been leaving.

Davies was tall and thin and gray as a badger. He looked tired and dyspeptic. "What can I do for you, Sergeant? Sit down, won't you?"

MacDougal said, "For various reasons which I can't tell you, Doctor, I'm looking into the past record of a Mrs. Josephine Slaney—"

"I'm afraid I never heard of the lady," said Davies blankly.

"Perhaps you'll remember when I tell you that she's a practical nurse. She nursed one of your patients, a Miss Mary Gilchrist, about three years ago."

Davies suddenly frowned. He took off his glasses and massaged his forehead. "I remember Miss Gilchrist, of course," he said wearily. "I did a lot of worrying over that case, and my conscience has bothered me ever since, I don't mind telling you I believe now I was wrong. I disliked the idea of any publicity— it's not a thing physicians like to invite—and she was socially prominent, you know. But I think I was wrong."

"What about, sir?"

Davies took his hand from his eyes. "I should have done an autopsy," he said.

MacDougal leaned forward. "You mean you think—"

"For my own satisfaction, I should have. It must, I suppose, have been her heart. It had always seemed sound, but these sudden failures do occur, and she was a trifle overweight. But she was recovering, you see. That was what puzzled me. Of course, it might be that the illness had imposed a strain. The nurse? I don't remember much about her. Miss Gilchrist didn't like hospitals, though she could afford a private room, but she still needed nursing. And there was no necessity for a registered nurse; you see, I admit to a prejudice on that—absurd to waste a trained nurse's time on a convalescent. I had the county agency send up a practical nurse. The only thing I remember about her is that Miss Gilchrist didn't like her. She said the woman's bad grammar and constant talk grated on her nerves."

"When was this? Had the nurse been with her long?"

"Oh, no—only a day or two. Miss Gilchrist was a very— fastidious woman, things like that annoyed her. I *should* have— for my own satisfaction. She had been a patient of mine for years, I knew her well."

"Were you going to dismiss the nurse and get another?"

"Eh? Oh, certainly, I said there was no reason she need keep the woman on if she disliked her. She was to have gone off the case the next day; I'd asked the agency to send another. But it was that night Miss Gilchrist died."

"The nurse—Mrs. Slaney—still with her," said MacDougal softly. "I see. What did the nurse say about her death?"

"It's been on my conscience," said Davies worriedly. "Looking back, I think it *must* have been a sudden heart failure, as I diagnosed it. The way the nurse described it. She called me, I remember, about nine in the evening. I went right over, and Miss Gilchrist was dead—"

"About how long?"

"Well, it would have been twenty minutes or so—the nurse called me immediately and I didn't lose any time on the way. The nurse said Miss Gilchrist had been sitting up in bed looking at a magazine—she'd just begun sitting up since she'd been home, she was still weak, of course—when suddenly she gave a gasp as if she was choking, and put both hands to her heart, and—just slumped over. She looked quite peaceful, oddly enough. Her lipstick was just smeared a little—I remember noticing—queer what irrelevant little things we remember. I suppose as she fell. I've known it happen like that before, where no heart disease was suspected. It does happen like that. And as I say, it isn't such good publicity for a physician, demanding autopsies. In the ordinary way, unless the family had a distaste for it, it would go through quietly—but with Miss Gilchrist, the papers would have got hold of it, and no telling what rumors would have been started. But I think now I should have taken the risk."

"Doctor," said MacDougal, "I think so too. I certainly think you should have."

"And then," he said to Valentine, "I went to see the lawyer who'd drawn up her will, and he handed me the motive. Your wild hunch sure seems to have hit the target. Are you going psychic? The X-ray eye to spot murderers? If the doctor and the lawyer had ever got together, this wouldn't have gone off so smoothly for Josephine. Both reasonably bright fellows—but one had half the story, the other the rest of it, and they never got together to add it up."

"All right, I'll bite, what was the motive?"

"In her will, a number of pieces of jewelry were specifically mentioned. And when they came to go through her personal possessions, three items couldn't be found. Not in her jewel case or the bank vault. A large diamond-solitaire ring set in platinum, a gold bracelet set with rubies, and another ring set with diamonds and sapphires."

"You don't say," said Valentine. "But, my God, didn't they even think about the nurse? The only outsider with opportunity—"

70

"Yes, sure. They also thought about the maid who came in to clean. But they couldn't find any evidence on either one, and there was no way of knowing whether or not those items had been there when Miss Gilchrist came home from the hospital. She didn't have a personal maid. It might have been a sneak thief while she was in the hospital. For all anyone knew, Miss Gilchrist might have sold those pieces, given them away. Nurse swore she'd never seen the jewelry. No evidence anywhere. So in the end it was just let drop, there was plenty left over. I saw the fellow on the Hollywood force who worked the case. They kept an eye on the nurse and the maid, sure, and neither of them tried to pawn the stuff. But, having the two halves on that story, I can almost see that little scene, can't you?"

"Clear as a live show on TV," said Valentine. "Josephine was slipping a few pretties into her pocket, and the society patient looked up and caught her in the act. Started to raise a fuss—reached for the phone, maybe, to call the cops. Doctor says she was still weak, and Josephine's a big heavy woman. Easy to push her back on the bed, shove a pillow over her face until she suffocates. Impulse, predilection to violence as they say, or just self-preservation? Maybe practical nursing is the only job she knows, and that charge would have blacklisted her. Oh, very easy that kill was—woman too weak to fight back. Then, set it up to look OK to the doctor. Quite a risk, but she got away with it. The woman's lipstick smeared, he says—so, probably, lipstick on the pillowcase. Change it, stick the stained one all innocent in the hamper— Yes, if anybody had gone looking, evidence all over the place—but nobody did. As she gambled. Set the stage, call the doctor, tell the story. I suppose the Hollywood boys were bright enough to search where she was living?"

"They did. Nothing. But Arguila—sergeant I talked to—says personally he'd swear she took the stuff, just after laying eyes on that kid of hers. If he ever saw a lout headed for a lineup, he said, that one's it."

"What, the ordained minister? Even of the Enlightened Believers?"

"Apparently there are two. This one is Mike. About eighteen then. The smart-aleck kind—and Arguila says he came out with a couple of proslang terms, talking to the dumb cops."

"Well, well, what do you know?" Valentine sat up, looking interested. "And you know as well as I do, there's just damn all in that for us. If that doctor had done an autopsy then—but there'd be nothing to get, on a suffocation, after all this time. And she stashed the loot away somewhere until it was safe to pawn it—or maybe she gave it to Mike to bribe his latest girl with."

"I got there ahead of you," said MacDougal. "It hasn't been recovered, no. But this does cast a little more light on Josephine, doesn't it?"

"You're damn right it does. I said I had a feeling. I don't say, not yet, that she's done any more killing. But she did that kill all right, and when it was for such a slight motive. It's past time she was caught up with." Valentine was looking annoyed. "There must be some way to trip her up— What's hit you?"

MacDougal just sat there, mouth open, and stared over Valentine's shoulder.

"Beg pardon, sir," said the voice of Sergeant Silver. "The lady says it's urgent—"

"For goodness' sake, *urgent!*" shouted Brenda Sheldon. Valentine turned. She came in at a trot, looking from him to MacDougal, who was still staring. "I tried to get you on the phone from Mrs. Cass's office, but the line was busy every time—so I caught the bus and it took *forever*—"

"This is Miss Sheldon, Dave," said Valentine. "Sergeant MacDougal, Miss Sheldon."

"Yes, how do you do," said Brenda breathlessly. "She's put the house up for sale! Just this afternoon—"

"Dave!" said Valentine loudly. MacDougal shut his mouth, but otherwise continued to look as if he'd just been hit with a sandbag.

"—Said she couldn't do that, she—Mrs. Cass, I mean—would want to hear that from Mrs. Foster, and so the woman opened her bag and showed her a power of attorney. So *that* was what she was signing that day, you see. Oh, Sergeant Valentine—"

Valentine walked around the desk and tapped MacDougal's shoulder. "Up!" he said severely. "You know enough to stand up when you're introduced to a lady."

MacDougal got up, still looking rather dazed. Valentine asked what was all this about a house?

"For heaven's *sake!*" said Brenda crossly. "I must say I never thought it was so, all the talk about the dumb cops, but are you deaf? This Slaney woman's put Mrs. Foster's house up for sale! With a power of attorney! Mrs. Cass was furious—

she spotted me coming home from work and called me in. Said she couldn't seem to make the woman mad, however insulting she was. She told her to her face we all knew she was a thief, defrauding a poor helpless old woman, and the Slaney woman just went on beaming and calling her dearie."

"Now calm down, Miss Sheldon," said Valentine. "Sit down and relax. This is very interesting, but—"

"But don't you *see?*" Brenda was flushed and angry. "She's going to take Mrs. Foster away somewhere—she *says* her own home—and she could do *anything* and nobody'd know."

"It's not so urgent as all that, you know." Valentine smiled at her. "Mrs. Cass isn't going to sell the house tomorrow, after all. If necessary, she needn't make any effort to sell it at all. And this says a little something more to me—do you see it too, Dave?"

MacDougal wasn't, apparently, seeing anything but Brenda Sheldon, a little disheveled but still remarkably pretty in a sleeveless yellow sundress and copper jewelry, her cheeks flushed and her mahogany-colored eyes bright.

"What?" she demanded.

"She's not very bright. Just as I said. She's got rudimentary cunning, and she's had a lot of luck. She's just smart enough to pick victims who aren't terribly important to anyone, but she's hardly the mastermind. She must be aware by now that several people who know Mrs. Foster dislike and distrust her, yet she puts the house in Mrs. Cass's hands. So much smarter to list it with a big company, stipulate no sign in front, and quietly sell it and melt away before anyone in the neighborhood realizes. And the way she let you in that day, too—the day the power of attorney was signed. That could have been dangerous—as it nearly was. If you'd rushed a doctor to examine Mrs. Foster, the way you tried. But she'd got the papers signed, she was safe—she thought. The neighbors aren't being kept out now, are they?"

"No," said Brenda. "No. How did you know that? Yesterday and today—she let Mrs. Hawkins in, and me—"

"Sure. She wants everybody to see how the poor old lady has failed, so she can't possibly take care of herself. What was it you told me Mrs. Foster said?—going to sell the house and go live with Josephine—"

"Yes, and that's what the woman said to Mrs. Cass today—"

"What she'd sold the old woman on by then. Be well taken care of, Josephine'll see to everything, dearie, don't you worry. Damn!" said Valentine. "And everything on her side—everything! Old people do sometimes fail rapidly like that, especially after a shock. And sure, we could march in with a doctor and get him to tell us—as I'm ninety percent sure he would—the old woman's being fed drugs. We can't even do that legally—and we don't want Josephine on a charge she'd get a year's probation on! I wonder what she's using—if she's got a prescription for it? But don't worry, Miss Sheldon, we're after her now. I think I've convinced Dave she's big game, and we might just put a few other men on it."

Brenda sighed. "I was so upset, I didn't see that right away—of course, you don't sell a house overnight. You're really trying to get something on her?"

"We're trying. And I think some of it—like her letting you in that day—is just plain cocksureness. She's so confident of her own position—the nice legal documents. Yes, I hardly think this is Josephine's third or fourth try at her little racket"—he smiled and quoted from *Puck of Pook's Hill*—" 'Lord, what a worn, handsmooth trade it is!' But we're working it, Miss Sheldon."

"I didn't mean to go all hysterical," said Brenda apologetically, "I just thought you ought to hear about it right away. But I do see, it might take quite a while to sell the house. Only—she could take her away before that."

"And we can keep an eye on her too," said Valentine.

"Yes, of course," said Brenda with a sigh, and stood up. "Well—"

MacDougal came to life suddenly and said, "Oh—er—now, hot day and all—you let me drive you home, Miss Sheldon."

Brenda looked at him and showed the unexpected dimple at the left corner of her mouth. "Oh, it can talk," she said. "Did you say, another sergeant? I didn't know you took recruits straight from junior high school—"

"It can talk," said Valentine. "It also has a very handsome new Mercedes sports car, which it had no business to buy on its salary. Let it escort you home, Miss Sheldon."

She went out smiling. MacDougal went out after her. On the threshold he turned and said accusingly to Valentine, "You didn't tell me she had red hair!"

Valentine sat down in his desk chair and laughed. It would be a very salutary thing if that confirmed playboy MacDougal had at last met Nemesis.

Valentine went home, collected Garm from the fenced back yard, and got himself a scratch meal which he shared with Garm. Then, after mental debate, he took Garm for a drive across town to call on Mary. After all, she might be interested to hear how Brenda's little problem was turning out.

She welcomed him in, made a little fuss over Garm; but was she just being polite? Valentine wished he knew; and he usually did know, about females, but Mary was different. A girl like Mary Fernald, a successful writer—not to mention those extraordinary green eyes—could do a hell of a lot better than an ordinary sergeant of cops. Since he'd met her, over that offbeat murder case involving all those detective novelists a few months back, she'd gone out with him when he asked—but he hadn't asked as often as he'd wanted to. *Was* she just being polite?

Valentine, who would hardly call himself a chaser but who

had, naturally, been around a little, wasn't usually so diffident. But with Mary it was different, somehow. It was the green eyes that had got him first; but there were other things about Mary too, once you got to know her.

Besides, she read Kipling. And she'd never once said that Garm—who had also been acquired in the course of that offbeat case—was a funny-looking dog.

She must meet a lot of men more interesting than Sergeant (first-grade) Dan Valentine.

But she'd probably be interested to hear about Josephine— as good an excuse as any, he thought.

She was. She stared at him, shocked. "But, Dan—it doesn't seem possible! Are you sure? For almost no motive?"

"The hell of it is, no, we can't be a hundred percent sure. But aside from usable evidence, I *am* sure—because of that Gilchrist thing. And that might not have been Josephine's first homicide, either—but that it was homicide I don't doubt. And that's why I chalk up some others to her, after thinking it over. As you say, it was a small motive. The threat of a charge of theft—and with the jewelry returned, probably only probation."

"I'm not following you," said Mary.

"She's a bad one," said Valentine softly. "The casual killer, the one who doesn't have to have much of a motive. Once in a while you get them, you know. And the hell of it is that in this particular case it's going to be, I think, quite a trick to prove it on her, if she has done some others. The deceased patients we know about how—except Gilchrist—were old, sick people. Old, sick people frequently die of natural causes. It also doesn't take much to shove them across the finish line, if you'll overlook the pun. A little neglect, just a trifle too much sedation, and that's that. We don't know what she's using—maybe different things—or where she's getting it, if it's something you need a prescription for. But barbiturates are volatile, you know, and you couldn't expect to find traces in an exhumed body. The latest one we could look at would be Mrs. Hall, and that's too long ago for traces."

"All right, I'll take all that for granted," Mary said hastily.

"I think as we go along we'll find a few more suspect cases, which will also be no good to us at all for building a legal charge. We check bank records, any records we can find, and we find three, five, ten or twenty grateful trusting patients have signed over their possessions to Josephine, and she's profited from it when—presently—they died. What's to prove she coaxed them into it with an eye on the profit? She'd say—if we accused her—that she just felt sympathetic to these poor old people, it was an inconvenience to her to take over responsibility for them but somebody had to and she felt so sorry—it was only right she should be paid back a little for all the trouble she'd taken nursing them, wasn't it? None of them had very much, after all! And sure, as that lawyer said, try to steal big money—but it wasn't. Accumulated savings, little nest eggs, what she'd get for the secondhand furniture and so on . . . I wonder if she did take Ferguson—or others—to her own place? That might have been a mistake. If she did that a little too often, taking patients home to die there—if any of them did, the neighbors might have begun to wonder. And damn it, any questioning around there might get back to her."

"But it sounds so wild, Dan—a real mass murderess."

"There's a saying about truth being stranger than fiction. I don't say for sure she is, I'd just like to find out. We could take a chance and walk straight in, find the old woman had been given drugs, probably find the nurse had got them illegally, and arrest her on that. Let her know she's suspected, anyway. But I'd like to get her on something carrying a heavier charge. She's a bad one, all right. And if she has done any more besides Gilchrist—remembering that one, there needn't be any illegal drugs involved at all. Very easy to suffocate anybody, especially anybody old and frail."

"Oh, I can't believe that part of it. But it's the cruelest thing I ever heard of, those poor old sick people."

"Yes, our Josephine's not a very nice girl. Damn it, I can't spare any more men to get through this list until day after tomorrow at least. But— Oh, and I didn't tell you about Dave and your Brenda." He told her about that, and Mary laughed.

"Now that I'd like to have seen! Poor MacDougal, I don't suppose he ever gets anywhere with a girl, looking about sixteen—"

"That's the funny thing," said Valentine. "They discount him, you know, just because of that, until he goes into action. Quite the playboy, our Dave. Very salutary if he's been caught up with at last. But maybe just a new quarry, at that."

"In that case," said Mary, "he won't get far. Brenda's a nice girl, and also she's half Irish. She'll cut him down to size."

Tomorrow he could spare two more men, Steiner and Powers, but in the meantime there was that court appearance, and the Brooks case. MacDougal would have to carry on with the list alone. There were a few other things he wanted to get started on today, too. He dropped in at the office first, and called all the banks and savings-and-loan firms in Venice, Ocean Park, and Santa Monica. Would they check to see if Mrs. Bella Hall, Mr. James Ferguson, or Mrs. Josephine Slaney had or had had accounts with them? If so, details, please.

The banks were very frosty. Banks always were. They didn't like giving out information about their customers. But sooner or later, when the police requested it, they had to part. Valentine got a reluctant agreement to call back with any information, told Sergeant Silver to expect the calls. He wished MacDougal good luck and saw him off on another day's hunt.

MacDougal drove up to the county courthouse and looked up the death certificates of Ferguson and Mrs. Hall, took down the names of the certifying doctors. Dr. Eugene Sylvester had

certified that Ferguson had died of asthma and aggravated respiratory disease, and Dr. William Lawrence that Mrs. Bella Hall
had died of cancer of the lungs. The doctors could wait a little.
One thing, he was collecting quite a list of people to call on—
doctors and lawyers chiefly, which was a change from the kind
of people cops usually called on. He hoped Mrs. Cass had looked
closely enough at that power of attorney to remember the
lawyer's name. If not, call every lawyer listed in this area to
find him?

The DMV had Teletyped information down from Sacramento overnight. Mrs. Josephine Slaney had held a California
driver's license for three and a half years. She had no record of
any accident in that time, four parking tickets and one illegal-
left-turn ticket. By their new policy, they had issued her a limited
license as a new resident—two years—to see how she was as a
driver; and when she went in to renew it, a year and a half ago,
her record was good enough that she'd been issued a four-year
license. Her present address was given; and on her application
form she'd said she was from Chicago, given her occupation as
a practical nurse. That was all they could tell him about Josephine; and that she was currently driving a blue two-door
Ford, ten years old, license plate such-and-such.

Yes, thought MacDougal suddenly, and how come? If they
were right in their premise about Josephine's little deals, she
must have accumulated a little capital. She didn't seem to be
enjoying it much—still putting up the front of the not-so-
prosperous hardworking nurse, still accumulating loot. Just
greedy? Some people were like that, just satisfied to have it,
safely tucked away. Or maybe she lavished it on her boys, Jason
the minister and Mike the lout.

Well, back to the legwork....

That day he pieced together a little more of Josephine's
past, and it began to make a pattern. A loose kind of pattern,
but a pattern. He thought the Widdemer case, her first in Hol-

lywood, had opened her eyes to how money might be made. For a while, apparently, she'd just gone on—for about a year— taking cases as they were handed to her; she'd be with this patient a week, that one a few days—he found one or two new mothers ("Oh, yes, that was after Randy was born"), surgical convalescents, and so on—all alive and hearty. Then he came across Mrs. Gwyneth Harding.

Mrs. Harding had lived in a modest middle-class apartment building in west Hollywood. She had been a widow, childless, in her middle forties, and had worked as a clerk in a large department store. The manager of the apartment building re- membered it all very well, because she'd been friendly with Mrs. Harding and was much shocked over the whole thing. She was still indignant.

"Talk about high-handed!" she said. "I'm not a bit sur- prised to know the police are looking into that nurse—should have been long ago, I daresay. It was disgraceful, but what could I do? I ask you! Such a nice person Mrs. Harding was too, it was a tragedy she should go so young—"

"What was it?"

"Her appendix it was. She put off going to the doctor, and then when she did go, it turned into peritonitis and was almost too late. She was real bad for a couple of days, and afterward the doctor said she shouldn't be alone when she came home from the hospital. So he got this nurse for her—a practical nurse. Great big fat slob of a woman, and common as dirt. Well, I dropped in at least once a day, to see how Mrs. Harding was, you know, and I sized that nurse up at first glance. All dearie and honey and not meaning one word of it—that kind. The doctor—Dr. Adams—came most days. She didn't seem to rally like she should, and about ten days after she came home, she— just died. Such a tragedy, her not fifty yet. Doctor said as her heart must've been strained. But anyway, she died. And such a poor little funeral—that was disgraceful too! There wasn't anybody to arrange things, and this nurse said she'd be glad to—I was going to offer, but by the time I did, it was all fixed up, see. Hardly anybody there—"

"You were going to tell me something about the nurse?"

"Oh, yes—outrageous it was! If you'll believe me, the very day of the funeral, that nurse turned up here with an old rattletrap of a truck and a young fellow looked like one of these delinquents, and they took every single thing out of Mrs. Harding's apartment! All her furniture—and she'd just got a new portable TV too—rugs, pictures, curtains, all her clothes—every single thing! I wasn't here when they first came, I got home just about as they were ready to leave, and I tell you, when I saw that truck I was wild! I called the woman a thief to her face, and I was going to call the police, but she never turned a hair. She says, cool as you please, Mrs. Harding left it all to her. A woman she'd known less than two weeks! So I said, I'd like to see some proof of that, and she opens her bag and shows me a piece of paper. It wasn't a will, it was—I can't rightly say what, but all legal, something to do with an attorney—"

"A power of attorney?"

"That was it, sure. Well, I hardly knew what to think, you can see. I will say, Mrs. Harding might have been persuaded into signing such a thing—she was a kind of meek, easygoing woman, and what with being so sick— But anyway, there it was. I couldn't do a thing about it. Disgraceful. Of course, Mrs. Harding didn't have much, she was just a working woman, and she hadn't a relative in the world, but it was the principle of the thing!"

"Yes," said MacDougal. "Do you remember what bank Mrs. Harding used, if any?"

"And that was another thing," said the manager. "I suppose, with that power thing, she could get hold of all Mrs. Harding's money. Yes, sir, I do, she always paid the rent by check and it was the Bank of America, nearest on Hollywood Boulevard."

MacDougal thanked her and went to check with the bank; luckily it was still a quarter of an hour before closing time. As always, the bank was reluctant but finally parted. Mrs. Harding had had a savings account of five hundred-odd dollars and a checking account of six hundred and something. Both had been closed out by a Mrs. Josephine Slaney, under authorization of Mrs. Harding's power of attorney, several days before her death.

Another nice little haul for Josephine. MacDougal went to see the doctor. Dr. Adams reminded him forcibly of Dr. Davies—saying, "It must have been a sudden cardiac failure, by what the nurse told me of the symptoms. She was having a difficult convalescence, and these sudden failures do occur, even in people her age. All the same, it surprised me a little—"

"Did you consider doing an autopsy, Doctor?"

"It crossed my mind—just for my own satisfaction, you know—but it was fairly clear, from what the nurse said, what had happened. But I don't understand why you—why the police—what's all this about the nurse? She seemed quite competent—"

"That," said MacDougal, "you can say again. A very practical practical nurse indeed."

From there on he began to find suggestive incidents. Josephine, sent out on a case that, presumably, offered no pickings, would (probably with some excuse like illness, family business) be off it in a day or two. Quite possibly she had told the agency (as she'd told the Santa Monica agency) that she preferred elderly patients; where there'd been a scattering of young mothers and so on, now he found a succession of older patients. He had time left, after the bank, to contact seven: three Josephine had left after a day or two, and four others who had been old people. Had been: significant. Only one of them was still living: an old man, on pension, living with a married daughter.

Of the remaining three—names had ceased to matter in this business—one old woman had died in her single rented room, another had been taken away somewhere by the nurse ("seemed like a nice woman, and good to the poor old soul") and an old man ditto.

No time left today to contact the doctors, the lawyers, fill in details. MacDougal looked at his growing pages of notes and thought abstractedly that he ought to be feeling more horror at this unbelievable business unfolding itself before them. Even as an experienced cop— This was one for the books, all right. Had Dan's wild hunch hit the target? Could it be that she'd taken all these patients off, all calm and cool? Oh, maybe some of them had conveniently died off naturally, but—considering Gilchrist—it could be, it just could be, that Josephine hadn't waited around long, taking loving care of these annoyingly helpless old crocks. No. The pillow over the sleeping face, the medicine withheld—and presently the doctor saying compassionately, Happy release for the poor soul, and signing the certificate.

Yes? If so, this was turning out to be really something.

He had covered about half the list by now. There were seventeen names left. He contemplated them and felt the hair stir on his neck. *All* of them, possibly? And James Ferguson, and Bella Hall? Besides Gilchrist?

It wasn't possible, he thought.

You did get them once in a while—the casual killers. The ones who killed to rid themselves of any small nuisance, to gain any small convenience, as a man might smack a folded paper down on a bothersome fly.

But here—my God, no, he thought. Dan's wild hunch—

I t was after six o'clock. He drove back to Santa Monica and found Valentine still in his office, growling over paperwork. Valentine surveyed him amusedly and asked, "By the way, I forgot to ask—did the impact of the famous mustache wring a date out of your redhead?"

"You go to hell," said MacDougal. "It's none of your business."

"She is a pretty girl. I noticed that. But I'm surprised at you—you always go after the buxom lasses. What was it you said once, a man likes to feel he can hug her hard without cutting himself on her breastbone? Very true. This one's a scrawny little thing, if she does have red hair."

"You keep your damn pornographic opinions to yourself," said MacDougal with dignity. "She's a nice girl."

"She won't do for you in that case, obviously."

"You just shut up," said MacDougal. "Did the banks come through with anything, before I tell you what I've got?"

"Quite a little bit." Valentine rummaged through papers on his desk. "Security branch in Ocean Park, on Hall. She didn't have a checking or savings account, but she did rent a security box. Came in about once a month. A couple of the tellers remember changing large bills for her—bills from fifty to a hundred."

"These fool women," said MacDougal. "Husband's savings and/or insurance, and instead of investing it, she sits on it in cash."

"That's what it looks like. No telling how much was there. One day Josephine comes in with a power of attorney, and kaput. We could have guessed that. Ferguson had two accounts at the Bank of America—checking and savings. The Venice branch. He doesn't seem to have been much of a miser—it came to a little over six thousand bucks. He closed out the accounts himself, but with Josephine in maternal supervision. Assistant vice-president remembered because the old man looked pretty sick, he thought. And Ferguson told him he was closing the accounts because he was moving—his nurse was taking him to live in a better climate for his asthma. Denver, he said."

"Oh, really. How charitable. My God, Dan, if your wild idea is so—this is a bad one. I don't like the feelings I'm having, either. Wait till you hear what I've got."

Valentine listened and looked shaken. "My God, no. Not *seventeen*—and Hall and Ferguson—it couldn't be! Not even Haigh or Christie—"

"I don't think all—it couldn't be, could it? But I do think some, Dan. This is one for the books. What about Josephine? Do the banks have any record?"

"Did they have a record?" said Valentine. "Brother." He scrabbled for another sheet of paper. "You may not believe it right off, but every bank in this town has got Josephine Slaney accounts. Security, Bank of America, California, Federal Savings, Coast Savings. She's got a little over eight thousand in the savings-and-loan companies, earning four and a half percent.

Checking accounts totaling roughly eighteen thousand in the other three. She pays in about eighteen hundred a month—rental checks, it looks like, same amounts and personal checks. And she's got two security boxes, at the Security and the California. It looks as if she's stuck some of the loot into real estate. It accumulates—she doesn't spend as much as she pays in."

MacDougal said, "Greed? Just the satisfaction of knowing it's there?"

Valentine was still thinking of all those names left on the list. "Could I be that right? I can't believe it—and how the hell to get any proof—"

"We've got to find a mistake she's made somewhere, sooner or later," said MacDougal. "She's not a brain, she'll have slipped up somewhere." He wished he felt as confident as he sounded.

Go delving into her history, see all the doctors and lawyers, the neighbors, get all the details. Sure. Which would take time, and men. And any little mistake on her part they did turn up might not be usable now. Like Gilchrist. She had taken some big risks there, and got away with it, just because the doctor and the lawyer had never got together.

And meanwhile, wondered Valentine, what plan was wandering around Josephine's mind for Mabel Foster? He felt depressed.

He went home, collected Garm, and took him out to a drive-in for dinner. Garm was passionately fond of hamburgers and ate two, pickles, relish, onions, potato chips and all, from his own tray. They went home, and Valentine settled down with *Plain Tales from the Hills*, but for once his beloved Kipling failed to hold him.

This fantastic business... Do a little legwork on it himself tomorrow.

He dropped by the office first and briefed Steiner and Powers. "Divide the list and off you go. See the doctors and lawyers as you go along. Keep it tidy. Just keep your fingers crossed that if it is so, we can catch up to her legally."

"What occurs to me on that," said Powers, a rather new ranker with promise, "is that if we find enough of these cases where she got away with loot, even if it was all legal, it'd be strong presumptive evidence."

"It would. But the D.A. likes something more than strong presumptive evidence. All those nice legal documents—"

Himself, he thought he'd go and see, for the first time, the quarry they were hunting.

He got to Mrs. Cass's office at a quarter of nine, and had to wait for her. He had told Brenda she could tell Mrs. Cass about the police being in on it now, if she was sure the woman could keep quiet about it. Brenda had assured him that she could; and when presently Mrs. Cass appeared, Valentine understood her confidence. Mrs. Cass, only a few inches below his own height and three times as broad, was everyone's friend at the instant of meeting. She had wavy silver hair and a pair of large and lovely soft gray eyes which rested speakingly on Valentine's; she clasped his hand warmly and drew him into the little office.

"I was never so thankful in my life as when Brenda told me, Sergeant. That woman! Who could ever imagine such a dreadful, dreadful thing? And to think that it was *me* who brought her to the Fosters!" She sank into the chair behind the desk. "I'll never forgive myself! To *think!*"

"Well, of course you couldn't know," said Valentine.

"Nevertheless, I'll never— And I quite agreed with Brenda, you know—she said the longer delay there is in selling the house, the longer we'll at least have poor Mrs. Foster in the neighborhood under our eyes—and I made up my mind I wouldn't make any effort to sell the house at all. But that woman! She had the brashness, come in here again yesterday and tell me she wanted the house put in multiple listing. Well, of course you are likelier to sell quicker. And what can I do? I'll tell you, what's more, she knows something about how real-estate agents operate. She said to me, You let me know when the big bus'll be around, so I can have the house fixed up. When a place is multiple-listed, you see, all the agents or their salesmen go round in a rented bus, to see over all the new places for sale. She's sold houses before."

"She has," he agreed.

"So I've had to put the sign out front and all, and I can't delay listing it above two or three days," mourned Mrs. Cass.

"Well, it can't be helped. Look, I'd like to take a look at her," said Valentine. "Can you take me up there, introduce me as Mr. Johnson the prospective buyer?"

"Why, surely—but do you think you *should,* Sergeant? I mean, she'd recognize you later on, if—"

Valentine laughed. "The way we're having to work this, I won't need an excuse or have a reason to get near the woman again until and unless we get enough evidence for a charge."

"Well, I suppose you know," said Mrs. Cass. "Do you want to go right now?" She rose. "We can walk easier."

She led him around the corner onto Royce and down four houses. The Foster house was the typical white frame bungalow; its front yard was neglected, the cement of the driveway cracked. "How much is she asking, by the way?"

"Twelve-five. It's worth about that. If this area was going into apartment houses like some, it'd be worth a lot more, just for the land—they come right in and knock these old places down, you know—but that hasn't happened here so far." She pushed the doorbell.

And presently there was Josephine, opening the door, beaming at them. "Beg pardon? Mr. Johnson—how-do—int'rested in the house? That's OK, Mis' Cass—I'm an early bird, don't matter to me. Only you got to excuse the breakfast dishes not bein' done."

"And how is Mrs. Foster?" asked Mrs. Cass formally.

"Oh, 'bout the same. I gotta patient here, poor old lady," she explained to Valentine. "Matter o' fact"—she gave Mrs. Cass a glance of injured dignity—"house is really hers, see, only she ain't able handle her own affairs no more, 'n' I'm takin' care o' things for her. I show you round, sir, come in."

Valentine said thanks and explained that he'd just been transferred out here, his wife wouldn't be coming until next week, and he was just looking around first. Trailed by Mrs. Cass, he followed the nurse's bulk through the long combination living-dining room to the kitchen. The nurse was wearing a white starched uniform, and he reflected that that uniform must be a valuable psychological aid to her. A white-uniformed nurse was not only Respectability, but Trustworthiness—with a touch of the mother-figure.

She chatted on amiably, pointing out all the amenities—she didn't seem to notice that Mrs. Cass, nominally the saleswoman, never opened her mouth. She was all friendly smiles and jolliness, and—as Brenda had said—her little eyes were quite empty of any emotion.

"Hafta ask you to be quiet, if you please, in here—my poor old lady's still asleep."

It was the second bedroom, and the shades pulled to darken it. "I'm real sorry, I want her have her sleep out, see. But you can see the size 'n' all, and when your good lady's here maybe you'll come back, see over it better."

Valentine stepped quietly into the room. He thought, there is an indefinable smell to old age. Not necessarily an unclean smell, but it was there. Old clothes too often washed, old bodies tired and tired of themselves. It was a small room, and bare of much furniture. Mabel Foster lay huddled asleep in the double bed, on her back. He had a glimpse of neat small features, a round face surprisingly unwrinkled, sparse tangled white hair. She looked small and terribly defenseless lying there.

He turned away and met the nurse's empty eyes and wide smile. "Poor old soul," she said. "The bathroom's right next door, sir."

Ten minutes later, Valentine at the front door thanked her, apologized for disturbing her so early, and said he'd consult with his wife. Of course he couldn't say definitely until she'd seen it.

"That's right, it's the ladies got to be satisfied, all right!" The nurse laughed her hearty laugh.

"Thanks again," said Valentine, and took two steps sideways through the screen door. He brought his hand from his pocket with a flat chromium cigarette case, and managed to drop it so that it skittered back toward the nurse.

He started after it a little slowly; as he'd hoped—she would be used to retrieving dropped objects automatically—she bent to it first, surprisingly agile for her size, and handed it to him. He thanked her.

As they gained the sidewalk, Mrs. Cass said shrewdly, "Was that to get her *fingerprints?* The way they do in books?"

"Melodramatic," agreed Valentine. Inside his pocket was an open cardboard box; the case had been slipped into that for protection. "Sometimes we have to do it that way."

"But do you think—"

Valentine shrugged. "I don't think anything—I don't know. Just, we'll try everywhere. She's not in our records, or L.A.'s. But she's only been here three and a half years, and people don't often suddenly go on the bent, as the pros say, in their middle age. Maybe she's in somebody's records, somewhere. You never know. If she's left some nice clear prints on this case, the FBI may be able to tell us whether she has a pedigree, and what kind."

91

* * *

He dropped the case in at the Prints office. "Mine will be on it, somewhere near the top here. I'd polished it before, of course. See what else shows, and if they look nice and clear, pass 'em on to the feds, will you?"

"Will do," said Sergeant Copley cheerfully.

Mrs. Cass had remembered the lawyer's name, but only the last one, which was depressingly ordinary—Wilson. There were four Wilsons listed in the relevant phone book; the third he tried was the right one.

Gerald Wilson looked alarmed at Valentine's proffered credentials and questions. He was a medium-sized colorless man about forty-five, all correct conservative manners.

"Why, yes, I drew up a document for— But why are the *police* interested?"

"What document did you draw for Mrs. Foster?"

The lawyer wet his lips. "A power of attorney. Is there anything *wrong?* The women were utter strangers to me, Sergeant, but by what Mrs. Slaney said—and I could see that the old lady's obviously growing incompetent, but she understood what she was doing, I'm sure of that. She was capable of signing her name—"

"Yes." Valentine thought that in a way Josephine was clever enough. The old woman coaxed and petted into committing herself to Josephine legally, and in this case (and probably others) the old woman vague about legal terms—it'd be, "This is just a lawyer's paper, dear, that says you want me to look after you." But the tranquilizer, the sleeping pill, as well, so the old woman would look plausibly incompetent to the outsider. "It was Mrs. Slaney who called you?"

"Yes. But she assured me it was Mrs. Foster's own decision, and I asked Mrs. Foster that, of course, later. I—look here, what is all this about?"

"I'm not in a position to say right now, sorry," said Valentine.

Wilson was no fool; he scented fraud, and was agitated. It is not good publicity for an attorney-at-law to get into the papers as Lawyer Who Drew Fraudulent Document. "But it was such an ordinary—it looked quite all right to me, Sergeant. Mrs. Slaney explained that the old woman was getting incompetent, and I could see that for myself, of course. I understood there are no relatives, and she obviously trusts Mrs. Slaney. It's pretty clear there isn't much money there, and the woman seemed kind to her—if I'd thought there was any *coercion*—"

"Well, maybe none we can prove," said Valentine. "Thanks anyway." He left the lawyer still looking alarmed.

Josephine might not have much education, he reflected, but she was smart enough to have created this nice little racket. And of course, any lawyer might exercise more care, in a case where it looked as if big money was involved; but in these cases—just as Wilson said, an ordinary thing. . . . And then, when the power of attorney let her clean out the bank accounts, sell the house if any, then— Did she? Shove them off so coolly to have them out of the way? There was no reason to—do it that way. So irrevocably. All she'd have to do would be to turn them over to the Welfare Board. On the other hand, as he'd said to Dave, not all of them would have been so docile; sooner or later one of them would have complained, and somebody would have listened. . . . And maybe she preferred the other way—maybe she got quite a kick out of it, out of exercising that kind of power. There were people like that. Not only motiveless killers, but random killers. The expedient thing. The easiest thing.

He thought it was past time Josephine was caught. And that indeed was going to be quite a little trick.

Well, see what Steiner and Powers turned up today.

He started for Hollywood, to take a look at the two ref-

erences she'd given the county agency. She had given the same
ones in Hollywood and Santa Monica: the Reverend J. H. Hoyt
and Dr. Bruce Rivers.

He took the doctor first. The address was on Fountain
Avenue. That almost said of itself, not a specialist or a very
successful doctor, financially. Fountain had run down a little.
Unless, of course, it happened to be the address of the very
exclusive Cedars of Lebanon Hospital, which was also on Fountain.

It wasn't. It was a house—an old Spanish-stucco house—
out east of Vermont. The doctor's brass nameplate shone on
the door. The house was recently painted, neat, with a mani-
cured lawn. Valentine was interested. Hollywood wasn't a town
where professional men used renovated houses as offices much;
there was too much cheap office space available.

He slid the car in to the curb and debated with himself.
Hell, he thought, it can't do any harm. He didn't think he had
"cop" emblazoned all over him. Go in, invent a few symptoms?
Size up Dr. Bruce Rivers.

He switched off the engine, jaywalked across the street. The
brass plate bore only the doctor's name, and below it was a
little cardboard sign with a movable arrow pointing to the line
DOCTOR IS IN. WALK IN PLEASE. Valentine walked in please, and
found himself in a comfortably if cheaply furnished anteroom.
Partitions had been removed, added in different places, to the
original living and dining rooms. The walls here were painted
light green, and the one window had a venetian blind the same
color. No curtains. Only a few magazines lay on the one table,
and they were, he thought, rather odd choices for a doctor's
waiting room: *True Love, True Romance, Screen Life*. There
was a plastic-upholstered couch and several chairs, and three
doors. None bore a label; but the opening of the front door had
rung a bell somewhere. The room was empty. Valentine stood
and waited.

The door in the rear wall opened and a woman stood on the threshold. She was not uniformed as a nurse, but wore an ordinary printed cotton dress, green and white. She was about forty, rather plump, with violently bleached hair and too-dark lipstick. She stood looking at him in silence for a moment before speaking.

"Yes?" she said, followed by, "Oh, you must be Mr. Anderson. Doctor said you'd be in about now." She smiled and came toward him.

First Mr. Johnson and then Mr. Anderson, thought Valentine. His day for aliases. He opened his mouth to deny it but she was still talking.

She was smiling at him in an oddly leering way, and her voice was subtly confidential. "Everything went off fine," she said, "you needn't worry. She can go home this afternoon. As long as— Doctor said you'd be in, with the rest of the money. It's five hundred altogether."

And what's this? thought Valentine incredulously. And then, Jackpot!

He hoped the sudden intelligence hadn't shown in his expression. He stared at her with dull incomprehension and said, "Huh? My name ain't Anderson, lady. I just come in, get an appointment with the doc, see. I been havin' these headaches—"

For a moment her expression tightened with apprehension; and then she looked at him more thoroughly, attempted a laugh, and said, "Oh, I'm so sorry, sir—what a silly mistake! But I'm afraid you don't understand—Dr. Rivers is a gynecologist."

"Huh?" said Valentine.

"A *gynecologist*—that means he just takes care of women."

"Oh," said Valentine. "Oh, I get it. OK, thanks, lady." He went out fast.

Behind the wheel of the middle-aged Chrysler, he began to smile. Talk about luck! And what was this, how did it tie up?

He was—where?—in the Wilcox Avenue precinct. He looked up the address and drove up there. Inside, a sleepy-looking desk sergeant was discussing modern art with a plainclothesman. "—Do for you, sir?"

Valentine introduced himself. "I'd like to see somebody in Vice, if possible."

"I think Zimmerman's in," said the plainclothesman. "Show him the way, will you, Jim?"

Zimmerman, a snappily dressed thin dark man with a cynical mouth, offered a firm handshake. "Well, what can we do for Suburbia, Sergeant?"

Valentine concealed annoyance. "Look, we're not L.A. but we do have nearly a hundred thousand population, you know," he said mildly. "No straw in our hair anymore."

Zimmerman laughed, apologized, and told him to sit down. "This isn't anything to do with me," said Valentine. "But I thought you ought to know about it, if you haven't got an eye on him already. I'm on something that—I think—if we get the breaks and crack it, is going to make headlines from here to

Moscow, but the point is, one name that came up is a Dr. Bruce Rivers—out on Fountain Avenue. Ring any bells?"

Zimmerman shook his head. "Never heard of him. Why?"

"I think you'd better take a look at him," said Valentine. "You might find him very interesting. I went in, with a nice manufactured set of symptoms, just to get a look at him, size him up. And this woman came out—not a nurse, blond by request, reformed Main Street—and says I must be Mr. Anderson. Before I can say no, she adds that everything's fine, some unspecified female can go home this afternoon, and Doctor said I'd be bringing the rest of the money, it was five hundred altogether. At which point I sketched out an impersonation of an illiterate ditchdigger, was informed that the doctor is a gynecologist—which it doesn't say on the sign in front—and got out fast. Like a good boy came straight to you."

"You don't say!" said Zimmerman. "You're quite right, I find your Dr. Rivers interesting. Address?" He scribbled. "Sounds very much like another abortion mill, all right. We'll devote some attention to him, Sergeant, thanks very much. Five hundred? He must have a reputation, that's kind of steep by the current rates." He looked at Valentine seriously. "Favors for favors received. Does he tie up so close to your Mr. X that it'd discommode you if we dropped on him?"

"I don't think so," said Valentine slowly. "I don't know, but hell, it's all up in the air. Would it panic her?" He thought of the empty eyes, the assurance as she showed him the house. Of all Brenda Sheldon had said. Of the way she had faced down that apartment manager, and Mrs. Cass. Cocksure? After all the luck she'd had— "No," he said. "No, and just possibly it might be a little help. Might rattle her just enough that she'd—" He grinned at Zimmerman. "You boys fancy yourselves as pretty hot, and with reason too. But if we break this one we're going to get some publicity too, and have an excuse to pat ourselves on the back."

"That so? What kind of caper is it?"

"What would you say," said Valentine, "to a killer for cold cash profit who's accounted for—just at an estimate—about fifteen people in the last three years? While looking as if she's competently nursing them to better health?"

Zimmerman didn't say anything for a minute, and then he said, "Good God Almighty!"

"I don't think He's got anything to do with it," said Valentine.

Valentine had a belated lunch. He failed to find any trace of Reverend Hoyt; the address he'd been given for him was an old one, he was not known there, and he did not appear in any of the phone books. Valentine headed back for the beach to find the Dr. Lawrence who had attended Mrs. Bella Hall. The address was on San Vicente Boulevard; it turned out to be a new brick and glass building, rather small, surrounded by its own convenient parking lot.

Dr. Lawrence seemed to have quite a practice; a pert blond nurse denied Valentine any hope of seeing the doctor today, until he produced his credentials. The small waiting room was full and all the patients necessarily also heard that a police officer wanted to see the doctor. They stopped talking or reading and stared at him.

"But what do you want to see the doctor *about?*"

"I'll explain that to the doctor, if you don't mind," said Valentine shortly.

He finally got in. Dr. Lawrence was a young man, and a handsome young man; he probably hadn't been in practice more than a couple of years. Valentine hadn't talked to him two minutes before he sized him up as a very cocksure young man, who couldn't envisage the possibility of making a mistake. He was The Doctor; he always had the answer.

"I can't conceive why you should be asking questions about

this Mrs. Hall. A very ordinary case. Is it something to do with her will? I wouldn't know—"

"No. Sorry I can't go into details at this stage, Doctor. I'd like to hear everything you can remember about the case, please. Medically and otherwise."

Dr. Lawrence stared, raised his handsome eyebrows, and said, "You know, I'm a busy man, Officer. I don't understand this at all, and unless you can give me some reason—"

"A very good one, Doctor," said Valentine, smiling at him. "It's every citizen's duty to give the police assistance when it's asked for. You've heard that." There was a suggestion of steel in his tone; he didn't like Dr. Lawrence.

"Oh, if you're going to make an issue of it!" Lawrence flung himself back in his desk chair petulantly. "Well, the woman came to me as a new patient, three months or so before she died. I'd never seen her before. It was a terminal cancer, she should have seen a doctor long before, of course. Nothing to be done. Naturally I didn't tell her so. I don't believe in wasting effort on a case like that—she was seventy-eight, and in any case she hadn't the money for it. Extensive hospitalization and so forth. She complained about my bills. Well, as I told her, if you want skilled advice you have to pay something for it." He lit a cigarette with a flick of the gold desk lighter, not offering one to Valentine. "Eventually the time came when she couldn't be alone, needed nursing, and I got her a practical nurse through the county agency. I couldn't say how long the nurse was with her before she died, a month or so, I think."

"Yes. Were you at all surprised at her death, Doctor? Had you expected her to live longer?"

Lawrence shrugged. "I must say, I hadn't expected her to go quite as quickly as she did, but there aren't any rules with cancer, you know. What *is* all this about, anyway?"

"What did you think of the nurse?"

"The nurse? Seemed competent enough—for a practical

nurse—as I recall. I only went to the apartment once, just told the nurse to call me for any emergency."

"I see. That was leaving a dying woman mostly in the hands of an untrained nurse."

"Are you implying that I neglected the patient? I don't have to take that, you know! I said the nurse was competent. There was nothing more I could do for the woman, beyond giving her prescriptions for painkillers." Impatiently Lawrence shrugged again. "She was seventy-eight, she'd had her life."

Valentine wondered sardonically how Dr. Lawrence might feel about that if and when he got to be seventy-eight. . . . And a sudden new nightmarish thought hit him. Prescriptions . . . If she was using barbiturates on her victims, to soften them up mentally, maybe she hoarded a supply by withholding pills from patients like Mrs. Hall. "What did you prescribe, Doctor?"

"I don't recall offhand, probably one of the codeine derivatives." Dr. Lawrence was both bored and annoyed. So filled with a sense of his own importance that he wasn't even curious. Another one like Dr. Robertson—waste of a medical man's time, these geriatric cases; you couldn't do much for them—and they'd had their lives, what did it matter? He wouldn't get any more here; Lawrence hadn't been interested, to remember any more.

He was stared out of the waiting room by the nurse and all the patients, and drove down to Ocean Park to see Dr. Eugene Sylvester. Dr. Sylvester had one of those renovated old houses on Commonwealth Avenue as his office; he was a middle-aged balding man with kind eyes and a quiet voice.

"Oh, Ferguson. Yes, I remember. Poor old chap," he said. "I only saw him twice, you know. His nurse brought him in the first time—a practical nurse, she was. Ignorant woman but she seemed kind enough."

For a moment Valentine was startled, and then realized that Josephine was taking no chances. The doctor Ferguson had been going to formerly would be asked to sign the death certificate. She had cannily let a new doctor see him, to be handy when the old man died. And that was strong presumptive evidence that there had been something funny about that death, wasn't it? Surely the natural thing to have done would have been to continue with the doctor who had been treating him, knew the case? Well, of course she had brought him down to her own place in Santa Monica, apparently after the house was sold; she could plead that it was easier to go to a nearer doctor. But it might indicate that the doctor more familiar with the case would have known that Ferguson wasn't quite at the point of death.

Sylvester was curious. "I suppose you can't tell me why the police are interested. Such an ordinary sort of case, I can't imagine— Well, he was a sick man, of course. I found no evidence of TB, but he'd been a chronic sufferer from all the allied respiratory and bronchial troubles—asthma, sinus congestion, retention of mucus, faulty lung intake, and so on. That wears the body down, over a period of years. The smog didn't help, either. And he was seventy-six. But he might have rallied, in a more congenial climate. He intended to move to Denver, taking the nurse along. She told me that. He was quite bad the first time I saw him. I had to give him oxygen."

"Yes. And the second time?"

"Oh, the second time he was dead," said Sylvester, blinking. "It was only a few days later. The nurse called me, very agitated, early one evening, and I went right over. He was gone when I got there. A bad asthma attack, and she hadn't any adrenaline or oxygen on hand. That was careless of her, with such a patient. She said her supply had run out and she'd meant to get more the next day, but as I say, she was an ignorant woman. She seemed genuinely upset. And of course, though I'd only seen him once, I could certify that his condition was what it was, and responsible for death."

"Did you ask why they'd come to you? I mean, if he was so ill, he'd probably been seeing a doctor regularly."

"I should have thought so, since the condition had worsened. I didn't ask, of course. He may have been dissatisfied with the man he was going to. Ethics—nothing was said about that."

Valentine thanked him and left. Here we go round the mulberry bush, he thought in irritation. Would they ever get anything usable on the woman? And damn it, she wasn't the big brain. A woman like Josephine, my God, symbolically thumbing her nose at this whole force of trained men! Nothing to show the D.A. Nothing.

He went back to headquarters and asked Sergeant Copley if they'd got any clear prints off the cigarette case. "Some dandies, three fingers and the thumb. I wired 'em off to Washington about ten o'clock—let's see, five and a half hours—we should hear pretty soon whether they recognize 'em."

"Good." Valentine went on into his own office and found MacDougal there. "Barring a miracle, we'll never nail her, Dave. There's just no handle. We're getting in a lot of information, but what the hell is it worth? I did run into one rather interesting little thing," and he told MacDougal about Dr. Rivers.

MacDougal was interested. "And she gave him as a reference. Even that's no help. Even if he is a lock-picker," he pointed out, using the pro slang term for an abortionist, "and when the Hollywood boys drop on him, Josephine will be the most surprised and shocked female in California—never suspected such a thing! Well, we don't know what Steiner and Powers will bring in."

"*I* know what they'll bring in," said Valentine bitterly. "They'll bring in details on a lot more cases like these we know about. And on at least half of them—maybe more—we can be sure it was homicide—and there'll be no more proof of it than we've got on the rest. How the *hell* can we show it, Dave? So the D.A. would buy it."

"It's a tough one, all right."

"It is," said Valentine abruptly, "exactly what Mary called it—scarifying. These people—all these people. We have the notion these days that we're kept tabs on by a number of people and agencies. Maybe even too much so, what with all the government interference, all the paraphernalia of urban civilization. But, just as that lawyer the Sheldon girl talked to said, there are a lot of people who aren't taken much notice of. By anybody. Not rich enough for the government to keep careful track of. Not young enough, or well enough, to be out among friends, noticed—soon missed from their regular routines. No relatives, at least no close ones, to keep tabs on them out of duty if nothing else. In the middle of nearly seven million people, they're alone, to all intents and purposes. They can—they have dropped out of life, and nobody's been much concerned about how. In a couple of cases, somebody's suspected Josephine of defrauding them, but it's never occurred to anybody, even the doctors, that she's also quietly murdering them. Because—why should she? We know the casual killers exist, but the ordinary person doesn't expect to meet one. These people were old and sick. Nobody was surprised when they died."

"I don't know that I believe that she did murder them," said MacDougal. "Sometimes I think yes, sometimes no."

"I don't say all of them. Maybe some of them did just die, but most of them died so conveniently for Josephine, didn't they? She cleans out Mrs. Harding's bank accounts, after having somehow coaxed or tricked her into signing that power of attorney, and before Mrs. Harding can find out and make a fuss, she's dead. She kindly takes over legal responsibility for Ferguson, takes him into her own home, and before he gets to be too much of a nuisance, or has time to realize she's got no intention of taking him to Denver, he's dead. There were others like that, you found yesterday—an old woman and an old man. She didn't have them with her long—in each case less than a

103

week. And we'll ask those doctors, and I'll bet it was the same sort of deal as on Ferguson—the doctors saw them only once or twice, to be handy to sign the death certificates. So very convenient for Josephine."

"There's Mrs. Foster," said MacDougal, thoughtfully stroking his mustache. "We're in on this one."

"What the hell do you mean, there's Mrs. Foster?" barked Valentine. "What do you suggest, that we wait till Josephine gets rid of her, pounce on the body, and hope that an autopsy will show suffocation or dope? Hasn't she killed enough people as it is?"

"I didn't mean—" began MacDougal mildly.

"So what did you mean? Watch her with an eagle eye? What could we hope to get? The only way we could catch Josephine doing something to Mrs. Foster would be by putting three men round the clock inside that house! As it is, Josephine can be doing any damn thing she pleases to the old woman, and nobody the wiser. I'll tell you one thing I think we should do. We ought to put a tail on her. She goes out sometimes, you know—to do the marketing and so on. I put Mrs. Cass on—because we can't show in the neighborhood—to find out if she has any regular time for going out. No sense wasting three men on it. She probably won't be out but a couple of hours a few times a week. I'd like to know where she goes. If she's getting prescriptions filled, for instance, we could learn something there."

"That's so, of course. We can try that. It's a tough one," repeated MacDougal with a sigh.

As Valentine had expected, what Powers and Steiner turned up from the rest of the Hollywood list was extremely suggestive, but legally useless.

Of those seventeen people, four were still living. Those four Mrs. Slaney had been with for only a short time; on all four cases she had made an excuse to leave the patient, and another nurse had been called in. They were all people with families.

The other thirteen had died while she was still with them. In three instances, it was pretty certainly natural death; she had not got anything, or much, out of them. An old man, ninety-odd and wealthy, surrounded by servants. He had not left her anything; but his lawyer said he had been in the habit of keeping fairly large sums of cash in the house, and none was found after his death. Not much had been made of that; nobody really knew whether there had been any cash around. An old woman, who had died too soon after Josephine came on the case—only three days—for Josephine to have worked on her. Another old woman who might have been too strong-minded for Josephine—she'd been with her a couple of weeks, but the woman died without signing anything for Nursie.

The other ten had all benefited Josephine, and passed out of the picture soon after. It was the same pattern. All elderly people without close relatives, and not much money—but some. Four of them Josephine had taken away "to be taken real good care of in my own home." Very shortly thereafter, a doctor had signed their death certificates. The other six cases had died at home.

Powers, who was getting intensely interested in Josephine, said he'd figured it out on paper that she'd taken an average of about three thousand bucks per head. In cash or value. It averaged out, very little from some, quite a lot from a few. The patients who owned a house were real windfalls. Most of them didn't. On some, she'd only got small bank accounts, the furniture, personal possessions. But out of the fourteen suspected homicides they had come up with (fourteen, my God), she had got four houses. Modest houses, but real estate was up these days. She had sold them for thirteen five, fourteen thousand, twelve five, and eleven seven hundred. A nice haul indeed. One of the houses had held a number of valuable antiques, on which she'd probably realized another thousand.

She had used different doctors and lawyers on each occasion.

Fourteen, thought Valentine. My God. Gilchrist, Harding, Hall, Ferguson, and these *ten* more—old people, alone and sick and largely friendless—sure, and being old, probably some of them not too mentally alert—cajoled and petted into doing whatever Nursie said was right.

Arrogant young Lawrence—*she was old, she'd had her life.* But she hadn't—these people hadn't. Whatever little piece of life was left to them, by God, or whatever made the plans, she had stolen. And Valentine wondered if maybe life (even a little piece of it) was worth more at that end of the trail than at the beginning. The old knew what life was worth, and valued it higher.

And nothing, nothing at all, to base a legal charge on...

Sergeant Silver stuck his head in the door and said, "Teletype from the FBI."

"Ah," said Valentine. "Let's have it."

And it was a very gratifying and interesting message. But even so, it handed them exactly nothing of any use as of now for the D.A.'s office.

What the FBI had to say was that the prints were those of a Mrs. Josephine Davenport (née Slaney), who had a little pedigree. She had first been picked up, twenty-two years ago, with her husband, Walter Davenport, on a charge of fraud. Davenport was a pro con man, not a very smart one. He was currently serving a taxi—five-to-fifteen—in Ossining, and had about eight to do. She had served six months on that first charge, and had been picked up next, six months later, on a Mann Act violation, accompanying a minor across a state line for immoral purposes. In this case, the performance of an abortion. That was why the FBI happened to know her prints; it was a federal offense. She'd served a year on that. She had been picked up in 1954 on another abortion charge; at that time she had been working regularly as a nurse-assistant to a Dr. Robert James Bradley, who was the abortionist—and it had been (reading between the lines) a land-office business—in Trenton, New Jersey. Somebody had tipped off Bradley that he'd been spotted, and he had run; they never dropped on him at all. But they'd got Josephine, and another nurse, and a couple of patients. Josephine had got a five-to-ten, and had served seven. The Davenports had two sons, Jason and Michael, who had been wards of the court while their parents were inside.

"And isn't this nice to know," said Valentine. "But, damn it, nothing to make a charge on her now! She hasn't even violated

107

parole—they let her out without it. All the same, it is nice to know more about Josephine."

And MacDougal said, "What do we do with it, Danny? Show it with our list to the D.A. and say, 'Don't you see, all this makes it look so probable?' The law doesn't deal in probabilities. Sure, sure, I like it too, *but*—!"

Brenda, walking down Lincoln toward home that Saturday afternoon, had a divided mind. Half of it was on Mrs. Foster, and the other half on Sergeant Dave MacDougal.

She must have been mad, she thought. When she thought about it, he must be at least her own age—a man wouldn't get to be a sergeant without some seniority—but he looked about nineteen. And that ridiculous mustache. Couldn't really be a false one, of course, but it looked it. She must have been *mad*, saying she'd go out with him.

And he'd probably take her to a hole-in-the-wall hamburger joint somewhere. The old black suede pumps quite good enough—why she'd made a special shopping trip for the new green sandals— Well, they'd been a bargain.

She'd always rather gone for mature men. Why on earth she'd said— Well, oddly enough, if you shut your eyes he *sounded* mature enough, but really— Any headwaiter would probably think she was having dinner with her young brother.

Of course it was always, well, flattering, to have a man act as if you'd made quite an impression on him. When he'd driven her home that day, he'd been stiffly polite at first and then a little easier—a certain amount of natural charm had shown through—even if he did look more like a college freshman than a cop. That mustache . . . Surely it couldn't be *dyed?* Ridiculous.

And why on earth was she having the vapors (as Gran used to say) about this perfectly ordinary thing? All *right*, she'd go out with him, see how they got along together. It didn't matter one way or the other, did it?

Probably they wouldn't get on at all. A career cop. He probably followed pro baseball, and liked westerns and beer and never opened a book except the Police Manual.

Oh, forget it.

Mrs. Foster. Were they looking, would they get anywhere? What Sergeant Valentine had said about—oh, God, that couldn't be true! Unthinkable. He had said, hard to make a legal charge. Could they ever, when she was so careful?

She turned down Royce Street. I'll go in, she thought. They had agreed—she and Mrs. Cass and Miss Devereaux—that the oftener they dropped in the better. Let the nurse see that people were concerned, keeping an eye on Mrs. Foster.

They were let in now. The nurse all smiling friendliness, welcoming. And Mrs. Foster not like her old self at all, vague and dreamy and forgetful. What was the nurse doing to her?

For a house, she thought. For the money from the house, and a little furniture.

She shifted the box containing the frivolous new sandals under her arm, turning up the walk to the Foster house.

She thought irrelevantly that he did have nice hands. She always noticed hands. His were long-fingered, square, strong-looking. But just meeting him once—

She pushed the doorbell.

It was not the nurse who came to the door, but a man. Brenda could hear the television in the front room, blaring loudly—a western or something, gunshots.

"Yeah, what you want, sister?"

Brenda stared at him. He looked about twenty; he was only a little over medium height, but very broad and muscular; he looked very strong. He had an unhealthily white face with a very narrow black hairline mustache and cultivated sideburns.

"I came—to see Mrs. Slaney," said Brenda. The other son—the lout, Mike, she thought. "Isn't she here?"

109

"Sure, come in." And as she stepped over the threshold, he looked her over coolly, not moving back; she moved sideways around him. "Say, quite a dish, ain't you? A real nice little heifer. I could go for you, honey."

"Where is Mrs. Slaney?" asked Brenda coldly; but inwardly she was queerly frightened. He's just an ignorant, insolent kid, she told herself; but something about him, about his eyes, put fear in her. Some aura emanated from him that said, Danger.

"In there with the old bag," he said absently, jerking a shoulder toward the bedroom. He was still looking her over. Brenda sidestepped carefully around him and started for the bedroom. He laughed and moved in front of her again; she was brought up short against him. "Don't you want to get acquainted, doll?"

She was afraid of his eyes. Dark eyes couldn't be cold, but his were. They were also oddly fixed and staring. He took hold of her arm.

"Let me go!" she said sharply. She had to shout over the noise the TV was making. She tried to pull away, and his grip tightened.

"Aw, now, don't be like that, doll. You're sure the first interestin' thing I seen around here. Lot o' fat asses comin' in, yak yak yak."

Brenda dropped the shoebox and slapped him as hard as she could. He swore, let her go, and stepped back. "You damn little bitch—" He reached for her again, but she had got past him, and ran across the tiny hall to the bedroom.

The nurse was there, back to the door, combing the old woman's hair. Mrs. Foster sat obediently as a good child on the bed, hands folded in her lap. "There, we're all neated up an' ready to have a nice glass o' iced tea, dear. But first we gotta take the li'l pill—"

"Mrs. Slaney," said Brenda. The woman turned with surprising agility.

"Why, it's Miss Sheldon." She smiled, but she wasn't pleased to have a visitor invade the bedroom like this. "Right kind o' you to drop by. If you'll just set a minute out front, we'll—"

"I have no intention of going out there again alone," said Brenda furiously, "while that insolent lout is waiting to grab me."

Instant uneasiness flickered over the nurse's face. "Oh, you met Mike—you don't want to let Mike worry you any—he don't mean nothin', just kidding."

"Scarcely what *I* call kidding!" said Brenda, who was trembling all over, to her own rage. "If I'd known I was going to run into a juvenile delinquent I'd—"

"Now don't you go miscallin' my boy, young lady—he's not neither—I don't s'pose he meant nothin'—" She was angry, but also uneasy. "Mike!" she bellowed. "You come in here!"

No response. Mrs. Slaney took Brenda's arm and almost dragged her out to the living room. For the first time Brenda realized how strong the woman was. Mike Slaney was slouched in a chair drawn up to the TV. "You shouldn't talk rude to Miss Sheldon, Mikie," said the nurse in an oddly pleading tone. "You didn't mean no harm, I know, but—well, maybe you oughta say you're sorry."

"She can go to hell," he said expressionlessly, not turning away from the screen.

"Oh, now, don't be that way," she said. She smiled at Brenda, but it was a rather nervous smile. "You don't want to mind Mike, Miss Sheldon. He gets moods, like, an'—an' I guess he's feelin' kind of low on account he just lost his job—"

"Job!" he said, and added an obscenity to that, and laughed.

"Oh, well—you know how men are," said the nurse. "An'—an' I gotta finish gettin' the old lady fixed up. We won't bother Mike—" She urged Brenda back to the bedroom.

111

Brenda, watching her, thought, she knows he could ruin the impression she's worked so hard to create here. The impression of the kind, competent nurse going out of her way to lavish good care on her patient. She's nervous about it, because she can't control him. He's a bad one. Something wrong with him. He's a wild one. Why does she let him come here? But of course, she couldn't prevent him. He'd just come, maybe to demand money. She doesn't like it, but there's nothing she can do about it.

And then she thought, I believe she's a little afraid of him too.

Mrs. Foster smiled at her and said in a thin voice, "Hello, child. Nice you dropped by."

"How are you, Mrs. Foster?" Brenda's knees were trembling, and she sat down beside her on the bed. The nurse went into the bathroom.

"Oh, 'bout the same." The old woman seemed very weak; she leaned against the headboard, her eyes vague. Not the bright, briskly normal old woman she had been. They all agreed there must be something wrong about it, because while she *might* have started to go senile after her husband's death, it wouldn't have been so suddenly—it couldn't have been. The nurse was controlling it somehow.

There had been mention of a pill. . . . And here came the nurse with it, a glass of water and something round and white on her palm.

"Here's the doctor's pill, honey," she said cheerfully. Mrs. Foster took it without protest; the nurse held the glass while she drank.

"Is the doctor coming to see you often, Mrs. Foster?" asked Brenda.

"Just the once that I seem to call to mind," said Mrs. Foster vaguely.

"Well, you keep on havin' them pains in your leg, we go see him again," said the nurse.

The old woman said after a moment, sounding a little fretful, "Don't reckon these pills do much good, somehow. There was some I took for arthritis—" She stumbled over the word, her tongue thick.

"These supposed to be better," said Mrs. Slaney. "If—if you care to wait a minute, Miss Sheldon, I make us some iced tea—"

"No, thanks," said Brenda, and got up.

"I don't like 'em," said Mrs. Foster to nobody in particular. "And that young fellow out in my front room, I don't like him either—who is he and what's he doin' here?"

"I quite agree," said Brenda. "If you'll—convoy me past him, Mrs. Slaney, I'll say good afternoon. I certainly didn't expect to find you behaving like this, as if the house is yours—already. Allowing your lout of a—"

Anger, uneasiness, some other expression showed in the woman's face. "Please don't think so bad of Mike, Miss Sheldon—he don't mean no harm—an'—he won't be here long, dear," she added to Mrs. Foster. "I'm sure sorry you feel that way, Miss Sheldon—I do my best, take care o' her good—I don't want nobody to think—" Talking, she followed Brenda to the front door.

Mike was still watching TV, smoking; he didn't look up.

Escaped, Brenda bolted for home. She met Mrs. Hawkins in the drive, cutting roses, and Mrs. Hawkins asked her what was the matter, so she had to stop and tell her.

"It's downright *disgraceful!*" said Mrs. Hawkins. "You should've called the police! And her always boasting about her son the minister! I never heard of such a—"

Brenda nearly told her there were two, but caught herself in time. Mrs. Hawkins, the innocent gossip, mustn't be allowed to know that the police were—looking.

She got away at last; she was more angry than afraid now, looking back over that little scene. Just an insolent kid—what

113

had frightened her so? And the pill—the round white pill.

She found herself dialing, presently asking for Sergeant MacDougal.

"MacDougal speaking," said an impersonal voice in her ear.

"It's B-Brenda Sheldon—I thought I'd better tell you—I just dropped by Mrs. Foster's, and—" She poured it all out at him breathlessly, and he had to interrupt to get a word in.

"Listen," he said. "You just listen." He was breathing heavily and seemed to be grinding his teeth. "You stay away from that house, understand? You just keep out of this."

"But how *can* I? At least when someone's calling most days, to let the woman know people are concerned. And *you* listen to me! I had the oddest feeling that she—the nurse—is a little nervous about that lout too. I don't think he's under Mama's thumb anymore, if he ever was. He's—I can't describe the feeling he gave me. Something—all wrong. All bad."

"You," said MacDougal, sounding anything but impersonal, "stay out of that house, you understand? You don't know what we've been finding."

"I'll do as I please," said Brenda tartly. "I thought you'd be interested to hear about the pill. I couldn't guess what it was, except that it was larger than an aspirin. And I had an idea— I thought if I went in one day and while I was there asked to use the bathroom, I might be able to spot the bottle in the medicine cabinet and steal one so you could have it."

MacDougal said something indistinct, and then, "Look, you just keep out of this. Yes, we are interested. Yes, we'd like to know what it is, but there are more important things, such as your neck. And we do *not* want the woman alarmed, for God's sake. My God, no. No telling what she'd— Look. You just stay put where you are and I'll see you at seven."

Brenda banged the phone down. She must have been *mad,* she thought. The natural-born autocrat. In spite of what he looked like—the pink-cheeked college freshman. Imagine. You'd never think to look at him—but, the natural-born autocrat. That mustache. Do this, don't do that. Ordering her around. And of all the obnoxious types, that was the *most*. She'd do as she damn well pleased.

Still furious, at Mike and his mother, and MacDougal and herself, she looked up Dr. Robertson's number, dialed, and was told what she knew, that the doctor wasn't in on Saturdays. But even nowadays, doctors had to leave emergency numbers, she knew that. "It is very urgent that I speak to the doctor," she said firmly. "It's about one of his patients. Please tell me where I can reach him. I just want to talk to him."

She argued for several minutes, and finally the receptionist gave her a number. When she got him on the phone, his voice was rough and rather cold. She tried to sound as businesslike as possible, to be brief. "I thought you should know, that someone should check with you. I don't know what the nurse is giving her, but she's claiming that it's by your orders, and I'd like to know if that's so. Mrs. Foster isn't at all like herself, and I thought if you could examine her—"

"Good Lord!" he said impatiently. "You ought to know, young lady, that I can't discuss my patients with anyone! Mrs. Foster—oh, that old woman, yes. For God's sake! So the nurse is giving her aspirin. You're heading for a slander suit, to do this. I've got no time to waste on hysterical women, sorry."

"Or old ones?" asked Brenda sweetly. "I wonder how you'd feel if you were eighty-eight and your doctor couldn't be bothered to waste time on you! If you ask me, I think you ought to be struck off the register!" She banged the phone down again.

She was still simmering when MacDougal called for her later that night. He was wearing a neatly pressed gray suit, and his tie was not quite so awful as the first one she'd seen him in. He smiled at her nicely and said he liked her dress, but Brenda wasn't deceived; she'd found him out. The autocrat—whatever

115

he looked like—and she wanted no part of him.

"I've thought of something else I need to do."

"We'll have no shop talk yet," he said firmly. "Later, maybe. I hope you notice I had the car washed for you." He went on talking about cars until she could have slapped him. How maybe Dan was right about this 300 SL Mercedes was too expensive for him, but it would outlast three ordinary cars, being built like a tank, and was such a nice one to handle, would do a hundred and fifty mph with a push, not that he had ambitions that way—

"Yes, it's a very nice car," said Brenda between her teeth. "But I think you ought to hear—"

"You just simmer down," said MacDougal. "I see something's upset you, but you're in no state to talk about it very coherently right now. You've got a pretty low boiling point, haven't you?" He gave her a quizzical glance. "Must be the red hair."

She relaxed and laughed. "I guess you're right. But I couldn't help getting mad. Oh, all right."

He took her to the Black Cock on San Vicente Boulevard, a quiet, very good restaurant where there was no music to interfere with conversation, and all the waiters walked on tiptoe and apologized for rattling the silver. When preliminary drinks were before them, Brenda said, "Now. I'll tell you what occurred to me afterward. After I'd called you. That—lout—only thing to call him—his eyes looked so odd, and I wondered if maybe he takes dope. He's not normal, some way."

"Could be, yes. I wonder what we'd come across if we looked at him hard."

"But aren't you *going* to? At everything connected with her? I thought—"

"We don't want to rock the boat," said MacDougal patiently. "We haven't got one usable piece of legal evidence yet. We can't afford to let her get one hint that she's suspected of anything, Miss Sheldon."

"Oh," she said disconsolately. "I'd hoped—"

"What we have got—" He looked at her consideringly and said, "If I tell you—I know you're concerned about all this—

you've got to promise to keep quiet about it. You're not to talk about any of it, to anybody, understand?"

"Well, I'm not quite a moron, of course I see that."

"All right." He gave her the gist of what they knew—and guessed—about Josephine. Brenda felt herself going pale and then flushed.

"But that's—incredible! All those people? Nobody could—"

"People like Mrs. Foster," he said. "Alone. Nobody to keep track of them, to care very much. Now, don't look like that. Dan's sold on it, but I'm not just a hundred percent sure."

"We've got to get Mrs. Foster away from her," whispered Brenda. "We've got to."

"Finish your drink and quit seeing horrors," he said brusquely.

She finished her drink at least; she needed it then. "But what a horrible—and she's so, so defenseless! Oh, and another thing—I've never been so furious at anyone—I called the doctor, Dr. Robertson, you know, because I thought he ought to know about those pills, if they *aren't* his idea, and to see if maybe he'd examine Mrs. Foster. I finally got hold of him and told him about the n—"

"You *what?*" exclaimed MacDougal loudly. He leaned across the table, and she saw her own fury mirrored in his vivid blue eyes. "You damned interfering little—vixen! By God, I ought to give you a damned good hiding." He sprang up and almost ran out of the big main lounge in the direction of the lobby.

"Well!" said Brenda to her empty glass. Of all the obnoxious, impossible, *odious* men she'd ever—And looking like an innocent Cub Scout leader or something—

"Another cocktail, miss?" Deferential waiter hovering.

"Yes, please," said Brenda defiantly. "Yes, the gentleman too." Gentleman! He was a lout as bad as that Mike.

It was nearly ten minutes before he came back and sat down. He said grimly, "My God, I'm sorry as hell now I told you what more we've got! If you go around opening your mouth so wide—"

"I don't! And what on earth did I say to send you off like that?"

"If you could add two and two," said MacDougal rudely, "it might have occurred to you that what you let out to Dr. Robertson might send him straight over to question Josephine pretty sharp. Maybe he's not interested in the old folks, but he's an honest man so far as we know, and doctors are like Caesar's wife where reputation's concerned. He'd give you short shrift, but if what you said penetrated at all, he'd be apt to go and question the nurse, and very possibly let out the news that somebody is suspecting her of this and that. Damn it, woman, don't you see that we can't rock the boat? We can't let Josephine feel one minute's uneasiness about her position! She'd be off like a scalded cat, maybe out of the state, and we'd never stand a chance of nailing her."

Brenda put a hand to her mouth. "Oh, I didn't see—oh, I'm so sorry! I was a fool—of course, I do see what you mean. I'm so *sorry!* Have I spoiled everything?" She was filled with shame at her idiocy.

"We'll hope not," said MacDougal shortly. He looked at his new drink and drained half of it. "I've sent a couple of men hunting him, to impress on him that he mustn't go anywhere near Josephine with any questions. Whether they'll get to him in time—" He shrugged.

"Oh, dear, I feel such a fool, not to have seen that, but I was so mad."

"Exactly," said MacDougal. "You and your low boiling point. You get mad, and you don't *think,* that's all."

"Well, you went off like a rocket yourself."

119

"It was an occasion. About once a year I do. For a good reason. It's just not good sense to go round blowing your top every five minutes, my God."

"And that," said Brenda, rallying, "from a Highland Celt!"

"Let's keep the generalizations out. Besides, only on one side. My mother was a rational Smith. You're the one with the temper."

"I was a *fool*, not to see that. I'm sorry. I said I was sorry. Oh, Lord, if he did go and see her—"

"Can't be helped now, don't borrow trouble. Just hope not, that's all. Next time, for God's sake, count ten, will you?"

"Yes," said Brenda meekly.

He eyed her speculatively. "I think I'm a fool too," he said unexpectedly. "One like you, spouting off regular as the Old Faithful geyser whenever some little thing annoys you. Me, I like a peaceful, quiet life. Well, what do you want to eat?"

They were halfway through dinner when a waiter came and whispered in his ear; he flung down his napkin and ran out again. When he came back three minutes later he said laconically, sitting down, "OK. Gunn got to him with the warning. He won't be tipping Josephine off."

"Thank God. I'd never forgive myself. You've got to get her. Stop her doing all these horrible things. Do you think you will? Can you?"

MacDougal picked up his fork. Unexpectedly he grinned at her—his unexpectedly charming grin, that made him look his real age. "Gunn said Robertson was 'shook up.' Evidently he hadn't tumbled to the implications in what you said. He hadn't intended to do anything. As we know, he's not interested in old people anyway. Then when a police detective comes around, he's probably wondering very hard if he's going to be accused of negligence."

"Good," said Brenda. "Maybe it'll teach him a lesson."

"I'm not," said MacDougal, "what you'd call a religious

sort of fellow—had enough of Presbyterian hellfire as a kid to cure me of any tendency that way—but there's one little maxim I do believe—be sure your sins will find you out. He may be a little more careful in the future, even about these worthless old folks."

"I told him he ought to be struck off the register."

"You don't pull your punches, do you?" MacDougal laughed. "Well, I'm sorry I swore at you, but it was a damn silly thing to do."

"Yes, it was. I'm sorry. I said so."

"And as for Josephine, well, we're working on it. And now let's talk about something more cheerful."

He was the typical autocrat, impossible, of course—astonishing, considering what he looked like—but he could talk interestingly when he wanted to. And he asked questions, and so she found herself talking about darling Gran, and how she'd come to work at Garnetts', and so on. They sat for a long while over glasses of brandy, talking, and he was quite nice and polite, and surprisingly intelligent.

When he had driven her home, she started to say something conventional about enjoying the evening, but he took her arm and said calmly, "You don't think I'll have you walking down that unlighted drive alone? Just the place for a prowler," and went round with her, to the little three-room house.

"Well, thank you very much, but there's never been—"

"Always a first time. Now you listen to me. I know you're interested in this business, and feel you've got a right, because you're the one unearthed enough to convince us to look into it. But you just keep on the sidelines. I don't want you—and your damned low boiling point—anywhere near Josephine and that oddball Mike. You leave it up to us, and mind your own business."

"I'll do just what I please, Sergeant MacDougal!" said Brenda, firing up at once. "You can't dictate to me! I *detest* men

121

who think they can order women around like lords."

"I'm telling you," said MacDougal, "Detest away, but don't meddle. I may be a damn fool, but however this business comes out, I want you intact at the end of it." He bent and kissed her cheek, gave her a little shove toward the door. "You mind what I say now." He turned back up the drive.

"Well!" said Brenda to herself rather breathlessly, as she wrestled with the key.

Valentine had gone home that night too tired to get himself a meal, and went out again to the drive-in with Garm.

And he'd no business going to see Mary again, two nights in succession, but of course she would be interested, wouldn't she? In a way, she'd put him onto this case.

It had been a rough day.

Josephine, of course, wasn't the only case they had on hand at the moment; and every city police force in this year of grace was undermanned. There was an all-too-successful burglar taking toll of homes over in the east part of town. There was a teenager who had knifed another kid to death. There was the usual handful of involuntary homicides—all automobile accidents. There was that puzzling series of thefts from the best hotel in town. There was the former mental patient who had killed her own twenty-year-old daughter.

And there was a very great deal of paper work to be done on all those cases. Valentine had spent the last couple of hours that day taking down testimony on that girl's death, and it was one of the rare times when he'd wished he wasn't a cop. The whole thing so senseless, so tragic. A bright, pretty girl, in her second year at college, and doing well. She'd wanted to be a nurse. And because some educated fool of a head doctor had let that woman out of Camarillo—

Well, the excuse—that Mary'd be interested. He drove up to her apartment. She was nice, welcoming him, making a little fuss over Garm. She surveyed him and said sympathetically, "Tough day?"

"Very tough. Thanks, Mary, I'm feeling better already," as she led him out to the kitchen and handed him a bottle. He made them two mild drinks and relaxed appreciatively, across from her on the couch. She was wearing, this hot night, a bare-backed halter dress of vivid green. She smiled at him over her drink and he began to feel better yet. He started to tell her how the case was developing.

"It's not developing, in one way. We've got some rather horrifying presumptive evidence, but no legal handle at all. Not even a good excuse to ask for a search warrant—which probably wouldn't turn up anything else anyway." He sighed and groped for cigarettes. "That woman has put away fourteen people in the last three years, and we can't touch her."

"*Fourteen*— You're joking."

"No joke. Anything but. We've got the names and dates and details." He hauled out his notebook on the case. "You want to hear all about it?"

"I certainly do. It's—incredible. I can't believe it. Are you sure?"

"Little things all added up. All right, and maybe going through it chronologically will give me some inspiration. She got out of the pen and landed here three years and a bit ago. I don't for one minute suppose she'd decided to go straight—she probably started out practical nursing to eke out a living while she looked around for a racket. *Or,*" he said suddenly, "and didn't I say I might be inspired, she might have been plying her old trade on the side for extra money. Abortions. I don't know why she happened to settle in Hollywood, but it could be because her older son—the minister—was already there. He's ten years older than Mike, he's been on his own for some time. She brought Mike, who was still a minor then, with her. Presently she gets sent to nurse Mrs. Widdemer, and either she worked

123

on her or Mrs. Widdemer just felt grateful—and inherited all she had. Maybe that put ideas in her head. Maybe the side business—if there was one—wasn't paying off too well.

"Then we get Mary Gilchrist. The first one. First one out here, anyway—which is a nice thought. She acted very damned cool and calm there, anyway, for an amateur. The way both Dave and I read that, it was an impulsive kill to protect herself. Now we know she has a pedigree, we can figure that as a stronger motive. If she'd been charged with attempted theft, her prints would go on record and be checked, and when the Hollywood boys knew her history they'd have put her on probation, kept a close eye on her. Anyway, exit Gilchrist. She was very lucky there, that nobody put two and two together. I don't know whether that scared her, or if some profitable side racket turned up, or what, but she went on for about four months, apparently, just taking ordinary nursing cases as they came along. And she could have earned an honest living at any of several other jobs that are better paid, but it just isn't in the nature of a pro like Josephine to go straight all of a sudden. I don't know what else she was doing then, but I'd take a small bet there *was* a side racket. Then we get Mrs. Harding. That was, you might say, the prototype kill. After that she started to go to town."

"But, Dan—how did a woman like that conceive the idea of the power of attorney and so on? I shouldn't think she'd know enough."

"Maybe the minister son briefed her. Could be. But while she's uneducated, she's smarter than she looks. Just a little. Anyway, that established the pattern. It was a little over two years ago. Now, we don't know what her side racket was, so we'll guess a little here. Ten to one it *was* abortions, and of course that's a lot more dangerous than the racket she's devised for herself now. I think—" Valentine stopped abruptly and said, "I'm a fool. I do wonder—I'll call Zimmerman in the morning."

"Who is Zimmerman?"

He told her. "I should have seen that before. They never picked up that Dr. Bradley she'd been working with. It just occurs to me that Bradley might have turned into Dr. Bruce Rivers. His prints will tell, and he's still wanted on that charge back East. Yes, and if so her side racket could have been blackmail on him. Anyway, from then on Josephine seems to have concentrated on finding and working on suitable patients. It's from that time we find her making excuses when she's sent to patients who'd offer her no chance of profit—young people, or people with families and friends. In that time she was sent to a number of patients, and a lot of them she didn't stay with long. Made excuses to leave the case, or—in some instances—they were cases she wouldn't have to be with long. In fact, at one point the agency complained about it, told her she wasn't reliable. Reliable! But ten cases she stayed with. And those ten patients"—he put out his cigarette—"I swear she murdered, after getting all they had. Just to be rid of them."

"It's fantastic. Like something out of Famous Trials—" Mary made a dive for Garm, who had discovered a dish of chocolate mints on the coffee table.

"She devoted quite a while to some of them. Some of them would have been easier than others, you know. Old people mentally vague to start with. I can show you the list of names, from Harding up to Bella Hall. Five of them she moved away from where they'd been living—said she was going to take them into her own home. I don't know whether she did—we can't sniff around too close there, you see. Ferguson, a Mrs. Mazzini, a Sven Lundgren, a Mrs. Harkness, and a Mrs. Morgan. Altogether, fourteen people—fourteen people, my good God. All very much alike. Except for Harding and Gilchrist, all elderly people, from sixty-five on up. Six of them on old-age pension, the rest getting along in a very modest way on small savings, private pensions. Only one of them had any living relatives, and in that case—the landlady told us—it was a cousin in New York and they never communicated. In nine cases they died while she was still with them, in their homes. In five cases—those she took home with her, as she's apparently planning to take Mrs. Foster—those people died within *one week* of the transferral—and meanwhile she'd had two of them, Ferguson and Mrs. Mazzini, examined by different doctors, who later signed the death certificates. And did so with no question in their minds. Why not? Ferguson was seventy-six and a chronic asthmatic. Mrs. Mazzini was nearly eighty and had cancer. And their regular doctors hadn't any doubts about the others, either. Lundgren was seventy-three and had had several strokes, was partly paralyzed. And so on. Who's surprised when somebody like that dies? The doctor who saw the Harkness woman even said casually that he wouldn't have expected it to take her off quite so soon, but it was a blessing it did, saved her a lot of suffering."

"*Fourteen,*" said Mary blankly.

"Yes, takes some swallowing, doesn't it? But granted that you lack any scruples at all about it, so easy, you know. And all different doctors and lawyers—I didn't mention that. As far as any of the lawyers knew, it was the first and only time she'd ever held a power of attorney. And as I thought when Wilson said it—another little thing. None of them asked many questions, had any suspicions, because it was obvious there wasn't much money involved. In the majority of cases it was a cheap apartment, not a house—in four cases, houses, but old and small, not worth much. In a few cases they were pensioners, and that was mentioned. What lawyer would be suspicious? Especially when the old lady or gent was obviously attached to the nice kind nurse, and vice versa. Not one of the lawyers we've talked to had any glimmering that she was interested in the profit she'd make."

"But—Dan," Mary said suddenly. She was frowning. "Why did she take those five—just five—to her own home? If she did?

That rather—breaks the pattern, doesn't it? Why should she? It made her a little more trouble—you said she took two of them to a different doctor, and so on. And waited a little while."

"I've been racking my brains about that," admitted Valentine. "I don't know. There must have been some reason, but I've got no idea what it was."

"Well—" said Mary. She was silent, and then added, "Well, we know she's planning the same thing with Mrs. Foster. Maybe it was something about those particular patients? What's different about Mrs. Foster from the other nine she didn't take home?"

Valentine thought. "She's a little older than the average. I don't know, I can't think of anything—" He sat up suddenly. "But I can! You do inspire me! Of course I can. Mrs. Foster *has* several people who are concerned about her. Who are keeping track of her, as it were. Who, incidentally, distrust Josephine, but that might not have been the case with any others, of course. Just the fact that there was even one person—an old friend, or a neighbor—interested enough to be coming in, keeping an eye on the patient— She might have thought it'd be safer to do it elsewhere. Yes, I think after serving time Josephine's playing it very safe indeed. In some cases, I suppose, the presumed friend would be elderly too, not able to get around, so couldn't have called at Josephine's house to see the patient. And time goes on, and any mail sent in care of Josephine is dropped in the wastebasket, so the sender assumes it's been received OK. Yes...I'd even say, if Rivers *is* Bradley, that may be why she didn't go back to working with him here. She'd been picked up once on his account—she decided to play solitaire. Yes, I like this idea—except for Ferguson. He was one of them. And nobody seems to have liked Ferguson. And we haven't turned up anything like that on these other four."

"You haven't looked specifically," Mary pointed out. "I expect you've been asking next-door neighbors mostly? Well, they needn't have been the interested ones. It might have been anyone living within a block—even an old friend across town."

"So it could. And come to think, why a different doctor on just those two cases? Because maybe the regular ones knew those patients weren't likely to die so soon? This gives us a few new places to look. But it doesn't solve the main problem of getting legal evidence." He thought about that; a little silence fell. Garm filled it by scratching, making music with his collar and license tag.

"Dan," she said in a small voice.

"Mmh?"

"It makes me feel—all those old people alone—I mean, it does make you think. You know. Actually the only relation I've got is a cousin in Baton Rouge."

"I know," said Valentine, swirling ice in his glass. "I can't even claim a cousin. It does make you think." He looked at her and opened his mouth to say something else, and then didn't say it.

"Yes?" said Mary. "What were you going to say?"

"Nothing," said Valentine; and staring at his glass missed the exasperation in her green eyes.

Sunday was just another day when you were a cop on a case. The first thing Valentine did that morning was to call Zimmerman and tell him about his inspiration. "Bradley's still wanted in New Jersey for that job, and if you can collect Rivers's prints—"

"Much obliged," said Zimmerman. "But that may be quite a trick, Sergeant. The little work we've done on Rivers so far, he's a canny old pro who can smell cop a mile away. We sent a good-looking young female from Juvenile to arrange an ostensible job with him, and he took one look, threatened to sue her for slander, and turned her out of the office."

"Bad luck," sympathized Valentine. "And of course no reason to ask for a search warrant. The way the courts are leaning over backward to be fair to the pros these days. What that woman said to me *could* have a perfectly innocent meaning."

"You're so right," said Zimmerman gloomily. "But this looks more promising—if we can steal his prints. Even if we couldn't keep him, it would put him out of business. I'll send one of my bright young men out to trail him, try to get into conversation and offer him a lighter or something. Thanks very much."

"Good luck on it." Valentine went into the outer office to discuss this latest idea with MacDougal.

MacDougal was brooding over the results of their three-day tail on Josephine. Mrs. Cass had told them that if the woman was going out (so the neighbors, artfully questioned, said) it was generally about one in the afternoon. She was usually back by two-thirty or three. They had stationed a man in a car across the street from twelve on. One day she hadn't gone out at all. The next day she had come out about twelve-thirty and driven her blue Ford to a downtown parking lot. She had visited the Bank of America, a dress shop and a drugstore; collected the car and gone to her own home.

She lived on Larman Drive, which was above Sunset and a rather classy address. Powers, the tail, had said that most places up there, in a recently developed section, were new and expensive if not very big, but this one had probably been the only house up on that street for a long while. It was a big old frame house, a good way off from any neighbors. He also said there was a brand-new scarlet T-bird sitting in the drive. Mike. Probably. They knew by then that Jason the minister didn't live with her.

She had come out about ten minutes later and driven to a supermarket on Santa Monica Boulevard, and then straight back to the Foster house.

The day after that, yesterday, she had emerged at about one o'clock—not in uniform that time, but looking (Powers said) as big as a house in a red dress and high-heeled shoes—and driven downtown again. She had gone into an Owl on Santa Monica Boulevard and made a phone call from a booth there. Quite untraceable, of course. A phone call she didn't want to make from the Foster telephone, evidently. She had then had a prescription filled at the pharmacy counter. She had next driven up to Hollywood, to an address on La Brea. It was a house, a big old stucco house, but not a private residence: Sign over the door said Church of the Enlightened Believers. She had stayed about half an hour, come out, and driven back to Ocean Park to her patient.

The pharmacist at the Owl had been questioned, and warned not to gossip. Fortunately, he had remembered her— she was, of course, a noticeable woman—and in any case, he said, it wasn't the first time she'd come in. He had filled various prescriptions for her before, and this one several times. She'd once told him she was a nurse. The prescription she'd had filled that day was for Empirin Number Three. What *was* it? Well, it was Empirin compound—acetophenetidin plus aspirin plus caffeine, with codeine added. A painkiller, of course: much stronger than any nonprescriptive tablets obtainable. The prescription had been signed by a Dr. Bruce Rivers.

The Church of the Enlightened Believers, as expected, was incorporated as a nonprofit organization. Listed as officers were the Reverend John Herbert Hoyt, William Green, Jason Davenport (he'd kept his legal name, evidently), and Morris L. Ernest.

All of this was nice to know, but it didn't take them much further.

MacDougal listened to what Valentine had to say and at the end said, "So, we go back and ask questions all over again on those five, and we prove out your girlfriend's inspiration. So what? What more does it give us of any legal use?"

"I know, I know," said Valentine. "But being on it, we'll work it, Dave. In the event that we can ever charge her, the D.A. will want all the details." His girlfriend. Obnoxious expression. And was she? On any basis? Maybe just being polite.

"I'll say one thing. I hadn't seen quite so clearly before how it does tie up—all those cases so similar. You convince me, Dan.

131

By God, yes. Fourteen, altogether. My God. Yes, she did those kills all right. It's one for the books. I don't know how the hell we can do it, but this one we've got to catch up to." His tone was grim.

Valentine said, "Half the job's done—I've convinced Davy MacDougal." But he wasn't feeling as confident as he sounded.

As he stepped into the little grocery several voices were speaking at once, and all in Italian. This little two- or three-block area was an anomaly in most big towns these days. Changing economies, various factors had seen the Polish Towns, Dago Towns, Hunky Towns vanish into the past. But here and there one did find a block or two where the old clannishness that was half fear kept those of the same background together. This was one of those areas, where Mrs. Mazzini had lived: a middle-class street in Santa Monica, old frame houses and around the corner on a secondary main street a few shops. The name over this one was D. Ciapperi.

There were four or five women shopping and talking, a stout bald man behind the counter.

"Yes, sir?" said the man in English. "Can I help you?"

Valentine went up to the counter and introduced himself fully, speaking his rather halting Italian; he felt the stares on his back. Reason he'd decided to cover this one himself; his Italian was far from perfect, but at least adequate. As a rookie, he'd ridden squad cars quite awhile with Pete Vanni, and in the interests of ambition—it was always useful for an officer to have another language—had picked up a working knowledge of Pete's mother tongue. Damn, the time went—six years and more since Pete had been shot dead by that hopped-up hood...

"One of my men came to the neighborhood recently, asking about a Mrs. Mazzini who once lived up the block—"

"Yes, yes, he spoke to me!" said one of the women behind him. "She lived in the house next to mine. He would not say why he was asking questions—we have talked about it."

"Yes." He turned to her. A big stout woman, middle-aged, with suspicious eyes. That was why he had come himself. Steiner had described the neighborhood, and where you found that kind of thing anymore, people like these were probably immigrant or first generation, and not disposed to be overfriendly to Authority. "You understand, we are investigating a crime, and we cannot talk about the details as yet. I have a few more questions to ask now, if you—"

"You are of our old country, sir?"

"No, I'm afraid not." They were thawing a little now, for his knowledge of the language and his courtesy. "Did all of you here know Mrs. Mazzini? I had thought perhaps she had done her shopping here and Mr. Ciapperi would know—"

"But yes, sir, so I did."

"And I," said the stout woman.

"And I too," murmured a drab-looking young woman who balanced a baby in one arm.

"It was tragic, a very sad thing," pronounced the stout woman solemnly. "So old she was and not one single person of her own blood left to her. A pity, a pity!" She clicked her tongue.

"None of you knew her well?"

"As to that—well! She was old, she did not get about to see people. And she had not lived here long, you see."

"How was that?"

"She had a very sad life, that one. No more than one child she had ever, a daughter. A nice, pleasant woman that one was—Lucia Arrano. She was married, but she had never had even the one child—it was sad. Often I heard her say how she prayed to the good God—and the novenas she would make! Holy mother, half the time she was at the church! But it was all of no use." She shrugged. "And then there is this terrible accident. In the automobile, on the freeway. They are both killed, Lucia and her husband. And so Mrs. Mazzini, she inherited the house, and she is old, and a widow, and had not much money, so naturally she stops paying rent and comes here to live. It was perhaps six years ago."

"I see. She had no close friends at all? No one who was much concerned about her?"

"Oh, yes, sir," said another woman timidly. "Mrs. Pozzo over on Hope Street. They were friends, used to visit each other. They were about the same age, you see. And, well, people tried to be good neighbors to her, we were all sorry she was so sick. I know Rosa here would go in to ask how she was, maybe take something to her—I did myself."

"Yes. Where would I find this Mrs. Pozzo? Is she still alive?"

Indeed she was, they assured him, and consulted each other about the address. None of them knew it, but he could easily find it—a small white house, five houses down from the next corner, and a climbing yellow rose vine on the porch.

He thanked them elaborately and started out to find it. As he walked up the block toward Hope Street he wondered what Stewart of Hollywood's racket squad was turning up on the Church of the Enlightened Believers. He had dropped by to ask what they knew about it, if anything. It was a strange one to them. But when they heard that one of its officers was the son of pro parents, they were interested. "We'll sniff around a little," promised Stewart. "It's always a good racket for attracting marks, a new religion." It looked that way to Valentine too; he reflected that Jason might be following in his father's footsteps rather than Josephine's.

He had Steiner and Powers out looking more closely at the neighborhoods where the other four, whom she'd taken home with her, had lived. He had a hunch they would find at least one close friend, somebody concerned, for each one. Probably this Mrs. Pozzo had been the one for Mrs. Mazzini.

He found her, and she had been. When he introduced himself and began to ask questions, a torrent of words poured over his head.

"It is because of that terrible nurse you have come—well I can guess it! She has at last committed some crime that is suspected, and the police come hunting! Oh, she was an evil one, that nurse! And so I told her to her face—so I did—but she did not even answer me back! It was a very wicked thing, and not one thing could I or anyone do about it—I went straight to Father Stefano, he did not like it either, he went to see her, but she was gone—oh, a wicked, wicked thing!" She was a tiny wizened old woman, very dark, with bright little black eyes.

"How?" asked Valentine, and was answered in another torrent. The nurse had come when Mrs. Mazzini got so sick; the doctor said there should be a nurse. This terrible woman, speaking kind words and evil in her heart. And when she had been there a little time, she had—it had later been revealed—persuaded Maria to sign the lawyer's papers. The priest would know what they were. Maria Mazzini had spoken English but not very well, and she'd been very, very sick—it was not known how she had been persuaded to sign the papers, but she had. And the papers had given the nurse all her property and the money in the bank!

"One day I go to see her, and there is a sign that the house is for sale, and she tells me the nurse is taking her away—I did not like it, why need she be taken from her own house? It seemed foolish, but she was too sick for talking, and so I went to see Father Stefano. He said it looked strange to him also, and the nurse had no rights over Maria, to say come or go. And he went and saw this nurse, and she showed him the papers, and said she would take good care of Maria. He told me of this—but he thought there was evil in the woman's heart, and he went again, and they were gone. Gone! And a strange man showing the house to people. You must see Father Stefano—he will tell you—he found out where she had taken Maria— And she let her die

135

without calling a priest, such evil should not be!"

Valentine managed to detach himself at last, and set out to find the priest.

Father Stefano was fat and red-faced, with a booming bass voice. What he had to say was that it seemed obvious to him that Mrs. Mazzini was being victimized by the nurse. The nurse had worked hard to convince him that she was taking responsibility for the old woman out of the goodness of her heart; but there was the house, worth at least twelve thousand, and a little money in the bank—Mrs. Mazzini had been a pensioner. The nurse had shown him a power of attorney; there was no way to challenge this legally. But he had worried about it, and determined to keep an eye on Mrs. Mazzini.

The next time he had gone there, they had already left and a real-estate agent was in charge. But he had got the woman's address from the agent and a few days later—"in my first free time"—had gone to call on Mrs. Mazzini. Incidentally, the house had been sold almost at once; there was a SOLD sign on it that day. And when he found the address, the woman had told him that Mrs. Mazzini had died the day before. He had been very shocked— "Of course, we all knew she was very ill. But what shocked me even more deeply, Sergeant, was that she had not called me or another priest to administer the last rites! When she knew how devout Mrs. Mazzini was—she told me there had not been time, but surely with the type of illness Mrs. Mazzini suffered, she should have known—" He shook his head. "But as you can see, that nurse made quite a little profit from Mrs. Mazzini. I fear she is a wicked and dishonest person." And that, thought Valentine, was the understatement of the year. "Er—I suppose you can't tell me why—?"

Valentine said no, apologized, and thanked him. It was just about as he'd figured. Here, there had been a couple of people concerned about the victim. But Josephine had reckoned that Mrs. Pozzo, the one most concerned, hadn't the means to get

Sorrow to the Grave

far from home often, and that once Mrs. Mazzini was out of
the neighborhood, none of the rest would go to the trouble of
looking her up. She had got her papers signed, put the house
up for sale, announced her plans—and then Mrs. Pozzo had got
the priest to call. He thought that had rattled her a little. For
the priest wasn't just the casual acquaintance, and he was an
educated man who'd see through her postures and simperings—
probably had let her see he did. She got busy right away, moved
Mrs. Mazzini and hoped he wouldn't come asking further.

And what Powers and Steiner turned up showed the same
pattern. All except Ferguson. Nobody seemed to have liked
Ferguson. With Sven Lundgren, it had been the manager of the
small apartment he lived in. They were about the same age, and
liked to play cribbage together. The manager said he'd sized up
that nurse all right—out for what she could get—but hell, way
it happened, what could anybody do about it? If he'd had any
idea what her scheme was—but she had Sven sold on her, and
the manager never heard about the power of attorney until it
was signed. What could you do? And she took Sven off to her
own place to live, and that was that.

"I dropped him a line a coupla times, but he never wrote
back. Knew he got the letters OK though, because they wasn't
returned. Then I had my stroke, and I was sick quite awhile, it
was, oh, I guess four-five months later I called on the phone,
asked for him, and she told me he'd passed on, just awhile ago."
He had lasted at her house just five days. "Poor old Sven. He
had a little nest egg tucked away too, and that bitch got it all."

For Mrs. Joan Harkness, it had been an old friend who
lived with her married daughter not too far away; in fact, Mrs.
Harkness had taken the apartment to be near them. They hadn't
thought much of Josephine either. And they hadn't known about
the power of attorney until just before Josephine took her patient
away. They had tried to talk to Mrs. Harkness, but she was, of
course, very ill, and didn't seem to understand. The married

137

daughter worked, and it wasn't for a week or so that they managed to get down to Santa Monica to see Mrs. Harkness, when the nurse told them that the poor soul had died just yesterday and she'd been about to write them. They had been terribly shocked, but of course she had been very ill—another cancer patient—and nobody could do anything then about the nurse getting what little she had.

For Mrs. Margaret Morgan, it had been a minister—the minister of a Methodist church—and several church friends who were on a Visit-the-Sick committee. They came regularly—she'd had a stroke—and so did the minister, who was evidently conscientious. The minister hadn't liked the nurse from the start; he was a young man who had absorbed some psychology at college, and he said she was *too* demonstrative. He'd been very disturbed when he heard that Mrs. Morgan had signed a legal document of some kind. He had questioned the nurse; she said that as Mrs. Morgan was so ill she needed someone to take care of things for her, and she was happy to oblige, that was all. What could he do? It was done. Then she had taken the sick woman away, and there'd been talk about that. And when the committee located her address and called, they were told that the poor woman had just died. Well, it had been a sad thing, but nothing to be done about it then, of course. He didn't suppose the nurse had got much after all—Mrs. Morgan hadn't had much except a pension that died with her.

Valentine could have told him what Josephine had got. Mrs. Morgan had been another thrifty one. Out of her pension (a private one from her husband's employers) she had saved up a bank account of nearly five thousand dollars, and she had a little furniture, a little jewelry, and a fur coat.

Everything was grist that came to Josephine's mill.

And there they stuck for almost the rest of that week. Nowhere to go; nothing to do but keep an eye on Josephine. Valentine fumed. And Brenda, calling in every day to ask what they had, was worried. Salesmen were bringing people to look at the house—and the nurse might take Mrs. Foster away before it was sold.

But on Friday Zimmerman called Valentine jubilantly to report success. "We've got him—or we're going to have him, right now. Managed to lift his prints off his steering wheel. He's Bradley all right. New Jersey's very happy about it. Two men on the way to pick him up right now."

"Well, it's an ill wind, et cetera," said Valentine. "Congratulations." Suddenly he laughed. "And I've just thought of something—this may be helpful to us too. 'Fly forward, O my heart, from the Foreland to the Start—We're steaming all too slow—' Yes, indeed." (If Mary had been there she'd have picked that one up easily and said, " 'The Long Trail.' ")

"What are you talking about?"

"She has—our Madame X—been getting him to sign prescriptions for her," said Valentine.

"Oh," said Zimmerman, "I get you. Say, that might be a little help to us. We got one of the women he had in with him, plus a patient, but missed your blonde. She got away, cleared her apartment before we got there. It occurs to me now, even if your girl wasn't working with them, she might know that one—try to get in touch with her, maybe to locate another handy doctor. It'll be in the papers who was and wasn't picked up."

"Possible. I'll let you know if she does. Blonde's name?"

"Believe it or not, Diana Forbes. Sounds quite the aristocrat, doesn't she? Has a little pedigree—procuring and abortions."

"Yes, well, we'll see." Valentine went to pass this on to MacDougal. He listened and began to grin happily.

"Nice," he said. "So we can cut off Josephine's source of supply. Give ourselves a little time, anyway."

"If it's the only one she's got."

"Oh, sure. You going to see that pharmacist now?"

"I am," said Valentine, and went. They had been in touch with the pharmacist, who was curious and helpful. That prescription called for thirty tablets, and she had had it refilled about every week. That seemed to indicate that somebody was getting around four strong doses of codeine per day. Which, thought Valentine, would be enough to turn anybody vague, forgetful, and mentally dull—let alone a woman eighty-eight years old. He also thought that Josephine had been lucky, if she'd used this much, that nobody had passed out on her before she was quite ready; some people had an idiosyncrasy for that stuff, and anybody with a weak heart—

He saw the pharmacist and explained. "In the ordinary way, of course, you wouldn't know about Rivers being picked up—so his prescriptions wouldn't be legally good anymore—until you got the new police list of those doctors. But you know

now. Next time the woman comes in, tell her so. All nice and polite and regretful, you know."

"Yes, *sir!*"

"And I'll be interested in her reactions."

"So will I," said the pharmacist. "What you want her for, anyway? Oh, I know you won't talk, but I can make guesses, can't I? Sure, I'll do that—have to anyway, now I know about this doctor."

She had had the prescription refilled last Saturday; they wouldn't have long to wait. She went to the drugstore that next afternoon, with her little plastic bottle bearing the prescription number and the doctor's name....

"I did it really artistic," the pharmacist told Valentine later, grinning. "I said first, like we always do, Certainly, ma'am, like there's no question, and back I go to the back room. Then after a while I came out, looking serious, and said I'd seemed to remember the doctor's name and had looked it up—which nobody would, of course, reason crooked doctors get away with it so long, even when the police know about them and they're on that list. I mean, how many prescriptions do we fill in a day? You look at it to see what it is, that's all—my God, if you stopped every time to check the doctor's name with that list, you'd never get anything else done! It's only if some name on the list is unusual, sticks in your mind, that you're likely to remember it. You know. I remember one that really struck me— about two years back, it was—woman doctor, and her name, if you'll believe me, was Ima Fish! You'd think anybody'd change a name like that, wouldn't you?"

"You would. So you came back and told her Dr. Rivers's name was on the police list of doctors arrested and/or struck off the Medical Register, and you couldn't fill the prescription. What'd she say?"

"First she didn't say anything. Went all red, and then she looked mad as hell. She didn't say anything for quite a while,

141

and then she said that was terrible, there must be some mistake, Dr. Rivers was a respectable man, he'd never do anything wrong. But if you get me, Sergeant, it was—automatic talking. It was what she knew she ought to say, to look on the up-and-up herself. She was"—he groped for a word—"she was shocked, but she wasn't surprised. I mean, it shook her, but she rolled with the punch."

"Mmh, yes. Natural," said Valentine absently. "Thanks very much." He looked at his watch; it was three o'clock. He left the pharmacy counter, fishing out a dime, went to a phone booth and called Brenda's little house. Saturday afternoon, he might catch her at home. He did.

"When did you see Mrs. Foster last?"

"Yesterday, when I got home. Have you—"

"How was she?"

"The way she always is now. Vague is the only word for it. As if she's only half there. Nobody, even that old, would fail as suddenly as all that! She was always as bright and normal as—as anything, only slowed down physically. But now—"

"Yes. I'd like you, and Mrs. Cass, and Miss Devereaux, to drop in at intervals"—he calculated—"from about tomorrow morning on. I think you'll find Mrs. Foster much more like her old self. You see, she's been getting doses of codeine, but Josephine's going to run out sometime today." He told her about that.

"Oh, how *wonderful!* Yes, I see. And if she gets back to her old self, then we can talk to her, and she can understand, and ask for that power of attorney back, and—"

"Not so fast," said Valentine. "I know, Miss Sheldon—you're thinking primarily of rescuing Mrs. Foster. I'm afraid we're thinking first of getting a charge to stick on Josephine. And she's going to be busily trying to contact a new doctor to sign prescription blanks for her—or get hold of a few to forge herself, if she knows enough. I have a little idea that she blackmailed Bradley-Rivers into that, you know. Yes, and how'd she know he'd run to Southern California? Pro grapevine? Yes. And if she knows Diana who slipped out of the net, she might know somebody else to contact—but—"

"What do you *mean?* Who's Diana?"

"Listen, Miss Sheldon. Go and see Mrs. Foster tomorrow. And next day. But promise me you won't—however bright she seems—say one word against Josephine. Don't, as Dave says, rock the boat. And tell Mrs. Cass and Miss Devereaux. This is just so we can have some witnesses for later on—witnesses to state that at the time Josephine was prevented from getting hold of codeine, her patient improved in health mentally and physically. You see? All right. Sure, we could charge her now with feeding her patient a dangerous drug, when the doctor who signed the prescription had never seen the patient—we could probably prove that. But we don't want her on such a charge. On any little charge that might carry a fine or a three-month sentence. Do you see? We want her on a homicide charge, if we can get there. We're working on it. Will you do it that way?"

"All right," said Brenda. "I see what you mean. All right. But if it's not soon—I mean, it does seem like a wasted opportunity. But all right. I'll let you know how she is."

"I have an idea," said Valentine, "that Powers is going to be earning his salary now, keeping track of Josephine. And he'd better lie in wait for her earlier. She's going to be getting around, trying to arrange for a new prescription or getting the stuff under the counter."

MacDougal agreed, "Gives us a little time. But what do we do with it, Dan? You tell me. There's no way to get at her."

"Same old problem. But there are a couple of things we might do," said Valentine abstractedly. "She might, as Zimmerman said, try to contact that Forbes woman. I don't think she's been in intimate contact with Bradley-Rivers, or his office

143

staff, since she's been in California. But she'd know what that setup was, of course, and it could be she could make a guess where Forbes'd be hiding out. Could Forbes direct her to another doctor who'd sell her a prescription? We'll see. And of course we can prove some little things on her—it may be in the end we'll have to bring her in on that, Bradley-Rivers's prescription, and try to break her down into a confession."

"From what I know of Josephine, she wouldn't be broken down very easy or soon," said MacDougal, pulling his mustache thoughtfully.

"She would not," agreed Valentine ruefully.

On Sunday, Josephine had left the house at eleven o'clock. She drove over to Hollywood, to an address on Hobart Avenue. Stayed about half an hour, and came out, Powers said, looking kind of mad. Went to a hole-in-the-wall restaurant on Santa Monica Boulevard, and talked with the girl cashier. Evidently she didn't get anywhere there either; through the front window Powers saw the cashier shaking her head. Josephine walked down to the drugstore on that corner and looked in all the phone books, copied down a couple of addresses. Her next trip took her to a middle-class apartment on DeLongpre, where she stayed only a few minutes. Then she went to an address on Berendo.

Josephine's looking for somebody, Valentine thought, looking over the report. Or several somebodies. Probably for the Forbes woman. She may have known who the woman's friends were, who might be sheltering her, or she might be looking for any shady character she'd known or heard of who might help her out.

Josephine was in a little spot. Mrs. Foster's friends had reluctantly accepted the evidence of their own eyes and ears, to believe that the old woman had lost some of her mental faculties overnight, after her husband's death. That did sometimes happen. But now the codeine tablets that had turned her so dull

and vague were no longer available to Josephine. It would probably take a day or so, maybe longer, for the cumulative effect
to wear off, but then Mrs. Foster was going to be talking and
acting much like her old self—unless, of course, that cumulative
effect had already done some permanent damage. A woman of
eighty-eight—

But if she did get to be her old, bright self, that would be
disastrous for Josephine. If friends saw Mrs. Foster return to
normal or nearly so, they were going to wonder and talk about
what had caused her recent condition, and they might—knowing
about that power of attorney—put two and two together. That,
Josephine couldn't have. On this deal, things weren't going as
smoothly as usual for Josephine.

When she had visited seven addresses, and it was nearing
three-thirty, she had stopped at another drugstore and then
driven back to Ocean Park. "After I saw her go into the house,"
said Powers, "I went back to find out what she'd bought. Lucky
she sticks out like a sore thumb, people remember her. She got
four-five little bottles of that nonprescription sleeping stuff, and
a bottle of ten-grain aspirin."

"That figures." And enough of those— But Valentine didn't
think she could get the old woman—especially when she wasn't
under the codeine—to swallow more than two or three tablets
at once. Those nonprescription sleeping tablets were largely
psychological in effect, hardly stronger than aspirin.

He called Zimmerman, explained the situation, and gave
him the list of addresses she'd visited. "Any of them ring a bell?"

"Mmh. That one on Hobart. Where Forbes's sister lives.
We looked there. Also that restaurant on Santa Monica. Why?
Let me think.... Oh, sure. We picked up one of the busboys
there, awhile ago, for peddling reefers. Suppose she knew about
him? How?"

"Oh, really," said Valentine. "That's a funny one."
He thought, Mike? Brenda had wondered if he was an addict.

145

But what good would that do her? She couldn't get the old lady to—

Morphine, he thought. Not a fashionable thing to get addicted to these days, but a dope pusher could probably get it if requested. Yes, and at a price too. She must be feeling a little desperate.

Everything going along almost as smooth as usual—almost—and she was so near to finishing up this little caper! As soon as the house was sold—she had to keep things on an even keel until then, Mrs. Foster alive but obviously much deteriorated mentally and physically; and now that she'd been welcoming all visitors, it would look rather odd if she started keeping them out again. And with Mrs. Foster her normal self, noticing things—in that small house—she couldn't very well. If she let visitors see Mrs. Foster as her old normal self, it might look very odd indeed if, when the house was sold and the old woman taken away to Josephine's, she very shortly died, presumably of senile decay, even if, in the meantime, Josephine had managed to get hold of some dope again to put her back where she'd been.

A very awkward little spot indeed. Because, of course, this was another of her victims who had people concerned about her. And Josephine knew that at least one of them, Mrs. Cass, disliked and distrusted her. She couldn't have any oddnesses show.

She would infinitely prefer to locate a new crooked doctor and buy a prescription from him. That would cost her less than dependence on a pusher. But while she'd been in California, she'd been out of touch with the pros, except for Bradley-Rivers; it was likely she didn't know any other crooked doctors. It would be a rather difficult hunt, cold; she could hardly pick a doctor at random and if he was an honest man hope to close the conversation by thanking him and walking out.

Well. See what happened tomorrow. Meanwhile, Valentine

went to see Mrs. Mazzini's doctor—the one who had been attending her before Josephine removed her to her own place.

Brenda called headquarters at five o'clock. "Hello, Brenda," said MacDougal. "What happened?"

"And when did I invite you to say anything but Miss Sheldon?"

"Oh, I don't wait for invitations. Takes too long. Especially with standoffish redheads."

"I told you I detest autocratic men. But I suppose most cops are, or they wouldn't be cops. Whatever they *look* like."

"A certain air of authority is encouraged," said Mac-Dougal, "sure. How was Mrs. Foster?"

"Well, she wasn't as bright as she used to be, but more like her old self—she followed what I said, and talked about Mr. Foster and the nurse and so on. I was dying to tell her everything, only I'd promised and besides she'd have been so frightened. But listen, Sergeant—"

"Now, now. Turn about fair play. Dave."

"Has anyone ever called you Davy?" asked Brenda sweetly.

"Not unless they wanted a punch in the nose." He was still trying to break Valentine of that habit.

"Oh, fine," she said pleasedly. "You look like a Davy, somehow. The pink cheeks and—"

"I suppose I handed you that one. All right, what were you going to say?"

"She talked about that lout. As far as she remembered he's only been there twice. She didn't like him, said he was very rude to her, and she's disturbed about it. I think because—she still likes the nurse all right, you see—he's the nurse's son, and that—well, puzzles her. He's so obviously a delinquent."

"Too old for that now. Over eighteen."

"Don't quibble, Davy boy. And—"

"Listen, you try tagging that on me at your own risk. I

147

abide by a maxim my old dad taught me—never hit a woman with the open hand."

"That doesn't surprise me. As far as I'm concerned, I'll stay out of range. Well out of range. Will you let me finish what I'm trying to tell you?"

"Proceed."

"Well, she said he came again yesterday, and they're going to move all the furniture from the house, everything—he came to see what there was, how big a truck he'd need. And Mrs. Foster said he had a gun in his pocket. She saw him take it out, and the nurse made him put it away. She—Mrs. Foster—was frightened. She said it seemed funny a nice woman like her would have such a bad young fellow for a son. And the nurse tried to sell me she'd just imagined it, was seeing things, but I know better—though I didn't say so, pretended to believe the nurse. And I just thought, maybe he hasn't got a license for it and you could—"

"That could be. But getting Mike out of the way—and we couldn't hold him on that, you know—wouldn't solve any other problems," sighed MacDougal. "OK, thanks very much. If I don't get tied up unexpectedly—which, you'd better find out now, cops are apt to—what about dinner Tuesday night?"

"Well, of course," said Brenda thoughtfully, "we don't get paid the highest union salary at Garnetts'. I ought to take advantage of free meals. I'm saving up for a car."

"Only good sense."

"Mmh. Why, I might save as much as five dollars a week more; if I ate enough I could probably skip breakfast. It's very nice of you, thank you very much."

"Pure altruism," said MacDougal. "Say seven o'clock."

Mrs. Mazzini's former doctor, a lantern-jawed fellow who rejoiced in the name of Ucceletore, had been shocked to hear of her death so soon after the nurse had taken her away. He had gone over her thoroughly not long before, and would have confidently predicted that she'd hang on at least another six months. There were signs—

"Say so to the nurse?" asked Valentine.

Ucceletore raised his brows. "I believe I did, yes. Why?"

"Reason she didn't ask you to sign the death certificate. She let another doctor look the woman over once, so technically she'd be under a doctor's care at the time of death and he could sign the certificate."

Ucceletore stared at him. "Are you telling me—"

"That's what I'm telling you. But no talk about it, please. You can see, its impossible to prove."

"*Fuori!*" said Ucceletore softly. "I will be damned. . . . But why, in God's name? And what put you onto it, after all this time?"

"Oh, your Mrs. Mazzini was just one of a crowd, Doctor. One of a crowd of fourteen. We're just catching up."

The doctor didn't say anything to that. He just stared. Then he said, "My good God in heaven."

"Doctor," said Valentine, "if Mrs. Mazzini had died about the same time she did, still under your care, would you have been suspicious? Instantly suspected she'd been given a shove? Refused to sign the certificate?"

Ucceletore gave a massive shrug and said ruefully, "Of course not. Of course not. We don't know everything, after all. She was a dying woman. I expected her to live on that long, but if I had known she had died then, I would have thought, well, God in His infinite mercy has been kind, to spare her suffering—He takes them in His own time. . . . But what an incredible— And very difficult for you to prove anything, I see that, of course."

"Say it twice."

On Monday, Josephine took off again. Powers called in about an hour later. "I thought I'd better, Sergeant. First chance

149

I've had. The kid came—in that new red T-bird—and evidently stayed. I thought, maybe to see the old lady doesn't have visitors, keep her quiet someway until the nurse can get hold of more dope."

"Yes." Valentine considered. He didn't like that. That was the obvious deduction; and what he'd heard of Mike, he was hair-trigger and irresponsible. "Where is she now?"

"If you'll believe me," said Powers, sounding amused, "inside an old flea trap of a sixth-class hotel on Olive Avenue, which looks to me very much like a cover for a sixth-rate cathouse. You might ask the Hollywood boys if they know it."

"And a very good place to go if you're looking for a crooked doctor," said Valentine. "Address? . . . OK, thanks, Mark." He relayed that to MacDougal, dialing.

MacDougal didn't like it either. He thought about it while Valentine talked to the Newton Street precinct station downtown. "Bang on the nose," said Valentine, "they've closed it twice and were much obliged to know it's in business again. Could be that Josephine will have another codeine prescription inside a few hours. Where'd she get that address? Mike, possibly?"

"Possibly," said MacDougal absently. Valentine picked up the phone again. He called Mrs. Cass and asked her to call at the Foster house, and phone back to report.

Fifteen minutes later she did so. The nurse's car was gone, she said, and only that awful young fellow was there. He told her Mrs. Foster wasn't feeling so good today and was in bed, couldn't see anybody.

"What could I do? I tried to get in, I said she ought to have someone with her—another woman—if the nurse wasn't there and she was feeling sick—but he shut the door in my face! When I think of what they're *doing* to— And *I* was the one who brought her—"

"Yes, well, don't worry too much," said Valentine. "Josephine can't risk anything happening until the house is sold, you know. Thanks very much." He put the phone down. "And of course Mrs. Foster doesn't like or trust Mike, the little she's seen of him, so if he's watching TV in the living room she'd probably retire to her bedroom, maybe with the door shut. Wouldn't hear him telling lies to callers. It's probably quite all right. And in any case, nothing we can do about it."

Powers came in at three-thirty. "She's got what she was after," he said. "From the cathouse—was it?—"

"Looks that way."

"I thought so—she went up to Santa Monica Boulevard into an old office building just this side of Fairfax. It was kind of tricky, I didn't want to show myself, but there was nothing for it, I had to get in the elevator with her to see what floor she was going to, there wasn't an indicator. I kept my head down and stayed behind her. She went to five, so I got off at six and made time down the stairs. She went into a doctor's office— Dr. C. H. Wallis. It's a very crumby setup, dirty old building, rents probably dirt cheap. Room five-twelve, by the way."

"How long was she in there?"

"About forty minutes. I was peeking over the banister when she came out, and she looked mad as hell. I'd guess she probably had to pay through the nose for what she got. And she'd have had to pay whoever she saw at the cathouse for an introduction, too. She came back to the beach on the freeway. She was in a hurry."

"Naturally."

"Sure. Stopped at a Thrifty—that big new one on Wilshire—and had a prescription filled. Went straight home. So I went back and asked the pharmacist what it was. Same as before, Empirin Number Three."

"Yes. And how convenient that the new doctor will fall under Lieutenant Zimmerman too, same precinct area. Such a rigmarole to explain all over again to somebody else." Suddenly Valentine began to smile. "Maybe we're getting closer," he said. "Maybe we can start to play a little game with Josephine." He dialed Zimmerman, briefly explained the situation. "Know anything about Wallis?"

"Nothing. Obviously he's on the wrong side of the fence. We'll take a look. Thanks very much. You're getting around on this, aren't you?"

"And around," said Valentine, "and around. Yes. Look, if you get anything on Wallis, which you probably will if you look hard, hold off on him right now, will you? We may want to— arrange things. Set it up just right, to cut off her supply again at a psychological moment."

"That's if we get anything on him. OK, if you don't ask me to leave him alone till next year. Always happy to cooperate, Sergeant."

MacDougal looked at him as he put the phone down. "What's this about a psychological moment?"

"I'll tell you—just a little idea...."

He had a date with Mary that night. He went home, took a shower and re-dressed, fed Garm and took him downstairs to the young manager's apartment, where four-year-old Stevie welcomed them in gleefully. It was another reason Valentine lived in this particular apartment, not as large or comfortable as his old one. Garm was a gregarious dog, and left alone shattered the peace for blocks around with his powerful voice. Fortunately the manager liked dogs....

Settled at a quiet corner table of the Fox and Hounds, they ordered drinks. Valentine brought Mary up to date on Josephine. She listened absorbedly, green eyes fixed on his.

"I'm afraid I agree with Brenda," she said. "A chance to get that poor old woman out of danger, at least. I don't see why, with all you know, you can't charge her. I see that on just one or two or even three, you couldn't, but with this many, I should think the presumption would be so strong—"

"No. The D.A. and the grand jury have to abide by the letter of the law, and technically we've got no evidence here at all, on murder. But I have," said Valentine, rattling ice cubes in his glass, "a small idea how to get at Josephine."

"At last. You're usually smarter, but I knew you'd get there in the end."

"Don't be impudent," said Valentine, grinning at her.

"What's the idea?"

"I think maybe we can rattle her some. This deal hasn't gone as smoothly as usual for her. To start with, she had several people who were concerned about the old woman. More people, and more concerned, than she's had on any other case before. But it was irresistible, because here was another house—a windfall. She's been annoyed by all these people keeping tabs on Mrs. Foster, but she's worked damned hard at creating the good impression. However, Mrs. Cass, and also the Devereaux woman, have let her see that they don't like her, suspect her of defrauding the old woman at least. That's a danger to her— they might make trouble. Then, Mike has been around, for a couple of people to see, and made a bad impression, undermined the impression she's tried to create. From what Brenda Sheldon said, that's worrying her quite a little. And now she's had this annoyance—and further danger—of losing her tame doctor and having to scurry around finding another, getting more dope to keep the old woman looking as if she's in senile decay."

"Yes, I see that."

Valentine finished his drink. "Well, it occurs to me, it might be salutary to worry her a lot more. We could, for instance, take the pharmacist into our confidence, get him to substitute something harmless for the codeine, so that she wouldn't dare take the old woman to see a doctor—even Dr. Robertson. Remember, the law says that a doctor must have seen the patient within ten days of death, or an autopsy is mandatory. Puzzle Josephine like hell that her codeine tablets weren't working any more. . . . But on the whole, I don't think we'll try that yet. Men lurking near the house, all very visible and very plainly cops— yes, I think that would rattle her quite a lot. Dave's been saying, don't rock the boat, because we haven't got anything legal on her—but this could be one way to get it. She's very longheaded, our Josephine, but if we got her scared—scared that she's slipped up somewhere, got herself suspected— And then, if Zimmerman's got something on that Dr. Wallis, which he probably will get, let him lay the charge, and close down her source of supply again." His tone was dreamy.

"Yes. And then?"

"And then," said Valentine, beckoning the waiter, "when she's thoroughly alarmed and wondering what to do now, Dave and I ring her doorbell and very suddenly and crudely accuse her of multiple murder. Do you think, in panic, she might give herself away somehow? Come out with something incriminating? It's a chance."

Mary was silent, and then said, "I don't know, Dan. She's— longheaded, as you say. I don't know."

"It's a chance," repeated Valentine. "That's all."

On Tuesday afternoon, when Brenda turned down Royce Street, there was a Ford truck sitting in front of the Foster house and Mike Slaney was just piling one of the tapestry chairs into the back, on top of other furniture. Brenda's heart missed a beat. They were moving, today or tomorrow.

155

She did not speak to Mike, but turned up the walk. The nurse came to the door almost at once. "I see you're—really moving," said Brenda.

"That's right, Miss Sheldon." The automatic jolly smile. "Like you see. I figure I can make the poor old dear more comfortable in my own place, and then it's just common sense, see, she don't have much, you know, and what with the doctor bills and maybe hospital bills later on, and all, what she gets for the house'll—"

"Yes. I'd like to come in and see her."

"She's resting right now, Miss Sheldon. She's gone down something terrible since The Death, you know."

"She was almost like her old self when I saw her on Sunday," said Brenda, and had the satisfaction of seeing uneasiness in the woman's expression. She was still angry at what Mrs. Cass had told her—about the woman leaving that lout Mike here—on guard, yesterday, to claim Mrs. Foster was sick and keep people out. Valentine had said something about getting Josephine rattled. She didn't think it would do any harm to mention that—it would be natural. She said firmly, "I'd like to see Mrs. Foster, please. Mrs. Cass told me yesterday that Mrs. Foster was ill, and only your son was here. I don't call that giving her very good care, leaving her if she was—"

"Now I don't need you to tell me my job, miss—it was just a li'l upset like, she needed rest was all—and I'm sorry, you can see we're kind of busy right now."

Mike came up behind Brenda and instinctively she stepped away from the door. But he only looked at her insolently and said, "Hi, doll," and jerked open the screen door. Brenda went in on his heels.

"Where's Mrs. Foster?"

"I told you, she's sleepin', you can't—I can't ask you in right now, Miss Sheldon—" Her tone was almost pleading. "She's all right again, but she needs lotsa rest, see—you know how she is, she just seems to lie around, don't take notice of anything—and I take care o' her real good, you know that."

"Oh, hell, Ma, let her look at the old bag, she wants. 'Bout all she can do." He was no longer sullen or indifferent; he sounded almost happy, and he grinned widely at her. He shifted the TV table and bent to pick up the portable TV. "Carry one like that 'n each hand," he boasted. "*Two* like that." He heaved it up, grunting.

"You be careful." The nurse's tone was warning.

"Hell, I'm ridin' high!" he said. "Out o' the road, doll." The screen banged behind him.

Brenda wasted no further words, but marched into the bedroom. The old woman was lying motionless on the bed, eyes closed.

"Please, Miss Sheldon—"

"Mrs. Foster." Brenda laid a hand on her shoulder. Slowly Mrs. Foster opened her eyes. "How are you, Mrs. Foster?"

"I—I feel—so awful—tired," whispered the old woman. "Those—pills. Not like—ones I useta—"

"Now, honey—you can see, Miss Sheldon—"

"Ought—know you, child. I can't rightly—"

"I'm Brenda, Mrs. Foster—your friend Brenda Sheldon."

Suddenly the old woman clutched her arm. "—Hurt me," she muttered painfully. "My arms 'n' legs—hurt—still hurt—he—"

"Now, dear, that's that nasty old arthritis," said the nurse rapidly. "You know that, an' the pills are to help cure it. Nearly time for 'nother one, dear—you like your pillow plumped up, honey? Here—"

"He *did*—please—it hurts—"

"Jus' the arthritis li'l bit worse, honey." Outside, Mike was whistling, shrill and clear and happy. The truck door slammed. "Time take another pill now."

"Just had one, not so long—"

"Time gets away from you, dearie. Now you just lay down again and have a nice rest, 'n' we'll ask Miss Sheldon not to stay talkin'."

"Mrs. Slaney," said Brenda furiously, "will you please stop putting on the act with all the dearies and honeys! You aren't fooling any of us, you know! I know exactly what Mrs. Foster means to you—the money you'll get for her house and furniture! A nice little profit—" She hadn't known she was going to boil over like that; just, suddenly, it was intolerable, listening to that unctuous pseudo-motherly tone. Her own voice rose. "That's what you were out for from the start, anyone could see! You must think we're all fools. Well, maybe you've run into some fools before and got away with this sort of thing"—she hadn't really lost her temper, and she knew there were things she must not say, but it was a fine feeling to loose off at the woman—"because you've probably built up a nice little racket for yourself, this isn't the first helpless patient you've robbed! Is it? Is it? But just don't expect Mrs. Foster's friends to stand by and listen to all your damned dearies and sweeties and not—"

"Oh, now, Miss Sheldon, that's just not so, I'm sure sorry you think that way. I do my very best."

"Let her talk," said Mike from the door. Brenda turned. He stood leaning on the doorpost, smiling unpleasantly; his eyes were queerly excited. A lock of lank hair had fallen across his brow and his open-necked shirt was sweat-stained. "Just let her talk. Not one damn thing she can do, Ma. Never is anything they can do, is there? Way you—"

"Mike, you go 'n' finish the loading, boy. Miss Sheldon's just got things wrong, 's all— That ain't so, miss, you just think wrong about it because—"

"Hurts," whispered the old woman. Brenda looked down and saw that she had shrunk away to the opposite side of the bed. Her dull eyes were frightened. She was looking at Mike.

"Just let her talk," he said, and laughed, and turned away.

"Please, Miss Sheldon—"

"I wonder whether you have a police record," said Brenda, looking at her contemptuously. She was rather enjoying herself now. Only she must remember not to let out— "Several of us saw what your dirty little scheme was from the start, you know—we're not blind! How many other people have you robbed this way? Just don't expect us to stand by and watch it without doing something, that's all! And I'd like to be sure just what kind of good care you're giving Mrs. Foster, too. You ought to be reported to the police, and it just could be we'll do that. They might like to know a few things—"

"Please, Miss Sheldon—Miss Sheldon, you gotta believe me, you're all wrong, that's not so— I'd never— Why, I think the world of— I gotta make you believe me—just want take good care of her, 's all—"

"Well, I've said what I came to say," said Brenda coldly. "Don't waste time trying to convince me. But I warn you, people will be keeping an eye on Mrs. Foster—and on you."

"C'n I help it, she starts to get senile so quick? Some of 'em do go like that—I just try take good care—"

"And you'd better not try anything more!" said Brenda recklessly. She walked out fast; and the fat woman followed her, almost pleading to be believed, protesting her honesty and good intentions.

Mike was slinging the other tapestry chair into the truck, without much regard for its mahogany legs.

Mrs. Slaney didn't follow her out the door.

Brenda went on home, feeling alternately pleased with herself, angry, and speculative about what Mrs. Foster had said. Appalled, she thought, could that possibly mean—?

And she'd probably have another fight with the autocratic MacDougal about it. When you thought about it, it was very surprising, about MacDougal. Looking like a Boy Scout, and actually being the autocratic and, well, masculine person he was. When you knew him. That absurd mustache...He'd roar at her and say, Don't rock the boat and call her seven kinds of damn fool. Let him.

Why on earth she was going out with him again.

15

Oddly enough, MacDougal didn't roar at her. He listened to an account of that little scene, stroking his mustache, and said, "Well. It might be— I see that—about the only thing left to us to try. And you might have fired our opening gun."

"Don't tell me you approve!"

"I think so. You didn't mention that we *are* in it, or anything about suspected homicides?"

"I did not. I hadn't really lost my temper, you know. I just thought it might be a good idea to scare her. Sergeant Valentine said something about getting her rattled."

"Yes. And come to think, not the opening gun. Yes, just as Dan says, this hasn't been one of her easiest jobs. First, she's had to devote a little more time to it than usual. There was the old man first—I think she hesitated about getting rid of him right away. Mrs. Foster hadn't yet come under her tender care and was up and about, noticing things, and people dropping in. I wonder about that—whether he died naturally or she did risk finishing him off."

Brenda said, horrified, "Not Mr. Foster too."

"Well, you know," said MacDougal, "any doctor'd tell you about strokes. They come from slight to massive. And generally speaking, if a stroke's going to carry you off it doesn't waste time. We've got a good medical opinion that if a massive stroke doesn't cause death within forty-eight hours, there's a pretty good chance of partial recovery. And he lasted three weeks."

"*No!*" whispered Brenda.

"And all we can do about it is wonder. If it was suffocation—as I think the chances are it was, *if* she did"—he shrugged—"no traces now. Few at any time." He sipped his drink.

"But it's incredible."

"Sure. And then, neighbors and friends a lot more concerned than on her other victims. And then suddenly losing her tame doctor. This has been a jinx case for Josephine. Danny says, make it even more so. He may have something. Dan—he sees things sometimes." He lifted a hand to the waiter, who scurried to collect their empty glasses and proffer menus. "He says if we can get her scared—"

"Oh, I just remembered, I didn't tell you *that!*—and I had the most awful thought about it— Mrs. Foster was back to being the way she's been—"

"Yes, Josephine's got a new prescription."

"But from what she did say, and knowing from Mrs. Cass how that woman wasn't there yesterday and Mike *was*—"

He listened to that. "She said her arms and legs hurt. 'Still' hurt. And something about 'He *did.*' Well, well." Suddenly his blue eyes went cold and for a moment he looked the complete adult he was.

"And she was frightened of him, I could see. I had the most awful idea. You know, if you're right about those pills, yesterday she'd have been pretty well back to normal. The only thing I don't see—"

"Don't you?" he said. "Don't you, Brenda? I don't claim

to be the smartest cop in California, but I can add two and two, and I don't like the answer I get here, not at all. What you were going to say was that evidently Mrs. Foster is still sold on Josephine—taking her pills meekly, letting Josephine plan for her—so there'd be no danger that, restored to her normal self, she'd make any complaint, ask for help. Only of course they can't afford to let anyone see her back to normal. It's rattled Josephine that anyone did see her heading that way. But Mike—left in charge—could have put that sign back on the door, or made excuses. I don't think he considered going to the bother. He did the easiest thing, and tied the old lady up until Mama got back with the new pills. Probably gagged her too."

"Oh, no, I can't bear to think— And she was trying to tell me—oh, how *awful*—"

"And I don't think that was Mama's idea, either." MacDougal looked at his fresh drink. "Because now Mrs. Foster will be afraid. I'll bet Josephine had quite a time soothing her down, persuading her Mikie's just a mischievous kid, coaxing her to go on trusting Josephine. It's on the cards Mrs. Foster'd try to ask for help, complain now, if she could. She'll have to be kept pretty well under, but even so she might let something out. I'll bet Mama was damn mad at Mikie. And Mike—you said he was way up? Having a ball loading the truck?"

"Riding high," said Brenda. "He said that. Riding high."

"This I don't like for sure," said MacDougal, playing with his mustache and looking at her seriously. "That sounds as if maybe Mike's got himself on the big H. And that kind are—unpredictable. If he's anything like Mama in having absolutely no scruples— Don't look like that. . . . I never knew anybody before that had eyes and hair the same color. Did you know they are? Just the color of an Irish setter I had when I was a kid. You're kind of cute, Brenda, did you know? Don't cry."

"I'm *not!*" she said indignantly, blowing her nose. "And I can't help being little—if you knew what a nuisance it is! And

I loathe being called cute! Of course you're horrifying me, am I supposed to say, Isn't it terrible, and change the subject? What are you going to *do?*"

"Play it Dan's way," said MacDougal. "He's the boss, after all. I didn't see it at first, because we haven't got any evidence for the D.A. But sometimes, a tricky one like this, you have to go all round the back ways. And anyway, it's all we *can* do, as the thing stands now. What would you like?" The waiter was hovering.

"What does it matter? Oh, I guess the tournedos of beef with mushrooms...tomato juice...Roquefort dressing."

"And the sirloin. Medium-well...tomato juice...Roquefort." MacDougal finished his drink.

"*What* are you going to do?"

"First step is to safeguard Mrs. Foster. Tell all those real-estate agents to lay off. Don't sell the house. They won't like it, they're going to ask questions we can't answer, but they'll have to take police orders. You see, legally Josephine couldn't sell the house, having just the power of attorney, after Mrs. Foster was dead. That should relieve your mind a little."

"Yes, of course. But what she—they—are doing to her—! She's so old, and all those drugs might—"

"Tell you something else our tame medical man said. The old ones are the tough ones. Anybody who's lived to be eighty-eight has to be tough. Younger people, he said, often give up very easy, lose the will to live. But the old ones surprise you, the way they hang on."

"Yes, I know," said Brenda forlornly. "Gran— I don't suppose Mrs. Foster would have much longer to live, at eighty-eight. Though she told me once her older sister lived to be ninety-six, and her mother was ninety-four. And a lot of people think, what's life to anybody that old? Well, if they're senile, or in pain, or— But she wasn't! Her mind was working as well as ever, she was talking and feeling and liking life, she was—is—still a *person*, you know?"

"You take it easy. I said we'd try to save her."

"And then what, after the house agents?"

"Scare Josephine," he said. "I think you rattled her quite a bit today. She must have known that a couple of you people weren't quite sold on her, but you made it pretty definite, and what you said struck home. She's rattled already because of the extra trouble she's run into with Mrs. Foster. So now we ride her some more. First, Zimmerman's looking for something on her new doctor. If he gets it, we can shut down her line of supply again. May want to delay a little on that, until she's softened up. We put on the obvious tail. And there's another thing that isn't really hooked up to this, but is probably worrying her some more—Jason the minister." He told her about that, and won a small laugh. "And Mike. We'll have a little look at Mike, I think. If we find anything we can pick him up on, it'll seem like everything's going wrong at once for her.

"And then Dan and I walk in and accuse her. With chapter and verse, all the details we've worked out. She might just come to pieces and make some damaging admissions. It's a chance."

"Well, maybe," said Brenda. "But a good chance?"

"I couldn't say," he said soberly. "Just, we'll try for it."

What he'd had to tell her about Jason had showed up yesterday. Stewart of the Hollywood racket squad had called Valentine to thank him for the tip about the Enlightened Believers.

"Oh? They're not quite as enlightened as they should be?"

"We've got a little enlightened ourselves," said Stewart. He sounded amused. "It started to look a little funny when I sent a man over to attend one of the services, size the place up. They hold services Saturdays and Wednesday nights. Attendant wouldn't let him in—said he was sorry, but anybody wanting to attend had to be introduced by a member of the church. Well, generally churches are only too happy to gather new sheep into the fold. So I was interested, but you can see it was a little awkward to get at. I had a man hang around while members were flocking in, to spot license plates and find out who some of them are. As it happened, that wasn't necessary. In the crowd was one Mr. Adam Knapp, big as life—so then I *knew* it was a racket."

"Known pro?"

"Good God, Sergeant, if he heard that he'd have a heart attack! Most respectable citizen in town—and one of the richest. He's got almost all the money there is. He didn't make it, just inherited it, and he's a very nice guy for all of that. Gives a lot of it away. He's got no sense at all about hanging on to it. In my time at this desk, he's fallen for I wouldn't know how many con games, some of 'em nearly as crude as the pigeon drop—and he's always so shocked when the nice man turns out to be something different—and he never learns. The grifter's dream, I tell you."

Valentine laughed. "I see."

"So I know him—very nice guy, Knapp, democratic and all that. So I go to see him and ask about the Enlightened Believers. Why, Lieutenant Stewart, he says, all indignant, you can't be suspecting anything wrong about these dedicated men! He's thoroughly sold on the Believers. Says he's introduced several new members since discovering this wonderful faith—and mentioned a couple of the sillier society girls over forty. He was herded into the flock by, if you'll believe me, his stockbroker."

"Do tell," said Valentine. " 'Old is the song that I sing,/ Old as my unpaid bills—' " Kipling always had the right word.

"What? Well, you know the rules the con men go by: Never try to take anybody at his own game, but outside it the smartest guy at his job is frequently a sitting pigeon, and I do mean pigeon. It seems, from what Knapp says—oh, he's enthusiastic about the Believers, gave him a new lease on life and so on—

they put on a kind of glorified revival meeting, with all the trappings. And one of the rituals is their own version of—what do you call it, not a churchgoer myself—communion, and that comes at every service. Knapp was looking exalted as hell by the time he got to that. 'Lieutenant,' he says all solemn, 'I tell you the Reverend Hoyt is a man of great spiritual power. At the climax of our communion, invariably the most wonderful, indescribable exaltation enters one's soul, a feeling of being literally uplifted by God's hand.' I say that sounded nice and how much money had he given them? He looked offended and protested a lot more that there couldn't possibly be anything wrong, but I finally got out of him that he's laying out a very hair-raising sum on a fine new edifice they're building. So I say, will he take me in to see a service? He's only too eager to—says I'll see for myself how innocent and uplifting it is. Damndest experience I ever had," said Stewart reminiscently, chuckling. "Cut a long story short, it was a kind of super revival meeting— this Hoyt looks like the pictures of William Jennings Bryan. Flowing locks and a magnetic eye. At the climax of the service or ritual or whatever they call it, the ushers hand out little paper cups to everybody, with what looks like wine in them, and the silver-tongued orator delivers an impressive invitation to God to come and join the company, and everybody says Amen and drinks what's in the cups. It tasted a little bit like cough syrup."

"And did you feel mightily exalted?" asked Valentine.

"Brother," said Stewart simply. "I never was so damn exalted in my life. I was the greatest man on earth. I could do anything. Everybody else felt the same way; they started to sing and yell and a few people danced in the aisles. I yelled too. It was wonderful—I felt like God. Talk about exalted."

"How long did it last?"

"Oh, must've been a good fifteen minutes or so—though I wasn't keeping track of time. When I started to come out of it a little, of course I recognized the symptoms. They broke up

167

about ten minutes later. And old Knapp says, Hadn't I experienced this spiritual exaltation? I said I sure as hell had, and called one of the boys to drive me home because I still wasn't sure of my judgment. But is it any wonder all those nice innocent people are sold on the Believers? I tell you, it was wonderful—it was really something."

"I believe you. So you raided the premises. What was it?"

"Oh, bennies. Just plain old bennies. One to a customer. One thing," said Stewart thoughtfully, "I appreciate the psychology of junkies more—you can see how it'd be a temptation, when it makes you feel like that."

"Have you picked them all up?" asked Valentine, laughing.

"Warrants just about ready now. Infringe on your business?"

"Not in the least—in fact, I think it'll be a little help. Take Jason with my blessing."

Josephine moved her patient to the house on Larman Drive on Wednesday. Also on Wednesday, several men went to see all the real-estate people who had the Foster house on their lists, and gave them polite police orders to hold off trying to sell it. There were protests and questions, but in the end they agreed to the orders.

That was the first move against her. Mrs. Foster had to be kept alive until the house was sold: she'd know that.

Valentine dropped in to see Brenda at her office, Garnetts' Manufacturing Jewelers. It was a very classy firm, with offices on Wilshire Boulevard, and he apologized for coming, to reveal her acquaintanceship with such hoi polloi as cops.

"It's all right," said Brenda, smiling, "if it's not too often. Mr. Garnett senior can be stuffy about extended coffee breaks. What is it?"

"I want you and Mrs. Cass and Miss Devereaux to call at the house very often now. One or two of you every day. If just briefly. Asking to see Mrs. Foster. And about two days from now, I want one of you—doesn't matter which—to let out something. It may be that Josephine will give you the opening, ask why you're coming so often, protest what good care she's giving her patient. But if she doesn't, make one. Make it sound as if you're letting it out unintentionally, hadn't meant to. And very obviously try to cover up."

"Let what out?"

"That you were asked to call often. Every day. By some unspecified agency. By that time, we'll have the obvious tails attached, and they'll have been noticed."

"Mmh," said Brenda. "*I* should think the best thing to do would be to get the pharmacist to substitute harmless pills. Then in a few days Mrs. Foster would be herself, and if Mike did tie her up that time she could—"

"I've thought of a couple of reasons against that," said Valentine. "First, we've no excuse to get into the house, and she won't be coming out, or allowed to use the phone. Second, it might be even more dangerous for her. Because now she knows she *is* in danger, from Mike at least, and with her mind working clearly again she might begin to wonder about Josephine—and those pills. And you see, they'd have to restrain her in some way from calling attention to herself, trying to get help. It's obvious that Josephine can't control Mike. He just might do something stupid."

"Yes, I see," said Brenda with a shiver. "All right, I'll tell Mrs. Cass and Miss Devereaux. We all want to help—anything we can do."

"This will be a big help."

Mrs. Cass and Brenda drove up to Larman Drive that very evening. They had a little trouble finding it; it was a short, winding street going up into the hills above Sunset. At its lower end it was lined with newish small ranch houses, but farther up there were many unsold empty lots. Mrs. Slaney's house sat squarely across the end of the dead-end street, and it was the only two-story house on the block. It was an old frame house, painted a violent Dutch pink with white trim; the light was just fading and they could see that.

"I don't *like* it," said Mrs. Cass. "Why, the nearest house is a good half block away! A person could go screaming her head off and never be heard."

The red T-bird wasn't in the drive, only Josephine's old blue Ford. The yard was neglected, the cement walk up to the house cracked. Brenda pushed the bell. After an interval she pushed it again.

"I'm comin', I'm comin'," said Josephine's voice. "Was upstairs—allus upstairs when the bell rings." She switched on the porchlight; the front door was open, this hot evening.

"Hello, Mrs. Slaney," said Brenda. "We thought we'd call and see how Mrs. Foster likes her new home."

For a moment the nurse looked taken aback; then she gave them her automatic jolly smile and pushed open the screen. "Why, I'm sure glad you did, come right in! I know you both got to thinking wrong about me, some reason, and I'm awful glad I can show you what a nice comfortable place I got for the old soul, an'—an' take the chance again, tell you I just want t' do what's best for her, honest to God. Come right in."

They went in. Like many houses of its period, it had no entrance hall, and they entered directly into the living room. Their hostess was busy switching on lights.

"Been gettin' her settled upstairs. Didn't reelize how near dark it was. There now, you set an' make yourselves comfortable. You can see for yourself what a nice place I got—*lot* nicer place than hers, I don't hafta go round—" There was naïve pride and triumph in her voice.

Brenda looked around and almost blinked. Next she wanted badly to laugh.

The big old room was crammed with furniture and ornaments. At first glance, there wasn't a single object of good taste or bearing any relationship to its surroundings or any other object. Money had been spent indiscriminately here, by someone lacking any taste, unerringly choosing all the wrong things.

She sat down on one end of an immensely long and heavy-armed modern sofa, upholstered in amber tweed with a black fleck. The coffee table was free-form, in blond finish, and sitting on it was a cheaply made china figure of a ballerina in pink and blue, a free-form ashtray in black glass, and an equally cheap milk-glass cigarette box with pink roses round its rim.

The wall-to-wall carpet was the same Dutch pink as the exterior of the house. Across from the couch was a maple-armed sofa in a colonial-print chintz of blue and white, with a ruffled flounce. An enormous blond-finished TV sat between the windows at the narrow end of the room, its Big-Brother-like eye staring. There was a large modern chair and ottoman in maroon plastic, a cheap modern platform rocker in green frieze, a reproduction mahogany piecrust table. On that sat a lamp. The lamp base was the head and shoulders, in black ceramic, of a Negro woman; the head was thrown back and the lamp standard rose abruptly from the forehead, culminating in a white cloth shade with pink ruching round top and bottom. Beside the TV sat one of those lamp poles, painted black, with white plastic cone-shaped shades projecting wildly in all directions. There was a grandfather clock in that corner too.

At the ends of the maple-armed sofa were blond steptables, bearing matching lamps. These were violently modernistic ceramic figures of kneeling Nubian slaves, bearing the lamp standards on bowed shoulders. The shades were dark blue with white ruching, many yards of ruching. There was a mantel of native cobblestone. It bore a row of ceramic ballerinas, twirling and toe-pointing, a large brass planter with a mass of ill-tended greenery trailing from it, and at the moment, a half-empty bottle of rye whiskey. Over it hung a very colorful lithograph of a young woman in a scarlet dress playing the harpsichord.

The curtains were sheer white nylon, held back in elaborate loops by coquettish blue velvet bows.

Brenda found herself quite literally speechless. She was aware that the woman had gone on talking proudly about her fine house, and that Mrs. Cass was making conventional replies. She wanted very much to laugh, and then she thought of what Josephine was, and had done, and the impulse left her. But in a subtle way, the naïvely horrible room lessened Josephine's stature for her; she was no longer quite so terrible a figure.

"We'd like to see Mrs. Foster," she said.

"Well, if you don't mind the stairs, o' course. She's just the same, poor dear. Gone down sadly. But then you know that. It's odd—I nursed so many old folk, I know—they'll be chipper as you please one day, bright as anybody almost—way she was a couple days last week—an' then they fail again." She talked steadily, putting that idea across, as she led them upstairs. There was a cross hall; three or four bedrooms up here, probably. She led them down toward the second door from the stairs. "Best room I give her, nice front bedroom—and the bed's brand-new. You see how comfortable she is, if she *don't* rightly know where, poor old soul."

It was a good-sized room, with a mahogany bed and dresser, an upholstered chair. Mrs. Foster sat in the chair and stared at them dully. She didn't seem to recognize them; she made no effort to speak, to answer their questions. But she looked fairly neat and clean.

"You can see how she is. This been one o' her bad days, an' then gettin' her in the car, bringin' her here, 'n' all, I guess was a little too much for her. But I see she hadda good supper, some nice soup an' buttered toast an' warm milk, an' she ate pretty good. Soon as you ladies leave, I get her washed up an' into her nightclothes an' into bed. Poor old dear, just settin' like that—it do make you wonder what the Good Lord has in His mind, don't it? You'd think He'd take them to Himself before they get like that—but there, just like my boy Jason's allus sayin', you oughtn't to criticize the Lord. Must be some reason."

Mrs. Foster just stared at them vaguely.

Outside at last, Brenda said soberly, "She'd been given a lot more than before. She was—right under, barely conscious."

"Yes, I'd say so," said Mrs. Cass with a little shudder. "Oh, Brenda, I do hope the police can get something definite soon! It just doesn't seem possible, a terrible thing like this."

"But that house!" said Brenda, sliding into the front seat. "That house! Did you ever see such a nightmare?"

"Nightmare's the word for this whole awful business," replied Mrs. Cass.

Zimmerman called Valentine on Thursday morning to report on Wallis. "I wouldn't doubt he's running a little mill and catering to a few houses and call girls on the side. So far, no usable evidence—but we probably will have eventually. The hell of it is, right now I'm too shorthanded to run a full tail on him. Two men off on vacation, one in the hospital. By Monday I'll have a couple free, I hope."

"Just the way it goes, I know. Well, when you get anything—"

"In time," said Zimmerman, "in time."

This was the first day of the very obvious watch on the Slaney house. Valentine was using men recklessly—Gunn, Steiner, Fisher, and Powers were on all day, sitting in their cars in front of empty lots down from the house. They were rather conspicuous there. It shouldn't take long for Mike and Josephine to notice them.

On Thursday night Miss Devereaux called to see Mrs. Foster, had the same hearty welcome, and reported the old woman to be as vague and speechless as Brenda and Mrs. Cass had found her.

Mike had been tailed by Gunn that day when he left the house: very obviously tailed, Gunn starting up his engine with a roar as the T-bird backed out of the drive, staying close behind. Mike had driven up to Hollywood to an address on Berendo, stayed a couple of hours; Gunn had parked openly outside and waited for him. Tailed along to a bar on Hollywood Boulevard. To another private address. And back to Santa Monica. He thought Mike had noticed him plenty.

On Friday, Fisher tailed Josephine when she went to have the prescription refilled. Mike came out on the porch and stared at the other three cars sitting there with men lounging behind the wheels, and Gunn leaned out the window and put a pair of field glasses on him. "I felt like a Keystone Cop, no kidding. But that kind, they never find out we've got IQs over eighty these days. He looked mad as hell."

On Friday evening Brenda and Mrs. Cass went to see Mrs. Foster again, and Josephine wasn't quite so heartily welcoming.

When she forgot (Brenda told MacDougal later) to put on her jolly smile, she looked a little angry and a little worried.

She offered Brenda her opportunity at the door, as they were leaving. "You seen how she is, t'other night—an' that Miss Devereaux comin' last night too—I mean, it's sure nice of you, take so much interest in the old lady, I don't mean you ain't welcome—but I wouldn't expect—"

"Oh, well, of *course* we're all interested," said Brenda, "and besides they told us to come every—" Mrs. Cass gave her a very obvious nudge and she caught herself, looked confused, and went on hurriedly, "I mean, all her old friends there asked us to come, and tell them how she was."

And in the car she said to Mrs. Cass, "Do you think it was too obvious? Of course, she's not very—sensitive, she mightn't have got anything more subtle."

"I only hope they know what they're doing," said Mrs. Cass despondently.

On Saturday morning Mike backed out the T-bird, and as he swung the wheel Gunn started up the engine of his old Chevy and waited, and followed close down the hill. A block down, Mike braked violently—so did Gunn—got out, slamming the door behind him, and stalked back to the Chevy.

"What the hell you doin', tailin' me?" he demanded. "Who are you, anyways?"

Gunn looked surprised. "Tailing you?"

Mike uttered obscenities. "You the fuzz?"

"The fuzz?" asked Gunn blankly.

"What the *hell*—" said Mike, jerked open the door and laid hands on him.

"Now don't start anything, mister," said Gunn, shoving him off. "What the hell are *you* doing, assaulting a private citizen?"

"Private citizen my ass!" Mike yelled, and pulled him out of the car. Gunn let himself be pulled. He was an inch under

175

Mike and ten pounds lighter, but what Mike didn't know was that he was also the top man of the police boxing team. Mike took a swing at him, and Gunn caught him with a neat left and put him flat on his back. Getting up, Mike called him names.

"I ought to report you to the police, young man," said Gunn with dignity, getting back into his car. "Assaulting me for no reason—are you drunk at this time of day?"

Mike called him more names, got in the T-bird, and gunned her. For the next hour he tried all he knew to shake Gunn, and failed. "He's just a punk," said Gunn. "Easy." Then he holed up in a bar on Third Street.

On Saturday evening Mrs. Cass went alone to see Mrs. Foster. MacDougal had taken Brenda to dinner; they met Mrs. Cass at her home, at nine-thirty, by appointment.

"Is she worried?" asked MacDougal.

"I think so," said Mrs. Cass. But her lovely gray eyes were troubled. "But it hurts me, to see that poor sweet old thing. She was always such a cheerful woman, wasn't she, Brenda? Such a bright old lady. Yes, she—that nurse—didn't like it, my coming again. She wasn't nearly so welcoming, and she looked—what's the word I want? Wary," said Mrs. Cass. "Suspicious."

"Scared?" asked MacDougal.

"I wouldn't say. I don't know. She talked a good deal—in a smarmy sort of way—about how she hoped I could see now what good care the old lady is getting and how we could all see how wrong we'd been suspecting she had any wrong intentions—like that. Telling me she just feels so sorry for old folks and just wants to be sure she has good care."

"Scared," said MacDougal in satisfaction. "Yes, everything's turning sour for Josephine. And while Jason isn't in this business, she's been worried about him too. Put up the money for his bail, you know—a thousand bucks. Yes, well—we'll see."

Brenda was silent all the way home to Royce Street. At the

176

door of the little frame house she said, "Dave? Do you think there's a chance?"

"We're trying for it. She might panic."

"I don't mean that. For getting Mrs. Foster out safe."

He put a hand on her shoulder. "That too, Brenda. We'll have a damn good try for it anyway." And she raised her mouth willingly, for comfort, but he kissed her only lightly and told her not to fuss, leave it to them.

And in spite of all her worry— Well, it was the first time, come to think of it, she'd ever been kissed by a man with a mustache. You could say—when you knew him—he just *looked* so absurdly young. Immature. There was some old proverb about it— Vaguely she remembered Gran chuckling and saying—

That ridiculous mustache. Why it should come out platinum blond when his hair—

Brenda creamed her face vigorously, reminding herself that he was that obnoxious thing, the complete autocrat. Ordering people around.

And remembered Gran's proverb—the egg without the salt. She blushed at herself in the mirror, wielding Kleenex.

The little mob of men they had set patiently watching the house was not necessary, of course; two would have done. But the psychological effect was the important thing, and four cars were a lot more noticeable than two. Valentine figured that both Josephine and Mike were doing a lot of staring out of windows in the last few days.

The men in the cars put on a little show for them. Rather often one or more of them stared up at the house through field glasses. One would leave his car, cross to another, and talk, gesturing, with the man behind that wheel; both would crane their necks up at the house.

177

Whenever Josephine or Mike left the house, one of the men tailed along. The nurse was not going out much these days. Mike was getting around, all over the place. A few of the places he went hadn't very savory reputations; and he seemed to have a lot of friends up in L.A.

On Tuesday morning, about eleven o'clock, the nurse came out, backed the Ford to the street, and started down the hill. She glanced at the two cars on the left side of the street, in front of those empty lots, just once as she passed; she was too far away from them for her expression to be read. Fisher turned his ignition key and started after her.

Fifteen minutes later Mike came out. He did no glancing around; he shot the T-bird down the hill like a rocket, and Gunn took off after him.

Leaving Steiner and Powers holding the fort alone, with no audience to put on a little show for.

Powers strolled over to Steiner's car and leaned on the window ledge. "Funny," he said. "They've never both been gone at once before. They've left the old lady alone. I don't like that. She might burn the house down."

"More likely she's too full of dope to move, what Dan says. But it is funny, at that. I'll bet the Slaney woman didn't know Mike meant to take off."

"Damn it," said Powers, "I know we've got to do it the legal way, Joe, but isn't it an awful temptation—both of 'em out of the way—to go up and get in that house! I bet you we'd find the punk's got some foolish powder stashed away—or maybe only reefers, but on that we could pick him up. And we just might get something out of the old lady." He looked wistfully at the pink house.

Steiner agreed, yawning and tossing away a cigarette butt. "Know what you mean. I wonder how long they'll be gone. This is a damn dull job."

About then it ceased to be dull.

There was a double snarl of engines racing up the hill. Two cars—and the two plainclothesmen weren't given much time to notice details. Two nondescript, beat-up cars, closing up fast, squealing to a halt, and men pouring out of them fast.

Powers had his back to the street, and by the time Steiner's face told him there was something wrong, the men were out and moving. He whirled, saw, and went for his gun, but before he got it out he was struck on the head and went down. He never got up again; they just fell on him.

Steiner was at a disadvantage, being behind the wheel, but he was quicker with his gun. He saw the men—seven or eight of them—moving in, one little crowd on Powers, the rest round the front of the car toward him. He fired through the windshield; a .38 carries a heavy kick and he saw one man go down. Then they had the door open and he was dragged out. He fired again without aiming, into the pack, and then he was down, blows raining on him.

Four against one, it didn't take long.

The two shots were heard by Mr. Ben Tismore, who lived three quarters of a block away down the hill, in the newish redwood ranch house owned by his son-in-law. Mr. Tismore was the only one of the family home that morning. The shots were also heard by nearby housewives busy at morning chores, all of whom said to themselves, Backfires, and didn't investigate. But Mr. Tismore knew gunfire when he heard it. He wondered about it, and finally—he was a deliberate man, slowed further by his seventy years—he got up and went to look out the front door.

Up the street was a little crowd of cars, two of them slewed around at crazy angles. A handful of men seemed to be doing something to something in the road—there were others at the side of a car parked along the curb. He saw one man jumping up and down. Then somebody yelled an order, there was some loud talk—he couldn't make out the words—and they bent over

179

whatever it was for a couple of seconds. Then, as if at a signal, they were all piling into those two cars, and down the hill they came, engines roaring.

Mr. Tismore had good eyes, and he made out with horror that the thing lying in the road up there was the body of a man. He ran to the phone and called the police, and then started up the hill himself to see if he could do anything until they came.

The man lying in the road looked quite dead—half the clothes torn off him, and bruises and blood—but the blood was flowing freely. Flowing too freely: For the savage slash of a blade had severed the big artery in Powers's left arm. Mr. Tismore, who had seen service in the first war—the big war—knelt and tore away the jacket sleeve. He was still there, valiantly twisting an improvised tourniquet, when the first patrol car arrived.

"By God, by God, I'll get them for this!" Valentine was almost incoherent with fury. "That was a hired job and don't we know who hired it! This punk."

"Prove it," said MacDougal shortly.

"By Christ, I'll prove it—I'll turn this town inside out—"

They didn't know whether Powers would make it. He hadn't regained consciousness yet; besides the knife wound, he had a depressed skull fracture, four broken ribs, a broken pelvis and arm, a deep cut over one eye. Steiner had concussion, two broken legs, broken ribs, and numerous knife slashes. At four to one, a really savage beating doesn't take long.

They got what they could from Mr. Tismore. He couldn't tell them anything about the cars except that both were dark and not new—"looked dirty and sort of beat-up." He thought there had been eight men, maybe nine. "A couple in kind of loud-colored shirts, one orange and one green mostly. And the way they moved, like, and the voices, I figured they were all young. It all happened so fast."

Nobody else on the block had seen anything.

Valentine raged, and MacDougal helped him. His men—and two good men—one maybe dead and the other laid up for weeks. And he knew who was responsible, and hadn't a hope in hell of proving it. He was especially mad about Steiner, who was one of the best men he had and a personal friend. He went to see him before he left the hospital.

There was a nurse in the room. He asked her in a low voice, "No change?"

"No, sir. He may not be conscious for some time."

But Steiner was a very good cop. As he'd lost consciousness it had been in his mind, savagely, that he must remember—remember all he could, and tell—if he could. Maybe his subconscious reacted to the sound of Valentine's voice. As the nurse spoke, he opened his eyes. His mind felt fuzzy and he was conscious of pain—pain, and stiff bandages on his body. He looked up and saw Valentine's angry, grim face above him.

"You'll be OK, Joe," said Valentine.

Steiner made a great effort and heard himself say thickly, "About eighteen—medium height—long face and widow's peak, dark hair—no lobes to his ears—saw him clear—light eyes—thin—I got him, I think—shoulder maybe—I fired twice—"

"OK, take it easy, I've got that."

"How's—Mark?"

"Bad. We'll get them. Take it easy." Valentine came out to the corridor, to MacDougal. "Damn it," he said. "Damn it. They read about it in the papers, even the ones who're on our side, and they say, Too bad. They eat and sleep and live safe from the muggers and the rapists—on account of cops like Joe. Dedicated cops . . . He didn't even ask about Mark until he'd got out what he remembered. Damn it."

"He'll be OK, they said," said MacDougal tersely. "Sure, we can read this, but can we prove anything?"

17

Both men's wallets had been gone through, and both their guns were missing. It probably hadn't been a pack of hired thugs, probably just some pals of Mike's. Mike must have been fairly sure that the tails were cops, but he wanted to know; the going-over was for good measure. If they were private eyes, it might discourage them; if they were cops they deserved it.

"Tell you something else," said Valentine. "Josephine didn't know one thing about it. That was all Mike's idea. And I think she'd have been wild, hearing about it. She's running scared now, Dave, and all she's concentrating on is maintaining the status quo. She can think further ahead than Mike, and she'll see that this will just spur us on and direct suspicion at them both. She's got no idea why we're sniffing around, but I think she's hoping very hard that it's on Mike's account, some little private caper of his own, and nothing to do with her. She'll be racking her brains to think how she might have slipped up somewhere, and telling herself she hasn't, that we can't possibly have any hint of suspicion of her racket. So she wants everything kept quiet and smooth until the house is sold and she can get rid of the old woman. I don't think she's pleased with Mike."

MacDougal agreed with that. "And those thugs might've come from anywhere—Hollywood, L.A. We're going to look at every address Mike ever visited with his tail. Joe gives us a partial description, thinks he winged him. And we're going to haul in Mike for questioning—by God, we'll get him for this if it's the last thing we do."

They did that first, but of course it got them nowhere. He kept saying, No and I don't know and Prove it. They couldn't, without chapter and verse. Not until and unless they caught up with the thugs and Steiner could identify at least a couple of them. As Mr. Tismore said, it had all happened so fast. Then, if the identified ones proved to be pals of Mike's, or somebody decided to talk— But at this stage it was all up in the air.

"You ain't got a thing on me," said Mike contemptuously. "I didn't have nothing to do with it."

"I'm watching you, punk," said Valentine. "Don't think for a minute you'll get by much longer."

"Why the hell you running a tail on me, bloodhound?" Mike was belligerent. "I'm clean, you got nothing."

"Maybe we just don't like your face, little man. All right, go on—get out."

Mike moved over to Sergeant Silver's desk. "I'll take the stuff back, mac." They had gone over him; he didn't have a gun or anything incriminating.

Sergeant Silver told him equably to take it. He counted the money in his billfold ostentatiously and said to Valentine with a sneer, "You're a real savage, man, ain't you? You better cool off."

Now, in pro criminal slang, a savage is a police officer who is overeager to make arrests; and no word better described Daniel Valentine at that moment. With very little excuse, moreover, he'd have forgotten all the rules and regulations and gone

183

for Mike with all the explosive force in him, which was considerable. But he restrained himself; and he smiled at Mike and said very gently, "Little snake. Nasty little snake, get out before I step on you." A snake, in that cant, is a petty crook, one hardly worth a policeman's time.

Mike scowled at him and went. Valentine raved, exercising his vocabulary, for five minutes; and then he settled down to locate those thugs if it was humanly possible. He deployed men, he contacted all the L.A. precincts, he went out himself on it.

In their rage over the attack, both he and MacDougal completely forgot one small thing Brenda Sheldon had told them.

Brenda was spending Tuesday evening as she spent a lot of evenings, over a few necessary chores and a book. She had got into a housecoat, and washed her blouse and stockings.

She removed her nail polish, scrubbed her hands, used cuticle remover, and filed her nails; settled in the big armchair in her tiny living room, with her book, she carefully applied new polish.

Miss Devereaux was going to see Mrs. Foster tonight.

She knew it was no use worrying; they were doing all they could. Try to take her mind off it with a book.

The book turned out to be not a very good choice. It was all about a girl who'd happened on a dangerous secret and, threatened on all sides by unknown enemies, was trying vainly against various handicaps to escape and reach the friendly authorities.... At a particularly exciting moment, the suction-cup soap dish fell off the wall in the kitchen, and Brenda leaped from her chair as if she'd been shot.

And suddenly, for no reason, found herself wondering if the doors were locked.... It was the book, of course. She was not nervous about prowlers or burglars, perhaps because she'd never had any frightening experience of them. In the summer, when you wanted every breath of air you could get, she often slept with the front door open, just hooking the screen. It was like that now, this hot night; at least, she *thought* she'd hooked the screen. But the kitchen door?

She told herself to stop being a fool. With the Hawkinses thirty feet away. It was this damned book, that was all.

The next thing she found herself thinking was that it would be very nice, instead of sitting here alone, to have somebody in the opposite chair. Somebody, for instance, like Dave MacDougal, who might be an impossible autocrat—whatever he looked like—but had nice broad shoulders and a certain air of being particularly competent in any sort of crisis. When you knew him.

He might be quite impossible in some ways, thought Brenda, but what you could say—he was competent. You could just sit back and leave it all to him—and sometimes even a redhead with a low boiling point might feel that would be very nice.

Nonsense! Get on with the book.

She roused herself and turned a page. And heard the kitchen door creak, and soft footsteps cross the kitchen.

It was such a little house— She hadn't time to get up before he was there at the door of the living room.

Brenda stared at him. Her heart was thudding furiously and irregularly; she couldn't move.

"Hi, doll," he said, smiling at her. It wasn't a pleasant smile. "It was real nice of you to set the bloodhounds on us. Real nice."

"What are you doing h—" It was a very small breathless voice. Scream, said her mind. Scream. The Hawkinses only thirty feet away, all the windows open tonight— But she couldn't make a sound; she could hardly breathe.

He moved toward her slowly, hands hanging loose at his sides. His mouth was still twisted in a sneering smile. And he moved within his own aura that said, Danger.

"Bitchy little twist," he said softly. "Had to get in on the act. Why? I don't get it. What the hell's it got to do with you? Run to Johnny Law—brace the brass buttons. Why?"

She didn't know what he was talking about. She tried to say so, but he moved closer and closer, and her heart was pounding so— Under his words his voice said, Danger, Danger—

He's going to kill me, she thought, so far as she was thinking at all. He's going to— Scream! The Hawkinses— But she couldn't scream.

"Little copperhaired twist," he said. "What did you tell the bloodhounds, doll? What the hell did you know to tell them, anyways?"

He hadn't touched her. He hadn't shown her a weapon, but it was in his voice and his eyes—his oddly wide, fixed eyes. Violence. Danger. And he was coming closer and closer.

Somehow—she never remembered moving—she was out of the chair and backing away from him. She managed to get out, "I don't know—what you—I haven't—"

"Why, doll? What the hell business of yours? I was clean— we was both clean. An' now the goddamn savages turned loose. How'd you brace the fuzzes, doll? Fill me in, quick! What'd you know to—"

It was like another language. She shook her head at him dumbly; and in some deep part of her mind was conscious of contempt for Brenda Sheldon, who was showing up as such a coward here. She, who'd always been so confident of keeping her head in an emergency, of keeping her courage.

She had backed up against the wall. She leaned on it, and he was still moving in. "Talk nice, little bitch," he said. "Brace me—what'd you tell the bloodhounds? An' why?" He was within a foot of her now. His eyes were cold but oddly wild; he kept licking his lips. "Brace me nice, doll—"

Mrs. Hawkins rattled the screen door and said cheerfully, "Brenda? I've got a nice dish of ice cream for you here, had

186

some left over." And Brenda went off like an air-raid siren.

Even at the time, she was surprised and ashamed of herself. She wouldn't have thought she *could* make that much noise. She screamed and screamed, while Mike Slaney mouthed a curse and bolted for the kitchen. She was still screaming when she unhooked the screen door for Mrs. Hawkins—who said later she'd nearly had a heart attack.

It was Mrs. Hawkins who phoned the police.

MacDougal, on night duty up till midnight, happened to be in Communications when the call came through. He got there in a dead heat with the patrol car, owing to the Mercedes. By that time Brenda had calmed down and was beginning to feel like a fool. When he rushed in and grabbed hold of her she fended him off indignantly.

"I'm all *right!* Only it was so sudden—and so odd—and that d-damned book had got to me."

They got the story from her eventually, after he'd assured himself she *was* all right, and made Mrs. Hawkins bring her a couple of fingers of Mr. Hawkins's Scotch. "I don't *like* whiskey! I'm all right now—I feel like an idiot, but he— And I d-don't know what he was talking about."

MacDougal heard what Mike had said and told her what he'd been talking about. "You told Josephine you thought she ought to be reported to the police. So you did. That I'd forgotten, damn it. So when Mike finds cops lurking, he adds two and two. And when I get hold of Cahill—! How'd the damn fool lose him? Yes, Mike's a wild one all right—he's not thinking ahead."

"It was like a foreign language—he said fuzzes, and brass buttons—I couldn't—"

"Pro talk," said MacDougal.

"You feeling better now?" He looked at her anxiously.

"I'm all right. I don't know why I was so scared of him—it's just something about him. I can't describe it."

187

MacDougal, who had got a whiff of it this afternoon, could have told her what it was. Mike—still a punk—was entirely devoid of any responsibility, control, ability to see five minutes ahead. Like a child, like a savage, he let his immediate impulses govern him. And as with children and savages, there was violence in him.

And no foresight. No. Because he might have known—

"So long as you *are* all right, I like this quite a lot," he said softly. Though he'd lecture Cahill about it. "This we can pick him up on." And then he looked at her. "Did he have any kind of weapon?"

She shook her head.

"Make any threats?"

"N-not even that. I told you I was a fool—he just scares me to *see*. He just kept asking those questions—I didn't— He kept coming toward me, and I—it was like a bird with a snake. I was a *fool*. If I'd talked back to him or ordered him to get out, I think—"

Cold traveled up MacDougal's spine. Hair-trigger Mike. He said, "I'm damn glad you didn't, lady."

And damn it, damn the luck, it wasn't anything of a charge at all, a hundred to one they couldn't hold him, but—

He went straight out to Larman Drive with the patrol car, to pick Mike up himself.

They had to wait awhile. Mike didn't come home until nearly eleven. MacDougal met him in the drive, with the two big uniformed men behind him, and charged him formally.

"What the *hell*—" said Mike. In the glare of the headlights he stared almost stupidly at MacDougal. "You can't—"

"Breaking and entering, Mr. Slaney," said MacDougal. "If nothing more, which it ought to be. We're taking you in now." And again he felt a trickle of cold up his spine; he could swear that only now did Mike realize he could be picked up for what he'd done.

"You bastards!" said Mike, and bunched his fists and stepped forward.

"Oh, give me an excuse, boy," said MacDougal softly.

Mike obliged by swinging on him. Enthusiastically MacDougal took careful aim and knocked him cold with one clean punch.

He didn't often lose his temper, but when he did he lost it all the way. And Mike had scared Brenda.

They probably couldn't hang on to him, because he hadn't stolen anything after breaking and entering. He'd be brought up in the morning, and there'd be bail. But in the meantime, this gave them a little something, because it made a reason—of a sort—to ask for a search warrant.

MacDougal called Valentine, who'd just gone to bed, and Valentine said that was very nice, but did he intend to do it right now? "It'll worry her a lot more, but I think that's its chief value. Unless, of course, we come across a cache of foolish powder, something like that."

"I know, I know. I just thought you'd like to hear. We'll make it first thing tomorrow."

He got the warrant overnight and went up to the house at nine with Gunn. Valentine, of course, she'd recognize. They were both still feeling a little grim; the doctors refused to say one way or the other about Powers as yet. He'd had six pints of blood and was only slightly improved, still on the danger list.

Josephine knew about Mike; Mike had called her from headquarters last night. MacDougal could have guessed what her attitude would be. It was Josephine who couldn't afford to rock the boat now. All she wanted was to maintain the status quo. She would still be hoping very hard that they weren't interested in her, only in Mike.

She was in her respectable white uniform today. She stepped back from the door at once when MacDougal showed her the warrant. "Come right in, Officer. Naturally I was just awful shocked, anything like this—Mike's never done nothing bad so far as I know before, he's been a good boy—I sure hope he ain't goin' to turn out wrong now. But I do know, these days you fellows are fair 'n' all, I just want to go along with you, do anything you say, see. I know you got to look. But— But I hope you won't hafta disturb my patient, I—"

"You're a nurse, Mrs. Slaney?" asked MacDougal.

That put confidence in her. They hadn't even known that— so it was just Mike they were interested in all along—they didn't know anything about her. "That's right, I gotta sick old lady here, she's senile and needs lotsa care."

"We won't disturb her," said MacDougal. As he came into the room and she turned, he saw that she had a beautifully developed black eye. She put a hand to it self-consciously, seeing his gaze on it.

"I hadda li'l accident, turned quick 'n' fell over a chair," she said. "Where d'you want to see first, Officer? Mike's room—"

Fell onto Mike's fist, thought MacDougal with an inward grin. And he knew why, too. Yes, Josephine would have been upset as hell about that beating-up. She'd know what consequences it would have; she'd have pitched into Mike about it—and evidently he'd pitched right back at her.

It was a big house, but they went over it carefully. She trailed along at first, developing her theme of eager cooperation with the police, who'd been only right in arresting her boy if he'd done something bad. MacDougal got rid of her by saying pointedly that they'd talk to her later.

"Well, all right, sir—only I hope you won't hafta disturb my old lady. She's still asleep, see. Not that she takes much notice of nothing no more, poor old soul, she's failing fast."

"We won't disturb her," said MacDougal again.

They started in Mike's room, and they really took it apart. It was a big room, crowded with things—expensive things bought, probably, on impulse and not taken care of. Fifty-buck sports coat tossed over the back of a chair—hundred-buck wristwatch unwound at the back of a drawer. Things like that. They found a pile of horror comics, and the usual dirty little collection of cheap pornography, and a postcard with an illiterate scrawl, signed Bill. They found a lot of things, but they didn't find any heroin or reefers or the appurtenant equipment.

But it was a big house.

Gunn said, "Hell of a good hiding place would be in with the old lady."

"He didn't know we were going to be looking—why should he hide it? Maybe he isn't a user after all—or only occasionally."

They went into the second front bedroom. It was a little darker—thin curtains were pulled.

18

MacDougal went up to the bed and looked down at Mabel Foster. A frail-looking little old woman, lying there deep asleep—in a drugged sleep. Yes, Josephine had known they would be coming, and she'd take no chances that they'd see anything but a sleeping old lady. . . . It was strange to think that this one old woman, so near death, had begun this whole business. On her account many men in different places and jobs were hard at work. Because of her, ultimately, Bradley-Rivers sat in the county jail awaiting an escort back to New Jersey and a prison sentence. And his recent patient and employee waited to learn their fates. And Jason was about to be arraigned, along with his fellow con artists, on several charges. Zimmerman was hunting for evidence on another crooked doctor. A pharmacist had an interesting little story to tell his friends; and several real-estate operators were growling about the highhanded police methods. Records in L.A. were hunting through their files for anybody there who corresponded roughly to that description Steiner had gasped out to Valentine. (They had found a few in their own files, but Steiner had shaken his head at them).

If—when they got this one tied up, he thought, there'd be the longest parade of witnesses ever seen in any court. All those doctors and lawyers— That is, if they got Josephine for the whole bunch—which was unlikely, barring a confession.

And if it hadn't been for old Mrs. Foster, he'd never have met Brenda.

"Poor old soul," whispered Gunn beside him.

"I'm almost afraid to remember," said MacDougal in an equally low voice, "that she might be our most valuable witness."

"How come?"

"If Mike did tie her up that day—and with Mike and Josephine talking, arguing, they might have let out some damaging admissions when she was in a state to understand what was said. If we can only save her—"

"God, yes, I didn't see that."

They didn't find anything there either. When they'd finished the house, they looked through the garage, poked around behind the garage. In the garage—a big double one—was stored all Mrs. Foster's furniture, carefully protected by plastic sheets. Gunn looked at the tapestry-covered set and said, "My mother's an antique hound. I think that'd be worth something. And there's the TV, too. She doesn't miss a bet, does she?"

They didn't find the reported gun Mike had had, though they almost got down to taking up the floorboards. There was nothing incriminating at all, to make a heavier charge on Mike.

So they went to talk to Josephine. She was in her nightmare of a living room waiting for them. If she was nervous, the only sign was in her spate of words.

"You didn't find nothing bad, did you? I sure hope Mike's not goin' to be gettin' into trouble this way. I tried bring him up good, why, his brother's an ordained minister, that'll show you! But Mike, well, he's not a little kid now, he goes off alone and maybe he got into bad company like they say."

MacDougal didn't sit down. He surveyed her leisurely and said, "Mrs. Slaney, you know why we picked him up, don't you?"

"He—he went into some house without—"

"Into the premises rented by Miss Brenda Sheldon. He accused Miss Sheldon of setting the police on him. Why do you suppose he did that, Mrs. Slaney?"

"I—I couldn't rightly—"

"You must have been a little disturbed, the last few days, to realize that the police have been keeping this house under observation?"

She fingered her injured eye delicately. "I—I didn't know it was—Mike said, but it mighta been he just thought so—I didn't—"

"And then," said MacDougal grimly, "to have him questioned, suspected of complicity when two of our men were beaten nearly to death just outside this house. Do you know that one of them may die, Mrs. Slaney?"

"I'm sure sorry to hear that, sir."

"You see, we understand elementary logic," said MacDougal gently. "How did those thugs know where to come, to find a pair of cops to beat up, unless someone in this house told them?"

"I don't know nothing about that at all, sir. Honest to God I don't. You think Mike's been doin' bad things, wrong things. I don't know nothing about it, sir. If he has, only right he oughta get punished. Maybe he did do that. Make that happen. If so, it's a terrible thing, no question, an'—an' I'd feel awful bad about it, but acourse he oughta get punished for it. But I don't know nothing about it, sir."

"Let's get back to Miss Sheldon," said MacDougal. "Who is Miss Sheldon, Mrs. Slaney? A friend of your son's? Of yours?"

She was silent; he could almost see her mind scurrying in circles. What should she say? How much? She didn't know what

Brenda had said—whether Brenda, unnerved by Mike, had poured out her suspicions to them. Whether they knew how Brenda was linked to the Slaneys. What, in the heat of the moment, Mike might have said.

But she had to say something; and it would be senseless to lie—Brenda would be coming here again, and they would see that, if the watch was kept on the house. Brenda almost certainly would have told them, at least, how she'd met Mike. She licked her lips and said, "I—I tell you something, sir. How it could be. I know this Miss Sheldon, sure. She's a friend o' my old lady, see? Lives inna same neighborhood as the old lady useta. She an' a couple other people int'rested, they drop by, see how Mis' Foster is, like that. An'—an'—well, one time when Miss Sheldon come—she's a nice young lady—I got to admit Mike was kind of rude to her, you know, makin' up to her. She didn't like it, she said some things to him, so—I guess when he found out you was—he figured maybe she'd—"

As a spur-of-the-moment production, that was pretty good. It explained Brenda naturally, suggested a halfway plausible motive, and kept Josephine and her old lady well out of it.

MacDougal pretended to consider that seriously. After due thought he said, "Well, now, that could be, Mrs. Slaney. Yes, we'd heard about that incident from Miss Sheldon. That's probably how it was."

She couldn't help letting out her breath in a little involuntary sigh of relief. "Excuse me, sir—but why *was* you watchin' him? You think he's done somethin' else wrong?"

"Well, now—we aren't just sure. Not yet. So I won't say. I guess that's all we want to ask here, isn't it?" he said to Gunn.

"I guess so," said Gunn, poker-faced.

She let out her breath again in relief. In triumph. It was all right; it was only Mike they were interested in; to them, she was just Mike's mother.

MacDougal picked up his hat and turned to the door; and

195

then, as if it were an afterthought, turned back and said casually, "I understand you're selling a house for your patient. Any luck yet?"

Her mouth sagged and twisted; he saw shocked, ugly fear in her little eyes. "I—" she said. "Where'd you hear that? Why should you—"

"Oh, Miss Sheldon mentioned it."

"No, it's not sold yet," she said. "Sometimes it takes awhile."

"So it does," said MacDougal genially. "Thanks again." As they went out, she was staring after them, her mouth working.

"She's running scared all right," said Gunn.

"And we'll scare her some more, with luck," said Mac-Dougal.

Valentine called the hospital as soon as he reached his office. The doctor said, "Well, he's hanging on. I won't say anything definite right now, but if he hangs on another twenty-four hours, he'll make it. If you're a praying man, Sergeant, you might direct a few in his name to the usual destination."

"I'm not, Doctor, but some of us might just do that. Thanks." He supposed he ought to be grateful that if one of them had to get it that bad, it should be the unmarried one. Steiner's wife was expecting their first child. On the other hand, Powers had a widowed mother to support.

Which was an unprofitable reflection.

MacDougal came in and briefed him on the search—nothing there. L.A. Records had called. "They've sorted out nine men who correspond to Joe's description," said Valentine. "They're sending some pictures over for him to look at. And I've been thinking. I think we ought to try to find Ferguson's doctor."

"I thought you had—oh, you mean the one in attendance in Ocean Park. Why?"

Valentine ran an absent hand along his regular profile. "I think he might just be very valuable to us. Those other four she carted away from their homes because there were people around who were concerned, who might get to suspecting something. But Ferguson had no close friends, nobody gave a damn about him. Nobody around there would have noticed or cared if she'd cut his throat and buried him in the backyard. So why did she take the trouble of removing him from his natural habitat? She got him to sign the power of attorney for her, told him she was taking him to Denver—didn't get rid of him until she had him safe in her own house. Why? Was it maybe so she'd have an excuse to take him—once—to Dr. Sylvester, so she could get Sylvester to sign the death certificate?"

"So?"

"So maybe," said Valentine, "the doctor he'd been going to, who knew the case, could say very definitely that he wasn't at all likely to die of what he had. Had said so to the nurse. Could say so to us now. It'd be another very useful little something, wouldn't it?"

"It would. Yes, I see what you mean. But my God, Dan, how'd we ever find him? None of the neighbors knew a name. It might have been any doctor in the whole beach area!" MacDougal pulled his mustache. "How the hell could we locate him? Sit down and call every doctor listed in the Santa Monica phone book?"

"Exactly," said Valentine calmly. "So there might be, what, a couple of hundred or more in the beach area—Santa Monica or Ocean Park, around where he lived. It might take a few days and a little sweat. It's lucky Ferguson wasn't too long ago, likelier that the right man would remember the case clearly. Wouldn't it be worth the effort, Dave, if the doctor could say very definitely, the man wasn't sick enough to die?"

"I don't know," said MacDougal gloomily, "I don't know that it would, Danny. Any jury—or the D.A.—might not believe that any doctor could be so sure, about a man seventy-six years old. And another doctor—perfectly reputable one—signed the death certificate in good faith."

"There is that," admitted Valentine. "But I think it's worth a try. We might be lucky, hit the right man after only fifty or sixty calls. Look, let Silver do it in his spare time. We may need every handle we can get, you know, on this one."

"On that I agree with you," said MacDougal with a sigh.

Mike had been up before the bench at eleven o'clock; bail had been granted, as he had no record and no theft was charged. He'd be formally arraigned sometime next week, and in view of those facts would probably be put on six months' probation or something equally mild. But at least now he appeared in Records.

For the first of, very likely, a number of times.

Sergeant O'Brien of LAPD's Records dropped in at head-quarters at three o'clock. "Here are some pretty pictures for your wounded warrior to look at, Sergeant. I'd better go to the hospital with you, see if he spots one of 'em. If he does, maybe we can fill in a little. And, my God, why do the tough ones always come in hot weather?"

"Ask me something easy," said MacDougal. "Why did I ever do such a damn fool thing as to join the force? I often wonder. Because I'm a damn fool, obviously. All right, let's go." He reached for his hat.

"That kind of day?" asked O'Brien sympathetically. "They come along, I know."

"That kind of case," said MacDougal.

"They come along," repeated O'Brien. "Anyway, you seem to have a good man in this boy with the sharp eyes. Middle of a fight, you're not usually in a state to notice details."

"Are you telling us, a good man?" said MacDougal. "Flat on his back for three months at least, and maybe the other one won't make it at all. Because a pack of thugs could be hired easy to have fun with a couple of cops."

"Hell of a thing," agreed O'Brien. He looked at the Mercedes and whistled, and said maybe he ought to switch forces. He'd thought the LAPD paid the highest salaries.

"So I'm extravagant," said MacDougal.

At the hospital, they found Steiner propped up, being fed ice cream by a very pretty nurse. He was, he said, feeling better. Well, not exactly ready to go back on duty tomorrow, but better. And they could see what kind of treatment he was getting. He managed a wink at the nurse. "Almost worth getting beaten up."

"Now," said the nurse in a no-nonsense tone. "Don't get ideas, I just happen to have a brother in the cops over in Pasadena. And," she added to MacDougal and O'Brien, "you can stay just ten minutes, Sergeant. No excitement." She rustled out.

MacDougal introduced O'Brien, who produced the mug shots. "It was the lobeless ears were the biggest help, we could eliminate a lot on that. Not very common, you know."

Steiner looked at the glossy prints as MacDougal held them up one by one, and on the eighth one said instantly, "That's my boy. Know him anywhere. I fired through the windshield, he was a little behind the rest—he had on an orange shirt—"

"Very positive, Joe?"

"A hundred percent sure. I think I even winged him. He went down—but I seem to remember I got a glimpse of an orange shirt in the pack—later—so maybe I didn't get him very bad. But that's the boy, all right."

"Well, maybe we have a little luck for a change. That's good—thanks, Joe. You've got everything you want? Cigarettes? Well, OK." The nurse came back and shooed them out.

MacDougal studied the photograph Steiner had so unhesitatingly chosen. Ralph "Bud" Stanger, nineteen, five nine, one hundred and fifty, Caucasian, male, eyes blue, hair black. "Why've you got him on file and who does he run with?" he asked O'Brien. "And while you tell me I'll buy you a drink."

"Thanks very much—today's great thought," said O'Brien. The nearest bar was a few blocks away, but the service was prompt. "Aaaah!" said O'Brien gratefully, putting down his glass after one swallow, and got out a cigarette. "I copied down all we've got on 'em, sure. Stanger has a little record as a juvenile. The inevitable grand theft auto, and petty theft, and an assault. From about five years back, since he was first picked up for lifting cars. He's from the Boyle Heights area, and he was, the last time we picked him up, running with a little gang. They were all picked up for robbery as minors, but you know how nice the courts are acting these days to these poor disturbed children. They're all out now." He looked at his notes. "Al Renfred, Miguel Moya, Bill O'Riordan—et cetera. Here you are. O'Riordan has a record of violence—he's older than the rest too. Another of 'em, Bailey, is wanted—he walked out of the County Honor Farm a couple of months back."

"What kind of capers, generally speaking?"

"Well, we've never been able to shove them inside except for a couple of days—it's been probation—but all of them except Moya have been picked up at least once for assault. They're just starting their careers," said O'Brien. "O'Riordan's the oldest at twenty-three."

MacDougal looked at his highball. "Who does Stanger live with—parents?"

"Thinking of fond honest Mama discovering he's got a bullet hole in him somewhere? No dice," said O'Brien. "Mama took off years back with somebody not so likely to get in jail so often. Papa's a pro—been dropped on for burglary and armed robbery. At present in San Quentin, due out in about three years. Stanger was a ward of the court until last year—he couldn't make it in high school. He was going to a trade school until he was eighteen. Then we couldn't keep tabs on him any longer, when he got a job—probably for the look of it, let the court see he'd earn an honest living. He's now living—or was six months ago—with Renfred, in a room in a hotel on Grand Avenue."

"Oh. Well, we would greatly appreciate it," said Mac-Dougal, "if he could be located, so we can see whether there is a bullet hole in him. And if there is, we'd like to round up these red-blooded American boys he's been pals with, to find out if they know Mike Slaney and maybe did a little favor for him—for fun or money. Come to think, with that kind, the fun would have been thrown in. What's the answer on them, anyway? How and why? I don't go along with the head doctors all the way, but there must be something wrong somewhere when we get so many of them."

"Now, Sergeant," said O'Brien. "Am I talking to a starry-eyed rookie? Some people just come equipped with bad characters. Fact of life. We have to deal with 'em. So sometimes it looks out of proportion—we see so many of 'em. Not really so. They're still in a minority. But, for God's sake, let's not kid ourselves it's anybody's fault but their own. So Mama did this and didn't do that, so Junior grows up to be a mugger. For God's sake. Some people just come that way. Leave Mama out of it."

MacDougal laughed. "How right you are. Like any cop, that I know. But on one like this"—he finished his drink, groped for a cigarette—"you get to thinking about people, what makes them tick. You do indeed."

"What," asked O'Brien idly, "occasioned the strong-arm stuff in the first place?"

"Some very quiet, private little homicides," said Mac-Dougal, and started to tell him.

O'Brien sat up straighter and straighter in interest and amazement. At the end he said in a hushed voice, "How are you going to prove it?"

"You," said MacDougal, "tell me."

19

On Thursday, things started to happen—good things. The doctor called Valentine at nine o'clock. "You can stop praying, Sergeant—he'll make it. Regained consciousness an hour ago."

"Thank God," said Valentine.

"It'll be a long pull, but he'll be OK."

Valentine had hardly put the phone down and relayed the news to MacDougal when it rang again and this time it was Zimmerman.

"We've got the goods on Wallis. He's not anywhere near Bradley's class, fell for the first policewoman we sent him. Details all arranged and money passed. So I've got a warrant and we're just about to go and execute it."

"Oh, fine," said Valentine. "Thanks very much."

"Likewise," said Zimmerman. "You've been very helpful pointing people out."

"So," said Valentine to MacDougal, "now we can cut off Josephine's supply again. This is going to be a little tricky. It'll have to be timed very carefully."

203

MacDougal agreed. They were coming into the home stretch now; and it was indeed going to be tricky. Deprived again of her codeine, Josephine was going to be very worried. Moreover, it would be even more dangerous this time, for it was very probable that when that had happened before, Mike, left in charge, had offered violence to the old woman, who might therefore have lost a little trust in her nice kind nurse. Not, apparently, to the extent of refusing to take Nursie's offered pills. But certainly, if she regained a more normal state, she'd talk about that. Josephine couldn't afford to risk that again. From what Brenda, Mrs. Cass, and Miss Devereaux said, the old woman was being kept even further under now, to the extent that she didn't understand what was said to her, didn't talk at all, only mumbled. And it was a tricky situation for Josephine in another way too; she knew Mike, and she knew that it was quite possible that, left alone with a Mrs. Foster who was troublesome or noisy without the drug, he might indulge in some casual violence that would result in her death. Josephine would lose the profit from the house then, and besides, that would be extremely dangerous, for no doctor had examined Mrs. Foster for a month or so, and consequently there'd have to be an autopsy and inquest.

And on the other hand, from the police viewpoint—talk about tricky! If, not given any more codeine, Mrs. Foster's mind began to work as clearly as it had—and if, as was at least probable, she began to realize that Josephine wasn't the nice kind nurse she'd thought—well, she didn't know that anyone else knew and was trying to help her. Unless she was completely broken down, she might make an effort to save herself—try to use the phone, call the police. They would have to restrain her somehow.

She was eighty-eight. She hadn't been strong when all this started, and she'd been having all that codeine ... but the police surgeon said, the old ones are the tough ones.

Valentine said, "Set it up now, get it started. I'll go see the pharmacist."

The pharmacist at that Thrifty was a tall gray-haired man with a prim manner. He kept saying, "Goodness gracious."

"Of course the name isn't on that list yet, but it will be. So if you'll—"

"Certainly, certainly, I should have to do so in any case, Sergeant, of course. Dear me. Goodness gracious."

"She'll probably be in tomorrow or next day to—" And Valentine thought suddenly, but would she be? Evidence that she'd been giving the old woman larger doses—

He thought afterward that it must have been sixth sense. Even as the thought crossed his mind, he saw the pharmacist's expression freeze, and without looking around, Valentine moved rapidly away from the counter to the next aisle, round that row of high shelves. After a moment he peered cautiously around a wire basket full of stuffed toys.

Josephine was standing with her back to him at the pharmacy counter. She was in her uniform.

Just in time, he thought. Are we getting the breaks at last? He hoped to God the pharmacist would put up a plausible act.

The pharmacist went away with the little plastic bottle. Josephine stood waiting stolidly, not looking around. Presently the pharmacist came back, and from what Valentine could see, put up a sufficiently plausible appearance—shocked expression, a hint of suspicion for anyone associated with a charged man.

And evidently Josephine was really caught off balance this time. The pharmacist stopped talking, just stood looking at her. And she just stepped back from the counter, and then turned and hurried away. Valentine watched her disappear into the crowd, and went back to the pharmacist.

"We cut that one fine," he said. "How'd she take it?"

"What—what has that woman done?" asked the pharmacist. He brought out a handkerchief and passed it across his mouth. "She didn't say anything. Not a word. But she was— very surprised and shocked. And then she looked— I never saw a look like that before. Like a—like a cornered rat getting ready to fight back. Vicious. I never— What has she done?"

"If we have any luck at all," said Valentine, "you may be reading all about it in the papers in a few days."

"Goodness gracious me," said the pharmacist.

Valentine drove over to Ocean Park, to Mrs. Cass's office. She was out showing clients over a house, so he left a note for her. He located Miss Devereaux at the drugstore, and briefed her. He drove on up to Wilshire, failed to find a parking slot, finally left the car in a private lot. He walked down to the big marble and glass building that housed Garnetts'.

He had to wait to see Brenda; she was taking dictation. When she came back to her little cubbyhole of an office and found him waiting, she looked excited.

"Oh, has something happened?"

"Something good," and he told her. A pretty girl, Brenda Sheldon: flushed and animated, listening to him. A time he might have gone for her—before he'd met Mary. But in a way he couldn't envy Dave—a redhead and probably quite a handful. He wondered if Dave was really serious about her.... "So now you lay off," he said. "None of you—I've let Mrs. Cass and Miss Devereaux know—are to visit the house for a while. You can see it's a very tricky little deal. Our doctor's opinion is that generally speaking it might take about three days for Mrs. Foster to get back to normal, for the codeine to work its way entirely out of her system. She'll be better tomorrow, and probably by the day after thinking and talking straighter, and by Sunday she should be more or less normal. Unless some permanent damage has been done by the drug, of course."

"Oh, no—" Brenda made a sick sound. "But I see it could have, of course. We'll just hope."

"Yes. I think, tentatively, we'll set it up for Sunday. Arrange details later. Meanwhile, all of you just stay away."

"Josephine is going to be worried," said Brenda thoughtfully.

"She is."

"And she'll be looking all over again for some way to get more. If she does that, and leaves Mike—"

"She won't," said Valentine. "She's realized how dangerous that might be." He explained, and Brenda shivered.

"You've got to get her. Just got to."

Valentine said, "We'll get her. We'll get her but good. We're feeling damn annoyed at Josephine, because indirectly she's responsible for that beating-up. We're on the warpath. Dave feels the same way."

"I can believe that," said Brenda, wrinkling her nose. "Quite the autocrat, in spite of his looks—if things don't go the way he wants, he'd start beating his chest and roaring."

"Oh, you've discovered that, have you?" Valentine smiled down at her. "Just a little advice, Miss Sheldon. Don't underestimate him. He may look like an innocent juvenile, but when he starts moving after something he wants, look out! You keep your fingers crossed that this comes off the way we hope."

Sergeant Silver was still patiently making phone calls to doctors. He had crossed about sixty names off his list. At his estimate, he had about a hundred and eighty still to call, and his left arm was getting stiff, he complained to Valentine.

They had kept the watch on the house, but in the normal way—unobtrusive. Gunn and Fisher were parked a block down, to pick up either Josephine or Mike if they left the house.

And what would be going on inside that house, the next few days?

But Thursday continued to be a good day.

At one o'clock, as Valentine got back from a hasty lunch, a Sergeant Kantor of LAPD's robbery detail called. "As per request, Sergeant, we've hunted up that Ralph Stanger for you."

"Ah," said Valentine pleasedly. "Found him, did you?"

"No trouble. Same address we had. We found Al Renfred with him."

"Don't keep me in suspense. Does he have a bullet hole in him?"

"He does," said Kantor. "A kind of nasty one, high up on the left shoulder. He also has quite a temperature, because he hadn't been to a doctor and it's got infected. Renfred says he got hit accidentally when they were fooling around with a gun a friend of his owns—won't divulge friend's name, all loyal, because he doesn't want to get him in trouble. And they didn't go to a doctor because a doctor'd report a bullet wound to the cops. They thought it wasn't bad, Stanger'd be all right. And of course neither of them has been in Santa Monica in their lives. They were with some other guys on Tuesday, up at Lake Arrowhead."

"The other guys being these pals who make up the little gang you know about?"

"Need you ask?"

"I suppose you've got him in the hospital."

"We have. I sometimes wonder why, but we're always so careful to give them anything they need these days, take such good care of them."

"Doctor have any guess as to what caliber, or—maybe the slug was still *in?* My God, if it was—" Valentine was excited.

"Don't have a heart attack," drawled Kantor. "We've just sent it down to Ballistics."

"Oh, God!" said Valentine rapturously. " 'And so the Little Less became Much More.' One of them's still got the gun it came out of— Look, let's drop on them right now! If they get wind of—"

"I don't want to sound superior," said Kantor apologetically, "but we didn't get to be the top force anywhere by needing things spelled out for us, friend. There are five men out now looking for the rest of the gang. And I shouldn't have spared that many, just to help out a neighbor, but we don't like to see cops beaten up any better than you do. Any cops. O'Brien said one of your boys was on the danger list."

"He's off now, thank God. But three or four months getting back on his feet."

Kantor said softly, "The bastards. These punk kids . . . But you'll be as happy as I am to know that they're now all over eighteen, so they won't be coming up in front of one of these softhearted judges as misunderstood kids."

"That makes me very happy indeed," said Valentine. "You'll let me know when and if you get any more."

"Ought to be hearing some news soon. I'll call you."

He called back an hour later. "We found the gun— O'Riordan had it. By the serial number, your man Steiner's gun. Haven't found the other one yet."

"Brother, I could kiss you," said Valentine emotionally.

Kantor laughed. "My wife might get jealous, Sergeant. We can hold them all—we've got them all—overnight without making a charge, and if Ballistics says yes on the gun, we can make a charge. They're all saying they were together all day Tuesday— we've got signed statements on that. At Lake Arrowhead. But if we can show definitely that Stanger was in Santa Monica collecting that bullet hole—after all, there's the serial number on the gun."

"Yes. When will you know?"

"Well, as I say," said Kantor, "nobody down here likes the idea of cops getting beaten up. When I left Ballistics just now, they'd all stopped work on several other things and were taking turns firing the gun into sandbags for specimens. At a guess, a couple of hours. Somebody'll let you know, and if it's positive you can come right down and take the whole bunch back for charging in your own stamping ground."

209

"And I don't give a damn," said Valentine, who had a date with Mary that night, "that I'd have to break a date with my best girl. Oh, boy. No way to say thanks."

They both hung around waiting for the call. Valentine called Mary to tell her he'd be late at least and possibly not there at all. The clock crept slowly on past five, five-thirty, to six; and MacDougal sat over the tedium of paperwork, chain-smoking. Valentine paced the office.

At ten past six a Sergeant Vandenberg of LAPD Ballistics called and said, "It's positive. Bullet out of Stanger was from your man's thirty-eight."

"I'll come down and kiss all of you," said Valentine. "Tell the county jail I'm on my way with the warrants." The warrants would take a little time; not long. MacDougal went off to start the machinery on that; Valentine called Mary again and broke the news that she wouldn't be seeing him that night. She was flatteringly sorry, but on hearing the reason nearly as excited and pleased as he was.

"You can really prove it on them? And Mike?"

"We really can. Doesn't say yes or no on Mike, but one of them might come apart."

"If you work them over," said Mary wisely.

"Now, Mary. You know we don't do that kind of thing anymore. Great as the temptation sometimes is."

None of them came apart right away. As was to be expected, they were all sullen and uncommunicative except for saying they were being railroaded. O'Riordan said he'd bought the gun in Pasadena six months ago. It was pointed out to him that its serial number identified it as belonging to Steiner up to last Tuesday. O'Riordan said that was just what they said and the cops had a down on him. After which he shut up.

All of them denied knowing Mike Slaney.

They collected four switchblade knives from the others,

and eventually found Powers's gun in Moya's hotel room. It tied up very nicely. The police would have a quiet word with the bench and try to arrange that the eight of them be held without bail.

When they'd seen them locked up for the night, MacDougal said, yawning, "Wonder what Josephine did today after she got the bad news? Reports weren't in when we left. I've got to report in anyway up to midnight."

They went back to headquarters, to see the reports Gunn and Fisher had turned in when the night men had taken over the tail.

Josephine had come straight home and stayed. Fifteen minutes later Mike had taken off, and gone up to L.A. He had visited four bars and one private address.

"She's sending *him* out to look this time?" speculated Valentine. "Doesn't trust him with the old lady, no. If he's a user, he'll know at least one pusher." He thought. "But these days, pushers deal almost exclusively with the big H or reefers. Maybe bennies. She couldn't use any of those on Mrs. Foster. They'd produce all the wrong symptoms. I don't think it'd be so easy for a pusher to get hold of morphine, do you?"

"It's out of fashion," agreed MacDougal sleepily. "No. Maybe a wholesaler— And how nice if we can show Mike contacting a known pusher. Yes, I think this gives us our little time, to hope the old lady will get back to normal. How do we set it up?"

"Sunday afternoon," said Valentine dreamily. "Tentatively. Unless it appears that Mike *has* got hold of some new dope. In that case, move in fast. But if he doesn't—and I don't think he will—Sunday afternoon. Josephine is going to be worrying, expecting Brenda or Mrs. Cass or Miss Devereaux to come, as they've been coming—to see the old woman better and brighter, maybe telling them how Mike bound and gagged her. She's going to be very damned relieved when they don't come—but

211

she'll do some wondering about that too. It may be that she won't be able to get even aspirin into Mrs. Foster, if the old lady *is* already suspicious and her mind starts to clear. Keep our fingers crossed and give it that much time. And time it all precisely, too. Say three o'clock Sunday afternoon, Brenda and Mrs. Cass arrive. If it goes the way we hope, by then she won't dare let them see Mrs. Foster, because Mrs. Foster will be almost her old self again. And quite possibly no longer sold on Nursie, with complaints to make—accusations. So Josephine will argue, tell them the old lady's asleep and so on, try to get them to go away. How long can they stall, arguing? Say fifteen minutes. So about then we arrive—in a squad car, for further effect—march in, accuse her, demand to see Mrs. Foster. Her morale might be just low enough."

"Yes. Well, keep our fingers crossed all right," said MacDougal with a sigh.

Mike got out and around on Friday, while Josephine stayed home. They asked LAPD Narcotics about all the addresses he visited, but drew blank; however, Narcotics said they'd have a look at them, see what turned up. Maybe something would, next week or next month.

Nothing else happened on Friday except the pack of thugs coming up in court for the formal charge. The bench had listened to Valentine and they were ordered held without bail.

Nothing happened on Saturday, on this business, until at four-thirty a weary and dogged Sergeant Silver located the doctor who had attended Ferguson.

He had called two hundred and eight doctors. The two hundred and ninth was the right one.

Valentine talked to him. His name was Silverberg and he sounded fairly young, brisk and competent.

"Certainly I remember the case. Why on earth are the police—? Oh, sure, sure, I know—you ask the questions. Well, I like to think I'm a respectable citizen. What do you want to know?"

"We know what his trouble was, Doctor. But would it have carried him off very soon?"

"It would not," said Silverberg. "Man was a damned old hypochondriac. Sure, he had respiratory trouble—hay fever, sinus congestion, but nobody dies of that. It's like the old gag about seasickness—not fatal but if you have it you wish it were. He fooled me for a little while, when he first came to me. He could fake a nice asthma attack. No—I'm wrong there, give the devil his due, he didn't realize he was faking. He didn't have anything to do but worry about himself, and he knew all the symptoms. He'd read all the books. You know? It was partially hysterical—he'd imagine he was having trouble breathing, and after a while he really would have trouble. But his heart was sound as a bell. That was what set me wondering, because with almost all true asthmatics the heart is eventually affected, at least by the time they're seventy-six."

"I see," said Valentine interestedly. "And his wasn't?"

"I did a bronchoscope on him too. It was completely negative.... Well, that's to test the mucus-absorption rate, that is, to see whether mucus is being retained in the lungs. You get that condition with asthmatics, to some extent, and it can be dangerous. But his lungs were clean as mine are."

"Interesting. Tell me, Doctor. If he went to a new doctor, do you think even a competent man would spot him as a fake on a first examination?"

"No, probably not. He *had* hay fever and sinus trouble, as I say. Plenty of people with asthma have hearts that sound all right through a stethoscope. As far as that goes, any heart can sound just fine through a stethoscope and yet be on the verge of sudden failure. Only an electrocardiogram— And other more thorough tests— What *is* all this? Tell you the truth, I wasn't surprised when he quit coming. After I'd done the bronchoscope,

213

I told him he didn't have true asthma, he wasn't nearly as sick as he thought. I've got no time to waste on patients like that. I have enough who're really sick."

"Yes. He had a nurse with him?"

"Which was quite unnecessary and his own idea. I don't think he has much money, you know. But he'd got hold of this practical nurse himself—big fat woman, talked like a hillbilly."

"Doctor," said Valentine, "we know all about her. Yes, and did you ever say all this to her?"

"I did," said Dr. Silverberg. "I told her he didn't really need the oxygen, the adrenaline—he was a tough old New Englander from long-lived stock, and he'd probably live to be a hundred if he didn't scare himself to death. Matter of fact, he's one of the few male hypochondriacs I've ever come across."

"Was, Doctor," said Valentine. "Was. We'd like a nice formal statement on all this, and I think eventually you'll be testifying about it in a murder trial."

"In a *what?*" said Silverberg. "What the hell—"

"It'd take too long to explain now," said Valentine. "Thanks very much."

20

Brenda waited outside Mrs. Cass's locked office, her impatience increasing by the second. Mrs. Cass was always so *reliable*, too. She knew how important it was that this plan be carried out according to the timing Valentine and MacDougal had arranged. Mrs. Cass was to have met her here, with the car, at two-thirty, which would get them up to Larman Drive at about a quarter of three. Valentine had said they must be obstinate in the face of whatever argument Josephine would give them, just go on demanding to see Mrs. Foster. At a quarter past three or so, he and MacDougal would be there.

And here it was nearly twenty minutes of three, and no Mrs. Cass. Where *was* she? She knew how important it was.

Brenda was sure her watch was right. Now it *was* twenty minutes of three.

(She couldn't know, then, that Mrs. Cass was sitting helplessly in a car with a run-down battery, waiting, fuming, for the man from the automobile club. That, she would find out later).

They simply had to be up there, to give that woman a last

demoralizing scare before Valentine and MacDougal came to try to break her down.

Brenda looked, for the fortieth time, hopelessly down Lincoln in the direction from which Mrs. Cass would come. She didn't see Mrs. Cass's beige two-door Dodge. What she did see was a lumbering green monster of a bus: a bus whose black-and-white sign said PACIFIC PALISADES. The right direction for—

They had to be up there—

She ran the few steps to the corner, to the bus-stop sign. She scrabbled in her coin purse for change. Outrageous, the way fares had gone up. The bus stopped and she climbed on, dropping coins in the meter.

She sat, staring out, silently urging the lumbering bus to hurry. She wasn't quite sure, either, where she ought to get off. This bus went in the right direction, through Santa Monica; but did it go up Sunset? Going to Larman Drive, you went up Sunset. She watched street signs.

It seemed to take forever. And there was a little distance to walk afterward. *Ten* to three, and the bus was just turning onto Sunset.

She watched signs and, about three minutes later, yanked the bell cord, got up to wait at the rear door. The bus sighed and groaned to a stop, and she was instantly down on the second step, the one with the little metal plate that made some connection and opened the door. The double doors folded back jerkily, noisily, and she was out.

She had to wait for the light; she must cross the street. But once on the other side, she hurried; she trotted as fast as she could up toward the corner of Larman Drive. It was nearly two blocks behind her, and then three more up the hill—

Three o'clock. She trotted faster, growing breathless. What *had* happened to Mrs. Cass?

But the hill, when she came to it finally, slowed her down. She didn't have the breath to trot up the hill, which rose steeply and moreover, like all these newly subdivided tracts, had no sidewalks. She walked—as fast as she could force herself to walk—up the rough blacktopped street.

After all, when she got there she'd need some breath left to argue, she thought.

She nearly hadn't. When she got to the pink house at the top of the hill, the fairly steep stone steps up to the door almost finished her. She reached the front porch, saw that the door was open, and stopped where she was a minute, panting for breath.

It was eleven minutes past three.

From inside, from the front room, she heard the nurse say, "But we gotta do something, Mike! Things can't go along like this no longer—you see that. You gotta find—" She sounded upset and frightened. Worried, at least.

"Take it easy," he said indifferently, almost happily. "I told you, this Clancy said he could get it, in time. Maybe sometime nex' week." His voice held that strangely lighthearted, careless tone it had the day he'd been loading the truck. And "riding high."

"Nex' *week!* My God, boy, them snoops might turn up here any minute! An' what am I gonna *say?* I'd hafta say *somethin'*. I been on tenterhooks—we gone too far, try to get out o' this one now—she—"

"*You* got too far in. Your racket, not mine. OK, then finish it off—cut your losses."

"I can't *do* like that! No doctor seen her, an' you know now she's got her senses back, I can't let a doctor—"

That was where Brenda pushed the doorbell. Her heart was thudding, and she thought that little piece of eavesdropping might be another knot in the slender rope of evidence against Josephine.

Instant silence fell in the room at the sound of the chimes. After a moment the nurse appeared on the other side of the screen door.

217

"Hello, Mrs. Slaney," said Brenda sweetly. "I've come to see Mrs. Foster."

The woman stood silent and motionless for a long moment. But as she'd just said, she had to say something. She said in a heavy, slow voice, "Hello, Miss Sheldon. I—I'm sorry, I can't ask you in, the old lady's asleep—I—"

"But I've walked all the way from the bus stop, and it's a hot day, isn't it?" said Brenda, and opened the screen door. Josephine did not move back, but stood there, a solid barrier. "I've come to see Mrs. Foster and I intend to see her. Please let me in."

"I—" said the nurse. "Listen, Miss Sheldon, I—you better not come in, see, there's—there's a quarantine, the doctor was here just today and says she's got something awful contagious."

"There's no quarantine sign. California law requires a sign, didn't you know that? I said I want to see Mrs. Foster, and I mean it. How is she?"

"She's—awful sick like I say—failed somethin' awful. You'd be terrible shocked, Miss Sheldon—an' now she's got to sleep, with the doctor's pill, I wouldn't want her waked up, see—"

"I can look at her without waking her up, can't I?" said Brenda.

"Now, why'd you want to do that? Listen, Miss Sheldon—"

"And what doctor do you mean? Just as I came up, I thought I heard you saying no doctor had seen her."

"I—I wasn't talkin' about her, somebody else. Now look, young lady, I know you think wrong about me, you said some awful rude things about me to my face. They was all lies, but you can't expect I like havin' you come round when I know what you think about me. Nor them other two neither. I just been gettin' sick 'n' tired, you all comin' alla time—there ain't no sense—what's there to *see*? She's failed awful, she's real senile now, don't even know you're there! I don't—can't expect me to act exactly happy, have you comin' wastin' my time—"

"And I'd also like to know," said Brenda steadily, "what you meant—and whom you meant—when you said, 'She's got her senses back now.' What did you mean, Mrs. Slaney?"

"I—I—"

She didn't hear movement from inside the room, but suddenly the door swung farther open and he was standing there beside Josephine. "You got good ears, doll," he said. "You better come all the way in."

"Yes, I have," said Brenda. She stepped into the room; dumbly, the nurse stepped back.

"Too good," said Mike. "Bitchy little twist. Bracing the law about us. Maybe you'll wish you hadn't."

"Mike—"

Brenda wasn't frightened—well, not very—because any minute now Dave and Valentine would be coming.

"What the hell's with this?" He said it to himself, looking at her.

"Listen," said the nurse rapidly—trying desperately to retrieve the situation somehow—"what I was talkin' about was somethin' different altogether, I don't know what you got in your head but it's not so, see? It's just like I told you, old lady's gone senile an' right now she's sick so I can't ask you in to see her—maybe sometime nex' week, I could phone you an' let you know—"

"What I've got in my head," said Brenda, "is that she isn't senile at all, but you've been giving her drugs to make it look that way."

The nurse's mouth worked convulsively. "That's—that's not so—I dunno why you'd—"

"Come farther in, doll," said Mike, and pulled her toward him and slammed the front door. "You use your brain too much, honey—you'll wear it all out."

219

Any minute now, Dave and Valentine would be here, she thought.

"You're real smart, little bitch."

"Yes," she said. "Yes, I am. But—" Let him know that others knew, and were coming. That odd, cold, bright look in his eyes again—

"Mike," said the nurse. "Don't—don't you—"

"Just like you said, gone too far," he said. "She guesses too goddamn much. Hafta get rid of her too, save both our necks. Hell, don't worry, it'll be OK—I know how to set things up so they look OK, I'm a real smart boy, didn't you know?" He laughed. "Just knock her on the head, see, 'n' drop her somewheres after dark—they just think, another muggin'—" He said it almost conversationally; and he took a gun out of his pocket, reversing it to hold it by the barrel.

"Mike, you can't—we can't—"

"Funny time for you to say, don't kill nobody."

Brenda stood frozen in his grip. *Where was Dave?* It must be long past three-thirty. She began to gasp it out, "The police know—they're coming—it's not only me—" But it wasn't penetrating his mind, she saw. He was "riding high" again, he wasn't listening to anything, and he—

She jerked free of him frantically, and ran. She ran the only way she could run—both of them between her and the door—for the stairs.

The phone call had come through just as Valentine and MacDougal were about to leave the office. Valentine had hesitated, and then picked up the phone. Said, "Speaking," and after a minute or so, "Could you speed it up a bit, Mr. Moore? I'm in a little hurry." But he had gone on listening for quite a while after that, and begun to smile broadly, while MacDougal made impatient gestures at him. "I see. Yes. Of course, this makes us very happy, Mr. Moore. Yes... Well, of course I can't promise anything like that. Up to the bench. We don't make deals.... Well, thanks very much indeed." He put the phone down.

"For God's sake, let's go!" said MacDougal. It was nearly twenty-five past three. "They can't stand there forever arguing— they'll be in a little spot—"

(Mrs. Cass was just parking in front of her office on Lincoln, looking around for Brenda.)

"That," said Valentine, picking up the hat he'd laid down, "was a very welcome piece of news. Seems that one of that little gang comes from a different background—Edward Charlton— family quite respectable, and substantial money. The black sheep. They got him a lawyer, this Moore, who's persuaded him that he might get off easier if he turns state's evidence. He's ready to talk. Sing us a very pretty song about how Mike Slaney briefed them for the job and gave them ten bucks apiece—"

"Very gratifying indeed, but we've got a date."

"Five minutes won't matter," said Valentine. "So we give the girls a little while longer to soften her up for us." He stopped at the sergeant's desk in the anteroom and told Sergeant McLeod, who occupied it on Silver's days off, to send a steno and a witness over to the jail to take a statement from Edward Charlton.

They went downstairs and got into the requisitioned squad car. "Use the siren," suggested MacDougal.

"Why? We're only about ten minutes late. What are you so nervous about?"

"Maybe I'm psychic," said MacDougal. "They've got only so much they can say to the woman—"

"So all right, in the end they can't get past her and have to go away. She's still been softened up."

MacDougal was driving, and he tried to hurry; but, dia- bolically, every light caught him. It was nearly twenty-five to four when he got to the corner of Larman Drive and Sunset.

That was where Gunn and Fisher were parked, and at Valentine's word, reluctantly, he double-parked alongside Gunn, who slid across the front seat to look out the window.

"See them pass?"

"Uh-uh. The girl came alone—in a hurry—walking. Probably took the bus. I didn't know whether to—"

"The girl, *alone?*" MacDougal's voice went up. He reached over and switched on the siren, gunning the engine.

Brenda ran up the stairs, hearing him swearing, running after. On the landing there was a little table with a potted plant on it; without hesitation, almost without thought, she picked it up and hurled it, plant and all, down the stairs. A crash, and more swearing. He had fallen, tripped.

She ran down the hall. Came to the door, and it was locked—but the key in the lock outside. She wrenched it around, pulled it free, jerked open the door and ran inside. With shaking hands—he was coming—she managed to lock the door from the inside.

Only then did she turn, leaning on the door.

Old Mrs. Foster was lying on the bed, and she wasn't asleep. Her ankles and wrists were bound with strong clothesline. Her eyes were frightened on Brenda; she moved convulsively.

Brenda's fright was swallowed by pity and rage. She ran across the room, knelt, and began to struggle with the knots. She murmured incoherent phrases, "It's all right now—the police know, they're coming soon—oh, what an awful—"

The old woman's eyes were intelligent on her. She made an effort to speak; she was very weak. "I heard them—talking about things—oh, Miss Sheldon, how'd *you* know? I been so afraid—kept me tied up since yesterday, and nothing to eat—I tried make someone hear me, but she said—said the house is way off from anybody to hear."

He was attacking the door methodically, with something

heavy. An ax? Please God, not an ax. She could hear the nurse's voice, frightened, pleading.

"Never mind now," she said, pulling at a hard knot. If only they'd *come*—where *were* they? "It'll be all right now—oh, Mrs. Foster, are you really all right? They've—"

"Awful stiff, and I feel so weak—arthritis and all—I been so afraid, since I *knew*—haven't rightly been myself, I don't know—I don't remember at all, even coming to this place, I don't know where—"

"No, I know—I know." Solid, heavy blows on the door. She looked around, and saw the gleam of an ax blade biting through the wood.

But there were men watching the house—Dave had said so—couldn't they hear, couldn't they—?

She looked around the room wildly for some weapon. There was a straight chair, a bench before the dressing table—

She snatched up the chair by its back. The whole middle panel of the door smashed in, and she saw his contorted face. *Oh, Dave!* she thought.

"Little bitch," he said. "Brainy little bitch. I'm comin'—"

Then she heard the siren.

She never knew whether he did, or whether it meant anything to him. His mind was fixed on one idea; anything else was extraneous. He went on breaking a large enough hole to get through.

The siren was very close—it was *here*. The lower panel of the door smashed in, and he crouched and was in the room. His eyes were wild and bright.

Brenda screamed, *"Dave!,"* and swung at Mike with the chair. It caught him on the head and he staggered back, dropping the ax. She hit him again and one of the chair legs snapped off. He was shouting curses, he was lunging for her again, and now he had the gun in his hand—

The top panel of the door disintegrated and MacDougal

was there. He fell on Mike and they both dropped to the floor; MacDougal got up, hauled Mike up, and hit him once. That was all that was necessary

"Wh-what delayed you?" asked Brenda.

He looked at her. Just looked, breathing deeply. "By God," he said, "I do believe if we hadn't arrived, you'd have brained him yourself. Redheads. Why in *hell* you came up here alone—"

"But somebody *had* to! We'd arranged—"

"My God," said MacDougal.

"And please, we've got to get Mrs. Foster to a doctor."

MacDougal unlocked the ruined door. "Now Dan's disappeared," he said. "What the hell—" There were sounds of combat from below, and they ran to the top of the stairs.

Valentine appeared at the bottom, looking up at them. "She tried to run," he panted. His jacket was ripped apart, his shirt torn, and there was blood on his face. "Hell of a thing—new experience for me—but she's as strong as a man, I had to knock her out."

"Suppose," said MacDougal mildly, "you go out to the car and call up an ambulance and some backup." He went back to the bedroom, put Mike's gun in his pocket, and looked at Mrs. Foster, whose eyes were closed.

"Oh, Mrs. Foster—please—are you all right?" Brenda was bending over her anxiously.

Her eyes opened. "I been so afraid—ever since— And she seemed so nice— Oh, Miss Sheldon, Brenda, I—I got to tell the police or somebody— I heard them talking, and they've done just terrible things! You wouldn't believe—"

"When you're feeling better, you can tell us," said MacDougal gently. "This is all very gratifying." He looked at Brenda. "Except that I think I'll get a collar and chain for you."

* * *

It all turned out to be even more gratifying, in the end. The nurse turned dumb to all approaches, coaxing or tough. But they found Mike's supply of heroin tucked away in the crawl space above a trapdoor in his bedroom closet; it appeared that Mike was a regular user, and after he'd been starved for a fix a few days he came apart readily and told all he knew. Which was a lot.

And it was just the way they'd figured it, trailing along behind, collecting facts and making deductions.

So they got Mike on an accessory charge. After discussion with the D.A.'s office, it was decided to charge Josephine on all of them except Gilchrist—that one was too hard to prove legally.

The headlines were quite something, and the trial made more, a couple of months later. Movie and TV magnates made fabulous offers for Nurse Slaney's Own Story; famous writers-up of real-life crime tales came to plead for interviews.

She stayed dumb. Maybe the shock of getting caught up with— She did not take the stand at the trial. Mike did, volubly, claiming that he'd never known until the very last, and she was his mother, he loved her, what was a guy supposed to do, run to tell on his own— He didn't get far with that.

Her lawyer, of course, tried for an insanity plea, but he didn't get away with it. And juries didn't like to send women to the gas chamber, but they didn't hesitate to send this one there. They gave Mike a twenty-to-life, which meant he'd be getting out—to make more trouble—in about ten years' time.

And Mary said thoughtfully, reading the headlines about the verdict, "Talk about offbeat homicides. Maybe, now she's convicted and couldn't sue for libel, an idea for my next plot ...But you know, in a way—all those poor old people alone— it almost makes me wish I'd married Ken."

"Who was Ken?" asked Valentine suspiciously.

"Oh, a man. A very nice man, actually, but I— Well, I mean, it does make you think."

"Don't be silly," said Valentine. "You needn't worry, nice girl like you, you can acquire a husband anytime."

"Well, it *is* a solitary occupation," said Mary. "Writers don't meet too many people, you know." She scratched behind Garm's floppy ears, he moaned pleasurably, and Valentine told her not to let him be a nuisance. "Don't you be silly, I like unusual-looking dogs." What was wrong with the man, anyway, she wondered. From what she knew of him, he wouldn't usually be so awfully backward with the opposite sex; but in the time she'd known him, he'd been friendly, companionable—and that was about all. He must have some funny ideas about writers if he thought they went around mingling with a lot of glamorous characters. After all, he *did* keep hanging around, asking her out—which seemed to indicate that he was interested at least. And she'd never turned him down. What else could she *do*, anyway, to let him know—?

"Yes, an interesting case," said Valentine. "Another offbeat one, all right." He wondered what Ken had been like. A successful writer—he thought a pretty good writer—she must meet a lot of men more interesting and attractive than a perfectly ordinary sergeant of police. He felt annoyed, at odds with himself; he wasn't used to feeling—diffident—with a girl.

"Yes, it was," said Mary. "I think it was awfully *brilliant* of you to get her." Maybe the time-honored technique of flattery would get her somewhere.

Valentine laughed. "Now, don't overdo the praise. As usual, it was just hard routine that got us there. 'Trust me, Today's most indispensable,/ Five hundred men can take your place or mine—' "

Mary said automatically, " 'The Last Department,' " and

looked at him exasperatedly. But he was looking at his empty coffee cup. What on earth was she to *do* with the man?

"That doctor was certainly right," said Brenda. "The old ones are tough. It's a nice place, isn't it?"

MacDougal agreed, opening the door of the Mercedes for her. It was a nice place, and Mrs. Foster was—remarkable.

It was one of those well-run private homes for the elderly where you paid over a lump sum for life care. Mrs. Foster had sold her house for twelve thousand five hundred dollars and thus become ineligible for the state pension, but on the advice of Mrs. Cass, had handed it over to this place and been given a new home.

She had a tiny, neat, private room, round-the-clock medical care; the food was good, she said, and the other old people nice and friendly. There was a comfortable main lounge, and TV, and sometimes special movies. She was settled and happy.

After a few days in the hospital she'd been almost her old self again. Physically slower and more frail, of course; but as mentally active as before. And she had rather enjoyed all the attention she'd got—Last Victim of Homicidal Nurse Escapes.

Brenda hadn't at all enjoyed being Heroine Who Rescued Elderly Victim.

"She's wonderful," she said now. "So—bright. Why, she might live for years more, and she's so happy and contented."

MacDougal agreed again, maneuvering out of the parking lot. "Makes you think," he said. "Of course, I've got some relatives, but they're all older than I am. Chances are I'd end up alone just like all those poor devils, unless I was such a fool as to marry a wife."

"We all have opinions," said Brenda tartly.

"Well, they might get changed," said MacDougal. "For one reason or another." He glanced at her.

"Always supposing," said Brenda, "that you could find a girl so hard up for male company that she wouldn't mind being ordered around like a—"

"Now, Brenda," said MacDougal, and stroked his mustache.